PENGUIN BOOKS

The Shiralee

D'Arcy Niland was born in Glen Innes, New South Wales, and spent much of his boyhood travelling with his Irish father. He began work as a copyboy on the Sydney *Sun* but soon left to travel the country, where he led an adventurous life, working in a wide variety of jobs – as an opal miner, circus hand, stevedor and woolshed rouseabout.

He married the writer, Ruth Park, in 1942 and they settled in Sydney where Niland worked as a writer, television and film scriptwriter and magazine editor. He died suddenly in 1967, two days after completing his last novel; he was forty-seven. *The Shiralee*, with its insights into fatherhood, confirms that he understood the human heart as well as he knew the country roads of Australia.

The Shiralee

D'Arcy
Niland

PENGUIN BOOKS

PENGUIN BOOKS

Published by the Penguin Group
Penguin Group (Australia)
250 Camberwell Road, Camberwell, Victoria 3124, Australia
(a division of Pearson Australia Group Pty Ltd)
Penguin Group (USA) Inc.
375 Hudson Street, New York, New York 10014, USA
Penguin Group (Canada)
90 Eglinton Avenue East, Suite 700, Toronto, Canada ON M4P 2Y3
(a division of Pearson Penguin Canada Inc.)
Penguin Books Ltd
80 Strand, London WC2R 0RL England
Penguin Ireland
25 St Stephen's Green, Dublin 2, Ireland
(a division of Penguin Books Ltd)
Penguin Books India Pvt Ltd
11 Community Centre, Panchsheel Park, New Delhi – 110 017, India
Penguin Group (NZ)
67 Apollo Drive, Rosedale, North Shore 0632, New Zealand
(a division of Pearson New Zealand Ltd)
Penguin Books (South Africa) (Pty) Ltd
24 Sturdee Avenue, Rosebank, Johannesburg 2196, South Africa

Penguin Books Ltd, Registered Offices: 80 Strand, London, WC2R 0RL, England

First published by Angus & Robertson Ltd, 1955
Published by Penguin Books Australia Ltd, 1975
This edition published by Penguin Group (Australia), 2009

1 3 5 7 9 10 8 6 4 2

Cover design by Claire Wilson © Penguin Group (Australia)
Cover image by Jacqueline Butler / Millenium Images, UK
Typeset in Fairfield by Post Pre-Press Group, Brisbane, Queensland
Printed and bound in Australia by McPherson's Printing Group, Maryborough, Victoria

National Library of Australia
Cataloguing-in-Publication data:

Niland, D'Arcy, 1920–1967
The shiralee / D'Arcy Niland
9780143180197 (pbk.)
Fathers and daughters – New South Wales – fiction
New South Wales – social life and customs – fiction
823.914

penguin.com.au

The swagman crawls across the plain;
The drought it prowls beside him,
A hundred miles from rim to rim,
And a shadow-stick to guide him.
The crow speaks from the broken branch,
And he replies, delirious;
But in the dark he drinks the dew,
Beneath the stare of Sirius,
And from his shoulder drops the swag,
The shiralee, the tether,
That through the cruel, stumbling day,
Drove all his bones together.
The load too heavy to be borne –
He cursed it in the swelter,
But now unrolls with humble hands
And lies within its shelter.

From *The Ballad of the Shiralee*
by Ruth Park

There was a man who had a cross and his name was Macauley. He put Australia at his feet, he said, in the only way he knew how. His boots spun the dust from its roads and his body waded its streams. The black lines on the map, and the red, they knew him well. He built his fires in a thousand places and slept on the banks of rivers. The grass grew over his tracks, but he knew where they were when he came again.

He had two swags, one of them with legs and a cabbage-tree hat, and that one was the main difference between him and others who take to the road, following the sun for their bread and butter. Some have dogs. Some have horses. Some have women. And they have them as mates and companions, or for this reason and that, all of some use. But with Macauley it was this way: he had a child and the only reason he had it was because he was stuck with it.

They'll tell you he took that child from the city when it was only three and a half and went into the backblocks and carried it on his shoulder, under his arm, and in a sugar-bag that swung as a balance to his bluey. And that's the truth. He still did it, for the kid was only six months older; though not so much – for it had been broken into walking and Macauley in desperate resignation had shaped his travelling time and means to suit it. They saw him coming into town with the child asleep in his arms, or thrown up with its head on his shoulder, bobbing with the rhythm of the walk, dead to the world. They saw it trudging beside him, the two of them such a contrast in size it made you laugh.

Wherever Macauley went the child went with him. It was his real swag. The one he carried on his back was a mere nothing. That swag when he hoisted it and strapped it about his thick shoulders stayed put and gave him no trouble. He didn't have to cook a feed for it. He didn't have to make an extra shake-down. If he put it on the ground it didn't walk away. He didn't have to wash it and comb its hair. It never had to have its buttons done up. It was never the burden to slow him down.

The mood was on Macauley again that day. There was nothing doing at Bellatta. He came out of the store and stood in the shade of the verandah, rolling a smoke. He was a man of thirty-five, built like a cenotaph, squat and solid. He had ridges on his forehead like a row of sleepers, a brassy look, and a wide hat that put evening on his face while the rest of him was in sunshine. His hands were huge.

Shouldering the swag, he stepped off the verandah and squinted back towards the dark cave of the store.

'Hey, you, come on,' he called as a man might call a dog.

The kid dawdled out, quickened its pace when it saw he had already set out on the road, and caught up to him.

'Look what the man gave me, dad.'

Macauley glanced down at the brown-paper twist full of lollies, hard, desiccated, and flavourless from long incarceration in the hazy showcase; and from there to the glossy dark-brown eyes and the one ball-shaped cheek.

'Want one?'

'They'll rot your guts,' Macauley said.

The child dropped back. At first glance it was hard to be sure of the sex. The stubby boots, the blue overalls, and the khaki shirt were a boy's. So, too, in a way, was the walk. In a little while Macauley heard the voice from some distance behind him, 'Wait for me, dad.'

He stopped. He sighed. Slowly, irritably, he turned.

He saw the slow fumble with buttons, then the figure squatting, and standing up all in an exasperating process of slow motion that maddened him.

'Hurry up,' he yelled.

'I can see the grass coming up already, dad.'

He didn't miss the excitement in the voice; it only annoyed him all the more with its time-wasting futility.

'I'm going.'

The little girl came running after him. She walked in his shadow, head down, stalking it, intent on keeping it under her stepping feet. She got tired of that, got abreast of Macauley, and pushed her hand into his. He clasped it gently, though unresponsively, aware of its stickiness, letting her bear the responsibility of keeping it there.

'Where are we going, dad?'

'Nowhere.'

'What are we walking for then?'

He didn't answer.

'If people walk they must be going somewhere. We must be going somewhere, too. Aren't we?' She shook his hand, ruffling his silence. 'Aren't we?'

'For God's sake, stop gabbling,' he snapped. 'Can't you see I'm trying to think? What have you got to be yapping all the time for? You give a man a pain.'

'Have you got a headache?'

'I sure have.'

'You want me to rub it for you?'

'It's all right,' he said gruffly. 'Just stop nagging, and it'll go away.'

She bobbed along at Macauley's side. He glanced down. All he saw was the large straw hat and each boot coming successively into view beneath it. It was like walking with a mushroom. He had worked it out from observation that she had to take three steps to equal his one. He slackened his pace with deliberate imperceptibility. He didn't want her to discover that it was a voluntary concession. That would have embarrassed him. Further, she was shrewd enough to latch on to the weakness, adopting it as a habit and profiting from it when necessary. The idea was to force it into her understanding that she had to toe the line. There was no compromise, let alone subversion.

The silence didn't last long.

'I know where we're going,' she said.

Macauley made no response.

'We're going to see our mother.' She announced it with the triumph of having achieved a solution to a puzzle that had been whiffling round in her own head. 'Aren't we?'

'No.'

'I think we are,' she persisted.

'Why do you keep asking? What's the matter with your nut? I told you we're not going back there.'

'Why aren't we?'

'You don't want to see your mother,' he said. 'She's no good to you, never has been.'

'No,' the kid agreed, with the emphatic, unfeeling articulation of a parrot, 'she's a silly old mother. She beats kids when they wet the bed and locks them in the lavvy when they eat all the cakes.'

'You forget about your mother,' he said.

How long did it take a kid to forget its mother, he wondered. That depended on the age of the child, and the younger it was the sooner it forgot, they said. Well, this kid was only four, and six months had gone since it took its last look at the old woman. Yet the questions still came, and the name still leapt to her lips. But what did she remember? Macauley couldn't be sure. He couldn't be sure whether the child remembered the form and shape of the woman, the dark cropped hair, the brown eyes: a pair of slippers trudging about the kitchen; hands turning the pages of a magazine, and sulky red lips with a cigarette between them; a cretonne apron hanging on the line in the poky backyard; a shopping bag stuffed to the craw and spilling out vegetables. Maybe it was the voice, often high-pitched, often harsh: maybe it was the smell of the gas stove, of garments drying before the open oven; the sight of wallpaper uncurled by the damp, stained with a mildewy pattern of its own, hanging from the walls; maybe it was the rattle of the windows and the whistle of draughts under the door, the jangle of the brass knobs on the bedposts every time the sleeper turned on the canoe-shaped mattress; and maybe it was the holy picture on the bedroom wall, The Light of the World, Christ crowned and the face flooded with the yellow glow of the lantern he carried; or the framed motto, Home is Love, hanging lopsided over the smoke-stained canisters on the kitchen shelf. But perhaps it was none of these things. Neither the entire vision of the woman, nor any of the images and figments. Perhaps it was no more than the memory of association, indefinite as a dream, a wisp of experience hanging in the mind.

They were walking across the Gallatherha Plains in the black-soil country, and Macauley foresaw a long dismal journey. The road was anything but smooth walking: it was caked hard and lumpy, making their feet feel uneven as though they were walking on stubble. There was nothing to see beyond them or about them but a vast wide-open space, without tree or habitation, nothing but endless flat plain. There was little feed. The black earth was a lurry of cracks, streaked and forked here and there like flashes of petrified lightning, and over its surface for mile on desolate mile was the brown decay of thistles.

And though the hours could go by the scene would not change. Time and place, and only time altered here.

Macauley kept his eyes ahead, sensing rather than seeing or hearing the small lap-dog beside him.

And he was thinking of this one and that one and of many things. He was thinking of a girl he used to know, and the way he saw her was like a picture on a postcard: with a cherry in her white teeth poised on a smile. He was thinking of the long man in the silk-lined overcoat and a face as black as an old billycan.

The one was Lily Harper: her father was an alderman, a church-warden, and the butcher down the street; her mother was all satin and silk and a parasol for Sunday, and Lily, she was just the rancy-tancy one for the refinement and culture. But they had no drawbacks that evening in the orchard. Her hair was like a copper coin. There was enough of it to stuff a sofa, all done up in bronzy braids and tied with a green ribbon. He undid it, and she let him, and it lay on the ground like a corolla, and her face was the centrepiece of it. She was so ripe, yet untried, aching for him.

Yet afterwards he heard her sniffling.

What's up now?

You know you shouldn't have.

What about you?

You're awful, she said. Just downright awful.

He looked at her and his eyes narrowed with quick anger.

You know, we've got a name for you.

What?

I wouldn't mention it.

Is that nice?

Nice or not, that's what you are. What the hell are you trying to give me? You're not blubbering because this happened. It's for something else. What? Come out with it.

She flared.

You think you're smart. Just because you come from Sydney, and just because you've travelled a bit, you think you're a man of the world. You think you know everything; just bursting with wisdom and knowledge. You think you can say anything to a girl. You think by being brutally frank you're honest. You mistake crudity for forthrightness. You wouldn't know tact or gentleness if you met them.

Now you're talking like a King's Cross queenie. Listen. I don't think I'm smart, and I don't kid myself I'm a man of the world. I haven't travelled. Not yet. This dump is the first I've ever been to outside the Smoke. I've never been away from home before. But, by God, by the time I'm twenty-five those things you say will be true of me.

Huh!

Huh all you like, but you'll see. I'll be eighteen tomorrow. Give me seven years and I'll show you. Yeah, look me up then and we'll see who eats their words.

You're rough and vulgar; you're nothing but a hoodlum. I'm absolutely stupid to have anything to do with you. You haven't any ambition. Any aspirations. You care about nobody but yourself – you're just eaten up with selfishness. You're good for nothing.

He was beginning to be amused.

Oh, I don't know about that. There are some things I'm pretty good at. In fact, I'd say I was a bloody first-rate performer.

You've been here a month. You've had three jobs and stuck to none of them. My father offered to apprentice you, but you turned that down, too. There's nothing worthwhile in you, that's all.

Hell, why don't you dig a hole right there and put me in it! I might as well be buried for all the use I am as far as you're concerned.

I thought, well – I thought there might have been some future for both of us together, but I can see it would never work out. I like you, but I can get over that. But I could never get over all the unhappiness that would come about if

I married you, or that will come about if I have anything more to do with you.

Marriage! What the blazes! Where'd you get the idea I was going to put the bit and bridle on you? God Almighty, I would be a bonehead. Tie myself down to one filly for life when I can have the pick of them from every paddock in Australia.

That's exactly what I mean – there's no life for a woman with you.

For a minute he was angry; then he shrugged his shoulders and grinned.

Anyway, how did all this start? We come out here, and it's nice, everything; I'm happy, you're happy; I get to giving you the best that money can buy buckshee, and you act as though you wouldn't mind paying for it, anyway. Then, bang, you start bashing the living daylights out of me. You sheilas pick the most peculiar times to have the guts-ache.

He looked at her, expecting the start of a smile, hoping the storm had blown over, still not apprehending the cause of it, and careless reasoning it out, anyway. She was sitting with her knees up and her dress pulled over them down to her calves. Her hair hung down her back like a copper waterfall. There was a look of aloof contempt on her face which only succeeded in giving it an aspect of seductive insolence, a haughty light in her eyes which only seemed to him a dare to his virility. She was overpoweringly desirable again. The fresh, detailed memory of her lusciousness boiled his blood.

You're a lovely thing, he said, the words choking out in a tumescent flood, the uninhibited compliments of passion. You're beautiful. I could eat you!

He covered her face and hair and neck with rough kisses. But there was no response from her this time. She did not yield; neither did she struggle. She turned her face, her cheek on the earth, biting her lips, crying bitterly. Her arms were outflung, unmoving. Only her hands kept clenching and unclenching. He had no pity. The tumult of his zeal left no room for it. Only when the fervour died in its own consummation did he begin to doubt the worth of it, feeling little now that it was over, and subdued by her wretchedness.

He didn't know what to do or say. He moved away, allowing her her freedom. He stood up. She arose, brushing down her dress, and glaring at him with a look of shock and pain and horror as though she had stumbled on the lair of a fiend. It made him uncomfortable. And the discomfort made him angry.

She turned and started to run through the orchard.

That's right, he yelled after her. Go home and blab in your old lady's ear. Put me in with your old man. Tell him to come after me with his cleaver.

He stood for a while brooding. There was a rustle like paper in the trees, a bend on the long grass. It seemed part of the reproachful sense of sordidness and unfairness. But no old man came with a cleaver. Not then or afterwards. Nothing happened. He did not see her again. He had one regret, but he didn't know why he had it. He wished he could have left her thinking sadly and warmly of him; not thinking of him with rage and hate. He knew he would have felt better.

'A man's a bastard,' Macauley said.

The kid looked up. 'What'd you say, dad?'

'Nothing,' he grunted.

That was Lily Harper, and she was a lady; she was quality and it made a man feel good that once such quality had had a bit of time for him.

And the other one he remembered, the one with the silk-lined overcoat, that was Tommy Goorianawa. He sat on a kerosene tin outside his humpy in the same town. He dozed in the sun with his hands on his lap and his chin on his chest. He was long and thin, and they called him the oracle of the north; he talked with all men on all subjects. He foretold droughts and floods and fires. They said he could read a man's fate in the sound of his voice and the lines of his face. They put a piece in the paper about him every year, on his birthday, and they said: Tommy Goorianawa is eighty-four today. Or eighty-five, or eighty-six, or whatever his age was. And the townspeople, many of them would turn up with little gifts of food for him, and he would thank them all with a little speech of thanks that showed he was a man of rough but true education, keen intelligence and inborn politeness. It was a gentleman of the town who had given him the silk-lined overcoat, and he wore it all the time, for his bones were cold in summer and colder still in winter; and he wore it, too, with pride as though he had some title and it was the insignia of his state.

He was nearly ninety when Macauley met him, and his head lifted at the sound of the approaching figure, and he called: What man is that? I do not know the footsteps.

Macauley halted but ten yards away, staring. The smile of welcome was already on the man's face. Rub that face and you'd get soot on your fingers, it was so black. The whiskers on the lean jaws were like snow-white splinters. Macauley gave his name.

Sorry to bother you. Just wanted to fill the waterbag.

Certainly. Give it to Nellie. She'll fill it.

A gin came to the door, one of the old man's relatives, only half his age. Macauley gave her the bag with a nod. He was still looking at the man.

Come here, boy. Come closer.

Macauley ambled over, dropped the swag, and sat on it. He wanted to stare and he knew now that he could. He took a good searching look. The old man wore a rag cap covered with patches, and though its peak was pulled down it did not hide the sightless sockets. The eyes even were not eyes. They were slivers of jelly, dull, opaque, and grey as oysters.

Dynamite did it, the old man said.

Macauley was taken aback, but he saw the smile come on the face and it was turned in his direction.

Tough luck, he said.

Where are you making, boy?

I don't know yet.

Tommy Goorianawa chuckled. He stretched out his long legs, leaned back, crossed his arms on his stomach and he said this to Macauley:

Some men are like a wheel. They were made to go round. They rust if they lie still, and they fall apart. You're like that. Some men, they can live in a box, but you're not one of them.

You're right, I'm not.

Yet such men are not always contented. They're looking for something, but they don't know what it is, and they often never find out. They climb up on the mountain and the valley looks sweeter below. They pitch their tent in the valley, and look up to the shining mountain. The man who lives in the box has what he wants and is content.

Yeah, the poor mug, he can keep it, too.

But there's another man. He's like a seed in an orange. He likes to be in the centre of the life that suits him encased by the skin and the rind. They hold him together. Without them he dies. His spirit goes and his body follows. You know what I mean? The sky is the rind of this man's world and the skin the green skin of the earth. They belong to him and he belongs to them; all part of the one heartbeat.

Macauley rolled his second cigarette. He could see the sense in what the old man said, but the talk was in the nature of a probing criticism that irritated him.

Come close, boy. Let me put my hands on your face.

The old man extended his hands, the palms pink and smooth as water-washed stones. The corded stringy wrists projected from the voluminous sleeves of the coat like saplings.

Softly, gently the fingers moved over Macauley's face, tracing the lineaments, feeling the strong jaws, the deep-set eye sockets, the firm cheeks, the resolute curve of the lips. Macauley felt a little foolish and, at the same time, a little uneasy. There was something uncanny about the old man and he sensed it. He felt the anxiety creep up in him as the translating fingers made their report. Macauley looked at the black face before him for some clue, but there was none. If the vision behind those sightless eyes saw anything, the face betrayed no sign of it.

The old man withdrew his hands at last and dropped them on his lap. He was silent. Macauley felt as though he had just been overhauled by a doctor and was now waiting for the verdict.

Well, what did you find out? he asked.

You want to know?

Sure, why not?

A man like you, said Tommy Goorianawa, he either dies quick with a knife in his gizzard or he lives to be a hundred.

Macauley was startled only for a moment.

Which is it for me?

I don't know. I'd tell you if I did. But I'll say this. You're a man, every inch of you, and there's a lot of good in you, but it's buried deep and it's twisted. It's like a wild animal that needs to be coaxed into the light and tamed; an animal that does not come willingly because it is frightened for itself. It will have its challengers and will rise in you like a secret. Try and not smother it. It's the stars and the wild wind for you, and the roads that tie the towns together, all right, but I'll say this – watch out for big trouble. Don't lead two lives or both will be unhappy; lead one and lead it well. And don't be too hard on them weaker than you. That's all I can tell you.

Macauley didn't say anything. He was blinking, the words still going through his mind. He couldn't decide whether the old man had taken a liberty or not. Confusion brushed with annoyance in him. He noticed the pot-bellied old gin at the door with the waterbag in her gnarled hand, and he was glad of the chance it gave him to make the next move. He nodded his thanks, and picked up his swag. He still didn't know how to get going. The wise old man helped him.

Good luck, boy.

Goodbye, Macauley said. That was all he could think to say. He stumbled across the paddock and got on to the road. He looked back at the humpy, a lopsided arrangement of corrugated-iron sheets and bag windows. There was a blue wisp of smoke curling from the tin chimney. The old man was huddled against the wall in the sun like a grotesque scarecrow. His head was down on his chest and his hands were in his lap. He was a black bundle like a twisted shadow; and that was the last he saw of Tommy Goorianawa.

Macauley was furious, but he didn't know why. He felt a burn in his face and a tautness in his nerves. There was steam in him and it couldn't escape. He didn't go on. He walked back the half-mile to the town, thinking of that old quack, that old black bull-merchant, Moses of the boongs; and a man should have hauled the cap off his head and chucked ninepence into it just to show him who was a wake-up to who: so that by the time he reached the pub Macauley was in a hurricane of a mood. He downed two beers, picked a fight, stretched out his man, and he felt a lot better.

But the man he stretched out chipped bits off him and left him only one eye to see out of; and he was only a young fellow like Macauley himself, and not the one to hold grudges and keep a tight face when he liked his face loose. His name was Lucky Regan, and he came up to Macauley and put his hand out and in no time they were rolling round drunk together, looking for flowers in the street, and singing that parody, 'It Was the Demon, Liquor,' and sitting down in the auctioneer's doorway fishing chips out of a hole in a lot of white paper.

Lucky had the money to bail them out next morning, and they set off together. They were mates on the track and they shared that first experience. And it was this road from Bellata.

This same road. They had ridden there in the backs of trucks, thankful for the lift when their feet became so sore and swollen they could do no more than limp like tender-footed horses, and the swags on their shoulders had put a ridge of aching stiffness right down the centre of their backs.

Walking it now, Macauley was walking in yesterday. The vivid images shot into his mind like images on a screen. They couldn't have picked a worse road to break themselves in on. Just like them in their rawness to drop on to the arse-end of Australia to start their maiden journey. They heard from every bone in their bodies, even bones they never knew were there.

A great circle, like the lid of a tin, and nothing alive or dead on it. No friendly tree to take rest under, and no waterbag to take a drink from.

We should have provided ourselves with a waterbag, Mac. But how were we to know?

That's right. How?

If we had of, we could have boiled the billy now and had a nice cuppa tea.

What would we use for wood?

Yeah, that's right. Not even a bloody skerrick of wood about.

A pair of green swagmen, they were.

The green swagmen plodded on, with the silence far and wide around, broken only occasionally by Macauley's whine or Regan's whinge. The sun fell upon them hot with the heat of metal. Thirst had become a built-in boarder with a grievance long ago. He threatened to get them down. Only their hearts kept them up.

Then Regan saw the tremendous sheet of water that was a mirage, but he didn't know it then and only kicked himself for a town lout later; so did Macauley, for he came in on the illusion, too. They doubled their pace and skinned their eyes. Their mouths felt like an ant bed. Water – they couldn't get it out of their heads. They talked water for miles, and their thirst increased with it, and their mounting thirst made them talk more water; they thought with delight of puddles and rain, and conjured up with acute clearness rivers and streams, cascades and waterfalls, the waterfront, boats building and people about drinking, swimming, sailing. They were reminded of pleasant places abroad, and tried to picture other places they thought they had seen in the magazines.

They even saw moving objects in that mirage, visionary shadows: sometimes a large army of people, other times moving vehicles, and once what looked like a big ship.

Their knowledge of geography was so poor and their enthusiasm so great that they started to conjecture excitedly as to what great river this might be. Macauley said he thought it was the Barwon, but Regan said he thought the Barwon was in Victoria. His pick would be the Swan or maybe the Murray. The Murray most likely, since it was the longest river in the world, so long in fact it met itself coming back. They plucked out of the geography of New South Wales all the names they had read and all the names they had heard, and Macauley finally settled for the Murrumbidgee. But Regan had changed his mind. It wasn't a river at all. It was the great inland sea he had been hearing so much about. And his great worry then was whether it would be too salty to drink.

Having come so far from where they first noticed the mirage it suddenly dawned on them that they hadn't got a yard nearer the vast sheet of water. By now they were nearly dead for a drink of lovely water if only it could be, sapped by their torment, debilitated by the frenzy of their enthusiasm.

Stumbling along, unable to talk and not wanting to, they were ready to drop when unexpectedly they came upon an artesian bore. Regan's limbs behaved erratically. He dropped his swag, flung out his arms, and, standing in one spot, lifted his legs like a man pedalling a bicycle uphill.

Look out, Lucky!

Macauley pointed at the two large snakes. Regan's legs worked again, only this time like a man pedalling a bicycle downhill.

They let the snakes slide away to safety, as there was neither stick nor stone nor anything else to kill them with.

Regan dipped the billy into the dam into which the water flowed from the pipe and rushed it into his mouth. He jerked, dropped the billy and sprayed it in all directions.

It's bloody boiling! He shouted. What the hell is this? Are we jonah'd or something?

Macauley put his hand gingerly in the water.

Ghost, she's hot all right.

Nearly scalded me gob off, that's all.

Macauley saw water running out of the dam along a bore drain. They followed it down some distance until they got it cool enough to drink. They poured bellyfuls of it over their heads. They gulped it greedily. In a while their bellies were leaden footballs. They belched and rumbled.

God, Mac, that water – you don't think it was poisoned?

They use it to water the stock, I heard.

Stock? What do you mean – rabbits?

No, cattle, horses, sheep. That's what them drains are for – they carry the water. That's what I reckon, anyway.

But Lucky Regan wasn't convinced. They poisoned waterholes to kill rabbits. He knew about that. And it wasn't long before he communicated his fears to Macauley.

I'm getting twisty pains in the guts, he reported. You getting them?

Yeah.

Regan stood up, wincing, grasping his bloated stomach. His eyes were wild.

I tell you, Mac, we've got a gutful of arsenic in us.

By God, you might be right.

Macauley stood up, too, grimacing, snarling, clutching his abdomen.

Just like the way your bowels knot up after a feed of porridge, he said.

But Regan wasn't interested in further identification. With panicky resolve he was thrusting his fingers down his throat, gagging and retching until he was sick. Macauley did the same. Both of them stood bent over giving the bore drain back its water.

After that, weak and wet-eyed, they lay down with their heads on their swags, their hats over their faces, and went to sleep.

Macauley woke first with the chill of shadow on him. The sky was overcast, all in a yeasty motion of sombrous hues ever darkening the earth. The lightning jiggled, sharp and brilliant as a blind shooting up against daylight in a black room. The ground shook with the rumble of tumbling thunder. The wind whuddered across the waste, scattering the roly-poly not unlike a lot of sheep making a stupid run for it. The resemblance was made more real the way one or two of the polys blew over the top of another.

Regan was awake now and surveying the cheerless environs with a look of incredulous disbelief.

Strike a light, anyone'd think we busted a mirror over a black cat on Friday the thirteenth. I think it's time I give my bloody name anyway.

No good of stopping here, anyway. Come on.

All they could do was keep moving. They must strike a town some time. The rain came with a few big drops, a hesitant rehearsal; then they heard it roaring over the plain, and saw it coming, a wall of grey between sky and earth.

It was all right for a while. They joked.

Who's moaning for a drink now?

Drink? This is no drink, Mac. This is a deluge. If I open me trap I'll flounder.

But they were soon in trouble. The road underfoot became greasy slime that changed to gluey sludge. It gripped their boots and plastered itself there in a cementy clog. It spread itself wide and thick on the soles and heels till they looked to be wearing mud snowshoes. Their feet grew heavier to lift, their walk became slower and clumsier. They were like flies on treacle. After a few hundred yards they were glad to stop and dig the stuff away with a penknife.

The rain was gone now, the wrath of an hour, and the sky was clear with a dustless purity. The sun was still hot, but the black soil seemed to become more sticky as it dried. Macauley and Regan began to grow several inches in height. The growth was picked up more on the heel than on the sole and gave them a slight tilt forward, after the fashion of a tall woman in very high-heeled shoes. Their soles became pads again, twelve inches wide. It made walking an agony, then an impossibility until they freed themselves of it once more.

Macauley was taking several hard kicks with the back of his heel against the toe of his other boot when suddenly the stilty mud heel, hard and pointed, came flying off and struck Regan on the shin-bone. It took the skin off and bled him. He gripped his leg with a curse and sat down. His seat dried like a black patch but with the stiffness of cardboard.

'When are we going to have some dinner?'

The same road, the christening road, the breaker-inner, but a pushover now; a pushover for a long time: and here he was walking it again seventeen years later with a kid of his own tagging along – a kid of his own tagging along like a bloody fish hook in his side. Who would have believed it? And what a ratbag situation, what a story to make the old hens in the giggle-house laugh.

'I want my dinner.'

'What the hell are you grizzling about?' Macauley demanded.

'I want some dinner.'

'You'll get it when I'm ready.'

The kid didn't say anything, and Macauley felt the tightness leave his jaws. He said gruffly. 'You can walk a bit further, can't you?'

'All right,' the kid said.

Macauley suited himself. Another hundred yards was far enough to satisfy him, to show the child who was boss.

'Okay, we'll boil the billy. I'll tell you what you do. See them thistles?'

'Which? Them big ones there?'

'Not them. They're growing. See all those rotten ones on the ground? Well, them. But I want the biggest stalks you can find, see? Not the little stuff. Righto – and hurry up.'

He dropped the swag, took out tin plates and tin mugs from the tuckerbag. He glanced up to see how his helper was getting on, and the kid had vanished. At least that was how it appeared. In his squatting position Macauley couldn't see her, but when he stood up he saw the small figure lying on its stomach behind a four-foot-high clump of thistle.

'Hey!'

The cabbage-tree hat turned. 'There's a funny thing here dad; it's got a striped jumper on and an awful lot of legs. Come and see it.'

'What about them thistles?' he barked.

The kid stood up. 'I'm getting them.'

'Ah, you're next to useless. I could have the billy boiled while I'm talking to you.'

It took him only a few minutes to gather the biggest of the sun-dried stalks and stack a fire. The glare of daylight was so great that the flames were almost invisible, but they licked up after the fumous haze and the hot dry wind fanned them. Soon he had a tight, low-set fire burning with gusty energy.

The thistles were the wood of this wilderness.

He opened the tuckerbag and took out a hunk of corned beef and a loaf of bread and some tomatoes. He sliced two rounds off the bread, stabbed each in turn with a long three-pronged fork made from fencing wire and stood them like hoardings against the fire. He buttered the toast and put the lid back on the jar, and put a piece on each plate with meat and halved tomatoes. The billy was singing, a little thrum, and the seething strings of bubbles were starting upwards.

'Hey, I thought you said you were hungry.'

'I am, too.'

'Well, it's ready.'

The kid dawdled across the cakey ground, staring fascinated at her hand. She lowered it in front of Macauley.

'Look, dad.'

'It's a caterpillar.'

'Will they hurt you?'

'No. But don't go picking things up. You might get bitten by something.'

'Can I keep him?'

'If you want to.'

The child's eyes glowed with pleasure. She threw her arms round his neck and kissed his hat with exuberance. 'Gee, thanks, you're a good daddy.'

'Never mind that,' he grunted. 'Get stuck into your tucker.'

He threw a handful of tea into the boiling billy, and lifted it off the fire with the toasting fork under the handle, and left it to draw by his feet. The kid ate hungrily, absently watching the tea leaves floating and sinking.

'What do you feed him on?'

'What?'

'The caterpullar. Do they eat bread?'

'Leaves.'

Macauley poured out the tea, the colour of syrup, and sugared it. He gingerly sipped. The kid waited for hers to cool. She had the caterpillar in the pocket of her overalls, and from time to time held it open to make sure that the grub was still there.

While they ate in the hot sun with the bush flies getting in for their cut, too, an old bundle of a man came down the road from the west. Macauley watched him approaching and recognised him at once for what he was, a flat country bagman, a type on his own.

'G'day, there.'

'G'day.'

'Hot, ain't she?'

'Yeah, warm all right.'

The old man dropped his swag and scratched his sweating head under his hat. The hat joggled but didn't fall off. He was like a smoked fish, dry, wrinkled and brown. His boots were the colour of an old cow pat. His palmer knapp trousers, with the pencil stripes rubbed out entirely here and there, were bent to the shape of his legs like a loose casing; they were caught on the hips and the hips stopped them from dropping. As it was the slack was down round his knees. The belt with the big buckle that was supposed to keep them up was girdled round his stomach, doing nothing except ornament his grey flannel. Frosty hair sprouted from the neck.

Macauley let the old man take the initiative. He could wait for the colours to show. In his time he had met plenty of these plain turkeys, as they were known. He had been in trouble with some, or rather they had been in trouble with him. None of them he liked. It was all to do with their professional character. They disliked the hillbilly bagman, these turkeys, as much as they hated his hilly country, and they treated him with contempt. They always avoided helping him. They were clannish and secretive.

They zoned themselves on the plains, wandering the roads and the backtracks among the sheep stations and the wheat farms, doing the rounds year in and year out. They did the rounds from shed to shed at shearing time, ate a couple of good meals, had the tuckerbag filled, and moved on to the next place. When all the shearing was completed throughout their run of the flat country they still moved about among the stations, obtaining some rations and camping in the bagmen's huts on the station property. If for a change they felt like some exercise other than walking they would take a job burr-cutting, walking about with a long-handled hoe, and not minding it, so long as the burrs were not too plentiful, as there was money for their trouble. They knew all the handouts and rest huts and all the familiar faces of their plain-turkey brethren.

The old man sensed the expectant atmosphere. He shrugged, smiled with friendly ease.

'Not gonna ask yer which way yer came. Don't matter to me son. Not gonna say, "How's the mountains these days?" Yer'd on'y bite, and next thing I'd be doin' yer over.' He chuckled.

Macauley squinted at him, went back to rolling his cigarette.

'Got a joey with yer, have yer? And what's your name, young 'un?'

'Buster,' said Macauley's kid promptly.

The old man straightened himself as with a shock of admiration.

'Buster, eh? Well, ain't that a knacky little name. Suits yer, too.'

'What's your name?'

'My name? Ah, I got a lotta names. But me mother called me Sam.'

'Where's your mother now?'

The old man wasn't quite sure how to answer that, and he was saved the trouble of thinking. Macauley had finished his summing up. He was satisfied.

'Drop o' tea there if you want it,' he said.

The old turkey looked at him wonderingly as if deciding the matter of whether he wanted it or not, when all the time, Macauley knew, he had decided.

'Ta.'

Macauley rinsed out his pint, handed it to the old man whose shaking hand filled it to the brim. He sat down on his swag with a sigh, put his elbows on his knees and cradled the warm mug in his hands. He glanced towards the child.

'You cart him about with yer?'

'It's a her.'

Old Sam looked astonished. In his mind that was even worse. He was curious about the relationship, the circumstances, the why and wherefore. The signs were as easy to read as a calendar. But Macauley wasn't saying anything.

'Puts a bit of spoke in yer wheel, don't it? I mean, movin' and that.'

'I get on all right.'

'Be pretty tough, I reckon.'

You don't know how tough, Macauley thought, but he didn't want anybody considering him a sorry spectacle, seeking out the clues and surmising the case-history with all its background of humiliation and unhappiness. Sympathy or gloating – he didn't want it.

'It's nothing,' he said. 'I've carried a swag bigger than both this and her put together,' he boasted. 'Smoke?'

'Ta.'

Macauley threw the tea slops on the fire and began to prepare for the road again.

'What's at Millie?'

'Bugger all. I just come through there. Tryin' to see if I can get a bit of burr-cuttin'.'

Macauley gave him a quick, hard glance. Old Sam didn't mistake its meaning. He said with some heat, 'Don't you worry, I can swing a hoe with the best of 'em yet. Give you a start, and lick yer hands down, young and all as you are. Me – I been a burr-ganger in some of the biggest camps in this country.'

'Why don't you get the pension and settle down?' Macauley taunted.

'Pension!' snorted old Sam. 'Settle down! That'll be the bloody day. They can stick their pensions up their jumper. When I go out I'll go out in me stride. And if I ain't dead enough when I fall down I'll get up and keep goin' till I am.'

Macauley laughed. He couldn't help it.

'How you off for tucker?'

'I'm right.'

'Weed?'

'I'll get some at Bellata.'

'Take that,' Macauley said. 'It'll see you there. I got another packet.'

The old man hesitated, looking up. 'I'll pay you for it.'

'Don't offer me money,' Macauley said, strapping his swag. 'I mightn't knock it back.'

'You think I'm a bludger.'

'Nobody said that. Well, we'll be getting along.'

Macauley had made his point. Nobody was going to put it over him. Whether the old turkey was guilty or innocent didn't matter. Either way, he was compelled to acknowledge Macauley's shrewdness. Old Sam thoughtfully hoisted his own swag.

'Where you makin', son?'

'Walgett way.'

'You ever done any cookin'?'

'Yeah, I've had that on,' Macauley said.

'I was just thinkin', if it's any help to you, there was a joker in Millie yest'y lookin' for a burr-camp cook at Boomi. Too far for me to go, but it might suit you.'

'Good.'

'O'Hara's his name. Nice feller, too. Tell him old Sam Bywater sent yer. He'll do anything for me.'

'Okay. Thanks.'

Old Sam put out his hand. Macauley considered it for a moment unprepared and slightly surprised. Their brief acquaintance in passing – nodding strangers – hardly justified the formality. There was warmth in the old man's half of the handshake, casualness in Macauley's.

'We'll meet again, boy, and I won't forget the drop o' tea and the bit o' weed you gave me.'

'Keep your legs together,' Macauley said.

He started off, easily getting into his stride.

'So long, Buster,' old Sam called.

'Goodbye,' Buster said.

They had walked for two hours, and Macauley couldn't help but observe, as he had been observing, the growing endurance of the little girl. It dragged from him some slight sense of gratification. He wasn't paying out tribute to the child: he was merely feeling the small but positive diminution of responsibility. But it wouldn't be long now. At the end of the third hour and a steadily maintained pace, Buster's feet were scuffling, and she was whining to be carried.

'Don't kid me,' Macauley said. 'You can go on a bit yet.'

'I can't. I can't,' the kid whimpered desperately.

'Come on.'

Macauley took her hand, and kept going. He felt the tugging weight. It got heavier and heavier. It was not brutality, but purposeful tactics. He stopped them short of the verge of exhaustion. When the child was swaying, leaning back from the mooring of his hand, the legs wobbling, the voice dreeing mournfully while the tears flowed unattended down the crumpled face – that was when Macauley picked her up.

She was asleep in five minutes, her head on his shoulder.

Pity crept like a little flame into the smoulder of his resentment, but the resentment was too strong for it and it was smothered. Macauley told himself this could not go on. He was vehement.

Yet when he saw emus he had a wish that she should see them; when he saw the wild pigs had been rooting up the ground he had an inclination to point it out; and when he came upon a goanna disgorging at his approach a kitten rabbit he had an instinct to wake her up and show her the sight.

But he did none of these things, though he stopped when he saw the goanna and watched the ejection of the rabbit buried to its hind-legs in the reptile's insides. The legs scrabbled as the rabbit, aware of the mysterious interruption, seized the advantage and struggled to back out. The goanna bolted with fright, and the rabbit, startled, weak, damp all over, made every attempt to run away, but failed. Macauley stepped after it and with one merciful kick put it out of its misery.

He came into Millie in the hush of sundown. It was so quiet it might have been a scene painted on a canvas. It was a pocket of civilisation – a few houses, a few groceries, a sort of post office: the vestiges of a settlement, so that you couldn't be sure whether it was just starting or just ending. By night a shut-up village, a huddle of buildings drenched in darkness. Or with moonlight on the rooftops shining like the blade of a knife. By day a cell of life set in the shadeless open amid the burning sun and the hot winds.

Macauley felt pretty worn, but a good feed under his belt, a rest, and he'd be right. Buster walked at his side again, refreshed and loquacious. She was hungry, too. Macauley thumped on a side gate, and the storekeeper came out wiping his mouth with a serviette and admitted them. He took them through into the shop. Macauley bought eggs, a tin of preserved pears, some rashers of bacon, and a packet of sweet biscuits.

'Old Tubby Callahan still the butcher here?'

'Oh, no,' the storekeeper said. 'Old Tubby passed on about three months ago now.'

'Well, you don't say!' Macauley was surprised and slightly shocked. 'I didn't think there was anything could ever knock him over.'

'No, you'd never think so to look at him. But he went pretty quick. Got crook one weekend. Went to Moree, and they bunged him down to Sydney. Just took a look at him there, sewed him up and sent him home again.'

'His missus still around?'

'No, she's gone, too. Living with her daughter at Tamworth. Will there be anything else?'

'That's the lot. What about the new butcher? Is he on the premises?'

'Oh, you won't get any meat there now.'

The storekeeper shook his head vigorously and let it peter to a standstill. He had a grave face, with sallow cheeks and eyes like the slit in a money box. His hair was slicked back on either side of a centre parting, in a way like the dark folded wings of a bird. He had a bit of Chow in him somewhere.

'That's too bad,' Macauley said. 'I was going to turn on a proper feed tonight. But never mind.'

He placed the money on the counter as the storekeeper wrapped up the goods. While he had been talking Buster was roving the store, peering at the rafters hung with hurricane lanterns, brooms, buckets, meat safes, mops, rifles, and other merchandise. The posts were draped with whips, belts, slippers, coat hangers, and cards of buttons. The floor space was mainly taken up with a rickety table on which were stacked bolts of cloth of many colours. There were open bags of potatoes, barrels of brown and white onions, behind the door and along the wall bags of sugar and flour. Pumpkins and marrows lay heaped in a corner. The place smelled of sultanas and spice.

'Just a minute,' said the storekeeper, and hurried out the back into the living quarters.

Macauley looked casually over the shelves, every alcove stuffed with goods. Hanging lopsided from a tack just above his head was the warning: A Clock Ticks But We Don't. Another placard farther along said: Come In But Leave Your Dog Outside. Another notice asked the customers if they had placed their Christmas orders yet, and notified them that a turkey on the lay-by was better than one on the go-by, and finished off with: For a few pence a week you can dine like a prince at year's end.

Macauley couldn't tie up the wit and humour of these notices with the humourless face of the storekeeper, but he didn't question its impossibility. Gravediggers could act like clowns; clowns like gravediggers.

The storekeeper came back with the change and a small parcel.

'There's a few chops there,' he said. 'I can't use them and you're welcome to them.'

Macauley said nothing, throwing silence over his embarrassment, and the necessity of framing an appropriate expression of thanks. If he offered money the storekeeper might not be offended, but some of the good would be taken out of his charitable gesture.

'I'll only be throwing them out, anyway,' he said.

'All right,' Macauley said, 'if you don't want them. They'll go goodo with the cackleberries.' He added on an impulse, 'Better give us a bob's worth of lollies for the kid. Mix 'em up.'

Outside, in the darkling evening, they walked round to the front of the store. Macauley looked up and read the owner's name: R. C. Cheetham. Underneath in smaller letters was the inscription: Only By Name, Not By Nature. Then followed the words: General Store.

Bit of a wag, Macauley mused.

A nippy nor'-wester was springing up. He pulled his hat more firmly on his head and strolled down the eastern end, looking for a place to camp for the night. He settled for a spot on the lee side of an old stable. While he grilled the chops on a small wire rack over a scraped-out table of red coals and hot stones, he baked the eggs in the hot ashes. The billy was simmering on the opposite side, lashed by the gusty flames.

After they had eaten, Macauley rolled a smoke and lay back on the spread blanket with his hands clasped behind his head. He was just beginning to enjoy the soothing torpor of relaxation when Buster jumped up and said, 'We got any paper?'

Macauley sat up, pulled the tuckerbag over to him, and tore off a piece of brown paper that had come from the store.

'Duck over there somewhere,' he said.

Buster was gone about ten minutes. Macauley was dozing when he heard a piercing yell. He leapt up like a cat, peering about him. The kid came running towards him out of the darkness in an outburst of sobbing, wailing incoherencies. He swallowed, alert with the impact of alarm and mystification. She stood before him, screaming and muttering.

'What is it? What is it?' He grabbed her frail shoulders and shook her.

He couldn't understand the lachrymal babble that poured out of her mouth.

'I can't hear a word you're saying. What happened? Did something bite you? Stop that yelling and tell me.' He was shouting.

'My caterpullar — ' she got out.

'Your caterpillar, yes. What about it?'

'It's gone!' she howled in a fresh paroxysm of weeping.

Macauley's shoulder's dropped. He let out a deep sigh of relief.

'Is that any reason to wake the whole neighbourhood?' he demanded. 'Anybody'd think you were being murdered. Cut it out.'

The loudness of his voice only reduced the volume of her hysteria, like a radio turned down; it didn't stop it. She fell on her hands and knees, crawling over the blanket and round the fire, peering, sobbing all the time. He saw the tears dropping from her eyes.

'Where is my caterpullar gone?' She was in a rage of grief, and as the search proved unavailing the rage mounted to an inconsolable dementia.

'Stop it!' bounced Macauley. 'You sound like a fire engine.'

He, too, went down on his hands and knees. They crawled about like a big dog and a little dog. Macauley gave up. The bitter agony of the lament was beginning to unnerve him.

'Listen, listen to me,' he commanded, 'I'll get you another one.'

'Want that one.'

'You'll have to cut it out,' he snarled furiously. 'Cut it out.' His words had no effect. He smacked her hard across the bottom. The sound came up with new and more hideous notes in it as the gas comes up when you put a penny in the slot. He thought of the lollies, dragged them from his pocket.

'Here, look – look what I've got.'

Buster glared at him with a crumpled face, keeping the emotion simmering, while she investigated his claims to captivation. They weren't strong enough.

'Don't want any.' She sniffed and went off again into an even more discordant bereavement.

'To hell with you then, you little bastard,' Macauley swore. He pulled his hat down on his head, dug his side into the hip-hole and pulled the blanket up to his neck. If nothing else worked, the dissimulation of sleep, the repudiation of interest in the child and her problem, might. Left to the loneliness of the hunt and the loneliness of the night with the wind whistling about the stable, and sensing the unpleasantness of ostracism, she soon relented. Macauley felt her scrabbling over the blanket, and then sitting beside his bulk, hooning to herself. But though she had relented, she had not surrendered.

He heard her get up. He raised his head. He saw her walking slowly, timidly, away to the blackness. He thought of a blind child groping. He thought of an apparition apprehensive of a strange listening world of darkness and prickling stars. She stopped, her courage run out, blocked by trepidation.

'Hey, where are you going?' he called.

At his voice she ran back, propelled by fear, to the haven

of his protectiveness. She fell down on her knees beside him, big-eyed, panting.

'You come with me?'

'Where?'

'Down to that man?'

'What man?' Macauley was raised on one elbow.

'The man in the shop. And find my caterpullar. My caterpullar's in that shop.'

The urgency of determination was in her voice, on her face. It was the first real insight Macauley had into the strength of her possessiveness.

'You can't go down there now. The man's in bed.'

'We can bang on the gate and wake him up.'

'If you did that,' Macauley told her, 'he'd come out and eat you, hat and all, he'd be so cranky. In the morning, eh? We'll go down first thing in the morning.' He was pursuing the promise of appeasing her: that's all that counted. 'If your caterpillar's in that shop he'll still be there in the morning. He can't get away. Be a good girl now, will you?'

'Where's my lollies?' she said.

He didn't care whether she was grafting or not. He gave her the bag of lollies and told her to get into the burrow: and not eat them all at once. He felt her get in beside him, and he went to sleep with crunching and schlooping in his ears.

If Macauley thought time, even a little time, would heal up the wound of deprivation, he was mistaken. The child was on his hammer from the moment he woke. She pestered him impatiently. He kept telling her they would have to wait until the store opened. He couldn't even persuade her to go and look for another caterpillar while he got the breakfast ready. She hung about, getting under his feet. She fidgeted with anxiety and boredom, and didn't eat anything.

'You better get something into you,' Macauley said. 'You'll be hungry later if you don't. We've got a lot of walking to do. And I don't want you grizzling to me for tucker. Eat that toast.'

'I don't want it.'

'Okay. But remember. You get nothing till dinnertime.'

He wasn't sure whether it was because of her distraction that she couldn't eat or because she had guzzled all the lollies.

It was still only seven when he had his swag ready for the road. But he wasn't ready to start straight away. He had something else to do. The feeling kept nibbling at him, tossing up memories of a big man with a chunky face and a laugh to shake the floorboards.

'We've got somewhere else to go first,' he told Buster. 'Store'll be open when we get back. Come on.'

Macauley found the cemetery and hump of soil. He stared at it for a moment. He heard the big booming voice down there. He saw the teeth like mile-pegs clamped on and wrenching the cap off a bottle. He saw the great figure in the Santa Claus outfit coming along in the back of a dray laden with toys for the kids of the place and presents for friends, and no man left out. Many things Macauley saw.

He knelt down and weeded the grave and left it clean. Best I can do for you, mate, he thought. Six feet down and dead, you're still a better man than a lot of them up here. He had a lot of time for Callahan.

Walking away, he felt better for having paid his respects.

Buster was curious. His brief answers to her questions in the cemetery had only raised in her mind a graspless conundrum.

'What's it called again?'

'What?'

'That place.'

'The boneyard.'

'What've people got to go there for?'

'Because they're dead.'

She had no understanding of the word, no comprehension of the state of death,

'Do they put them in a big hole and cover dirt all over them?'

'That's right.'

'Can they see?'

'No. They can't see. They can't hear. They can't feel. They're like a log of wood. They're finished. They're no use to anybody any more.'

'What do they get dead for?'

'I don't know.' He had had enough. 'Forget about it now.'

Fifty yards from the store Buster left Macauley's hand and ran towards it. She had seen the open doors. He let her go. When he walked in she was searching the floor, and as hope began to fade her face clouded with dejection.

'It's gone.' She started to sob.

'She's lost a bloody caterpillar she had in her pocket,' Macauley said, to Cheetham's puzzled inquiry. 'You'd think it was a million quid.'

The storekeeper's face was touched with sympathy. He studied the little girl's movements, the anxious scouting, the lugubrious face. He saw her sit down on a bag of sugar and weep mournfully.

'You know how kids get attached to things,' he said with understanding.

'All I know is I'm going to have one helluva picnic if she doesn't find it.'

Cheetham went round the counter and squatted down in front of Buster. She hid her face in her hands away from the public gaze. Tears slipped through her fingers. She inched the fingers apart, and, having seen that he was still there, shut them quickly again.

'Go away,' she told him.

'You know what I got for you?' he coaxed.

She stopped crying, and looked at him through her fingers.

'What?' she glared.

'Something real beautiful,' Cheetham said softly, enticingly. 'You dry those tears now and come and I'll show you.'

He picked up a corner of his apron and wiped her willing face: she took the white cloth and blew her nose. Cheetham took her hand and led her towards the end of the counter. There he pointed to a tilted cardboard box filled with rag toys. Buster looked with a grave face from the storekeeper to the box and back again.

Smiling, he picked up a teddy bear. 'You like that?' She shook her head after a moment's study, and he picked up a rag doll for her approval. She didn't think much of that, either. He had showed her four or five toys, but she wouldn't settle for any of them. Macauley felt embarrassed by the child's seeming ingratitude. He seemed about to say something, when Cheetham caught his expression and shook his head with a frown of warning.

'I know,' he said. 'I'll put that box on the floor and you pick your own toy. How's that?'

They watched Buster casting amid the medley, deciding and then changing her mind again, until finally she dragged out her choice, and beamed as she turned it upside down and this way and that while the rest of the classier animals and dolls stared in dumb astonishment wondering what was the matter with them.

Macauley, too, was puzzled as he gazed at the new addition to the family. He couldn't make out what it was. It was a thing of brown felt; it looked as though it had started out to be a giraffe, changed itself to a cat, and then called off the deal at the last moment in favour of camelhood.

'What made her pick that?'

He frowned.

Cheetham shrugged his shoulders, and smiled. 'No telling with 'em, is there?' He felt he had to explain the reason for the distinction between it and the other toys. 'Made by old Mrs Evis down the road for a church bazaar. About half a dozen there were. Different kinds. You know? But nobody'd have 'em on at the fete, so I ended up taking them off the poor old thing's hands. I thought I'd tossed them all out. Must have missed that one.'

'Thank God, you did.' Macauley grinned. 'What's the damage?'

'On the house,' Cheetham said. 'I wouldn't know what to charge you, anyway.' A thought struck him as he saw Macauley lift his swag. 'Say, which way are you going?'

'West.'

'Ah, what a pity. I was going to say, young Jim Muldoon is leaving this morning. You might have got a ride in his truck. But he's going the other way.'

'Where, Moree?'

'Through there, yes. He's going to Boomi. His father's had a stroke and it doesn't look as if he'll last. So they sent for Jim.'

Boomi. Macauley turned the word over in his mind. He said, 'I heard there was a bloke looking for a burr-camp cook at Boomi.'

'That's right. He was here yesterday. Apparently they're in a bit of a spot; can't get a cook for some reason or other.'

'O'Hara?' Macauley said.

'That's the man. He's been looking all over the place, he reckoned. He left here yesterday on his way back.'

'Sam Bywater told me. You know him?'

Cheetham gave a hooting laugh. 'Old Sam, yes. He was here yesterday, too. Put the nips into me for tea and sugar and tobacco in his usual style. The biggest bludger in the country, and can't bear it. Can't help it, but can't bear it.'

'What a helluva way to be.'

'Good old stick, though. Wouldn't do you a bad turn.'

Macauley was chewing over the prospect of going to Boomi. There was no urgent hurry to get to Walgett. In fact, there was no solid reason to get there at all. It was merely a destination and a speculation. There was the chance of a job at Boomi, though if he had to walk there he wouldn't have considered it. A ride there was a different matter. It was quick and convenient. Especially with the kid. He didn't overlook the conjunction of circumstances, either. There was a hint of predestiny about them, as though fate was giving him the nudge. Why not take the opportunity?

'I think I might be in it, that ride to Boomi,' he said.

Cheetham took him out on the verandah and pointed out Jim Muldoon's place. He stood there as Macauley and Buster walked off, and he was standing there again, as though he hadn't left the spot, when an hour later the truck passed with Macauley's swag in the back. He waved, and for a long time he saw Mrs Evis's monstrosity being waved in return.

It was eight o'clock that night before the truck rattled its way down Boomi's main street. Macauley and Buster got out, and Muldoon went on. Buster watched the red tail-light dwindling in the distance. He had another seven miles to go.

Macauley knew his way about the town, but he wasn't going to bother with home cookery tonight and he wasn't going to bed-down for a while yet. During the trip he had been thinking of the job at the burr-cutter's camp, conjecturing why O'Hara was finding it so hard to get hold of a cook. Muldoon didn't know, though he had heard of the man running round like a blue-arsed fly, as he said. Macauley intended to put out a few feelers.

He went into the Greek's and sat down in a cubicle. Buster sat opposite with the strange three-part animal on her knee. They ate hungrily and in silence. Buster made a mockery of giving her charge a bite of bread.

'Eat your dinner, Gooby,' she reprimanded.

Macauley looked up. 'What'd you say?'

'When?' the child looked inquiringly at him.

'Just now. What'd you call that thing?'

'Gooby,' she said shyly.

'Gooby?' he said unbelievingly. 'Gooby?'

'Yes, that's his name.'

'Gooby. Where did you get that name from at all?'

'I don't know,' she said. 'Nowhere. He just looks like a gooby, that's all. Don't you, Gooby?' She stroked her cheek on the animal's hide with love and delight. Macauley didn't know what a gooby was, but her obvious fondness for it and the happy expression on her face stirred a strange sentiment in him as though he had been cheated of something. He thought he should have been the one to give her something like that, and he wondered why it was that he hadn't thought of doing it. He was piqued with a nag of jealousy against the man who had beaten him to the punch.

When the young white-coated Greek came to take away the plates Macauley said point-blank, 'Who's O'Hara round here?'

'O'Hara? Aw, he's an auctioneer, and a sort of contractor.'

'He offered me a job,' Macauley said, 'as a cook out at the burr-camp.'

The youth looked at him with a quick, birdlike intentness, as though he thought Macauley was about to tell a joke. 'You didn't take it?' he asked.

'I did take it.'

The Greek ran a hand over his liquorice hair and grinned. 'Boy, you're game.'

'Why do you say that?'

'Aw, I don't know,' the Greek gestured, shrugging his shoulders. 'Not very nice – you know – men out there. Fights, trouble.

Every Saturday they come to town and get drunk: come in here and give cheek and make a mess. You know.'

Macauley's hard expression didn't alter. What was a pack of toughs to the brown-eyed, soft-bellied, pasty-faced Greek was not necessarily a pack of toughs to him.

'That all you know?' he asked.

'That's enough, isn't it?' the Greek said with a grin of very white teeth.

Macauley put down the money, threw his swag up. 'Don't ever be too frightened,' he said, 'of anybody, or anything. It only helps the other bloke.'

The Greek looked after them, his face squinched in thought. Outside Macauley looked up and down the empty street. There was nothing but a few lonely lights. He walked down the road. He paused at the door of the billiard room, looking in at the green baize tables under the brilliant arc-lamps, seeing men sitting along the sides of the wall, and players making their shots in the bluish smoke atmosphere.

'You got a smoke, mate?'

The voice came from the outer darkness, and as Macauley looked a dark shape detached itself from its leaning posture against the front of the building and slunk towards him. The whites of the eyes he saw first before he saw any other feature. Then he was glancing at the beanpole figure of an Aboriginal, dressed like a pauper, from the floppy hat with the new felt crown sewn into it to the boots without laces, broken at the seams so that the sides of the feet down to the little toe extruded.

'Sure. Help yourself.'

He watched as the long fingers rolled a cigarette the size of a cigar. He knew the score. It was the Abo's wily way of taking enough tobacco for three cigarettes. After a few draws and when away from his benefactor he would gut the first cigarette and take out the makings, or, preserving it intact as the repository, would pluck just enough weed from it to roll himself a match-thin cigarette when he needed it.

'Better take a few papers, too,' Macauley invited, letting the Abo know he was a wake-up.

'Thanks, mate,' the Abo said simply.

'Listen,' Macauley tossed off the question, 'what's the strength of all this trouble they're having with cooks out at the burr camp?'

'You goin' out there?'

Macauley didn't miss the tone of the apprehensive interest.

'I'm the new cook there,' Macauley lied.

'Geez, you wouldn't get me goin' out there.' The Abo spat eloquently. 'Buggersafellas, them out there. No good.'

'How many cooks they had out there?'

'They had three – no, four. Them fussy humps, you can't satisfy 'em. They had four cooks and they all went.'

'What, turn it in, did they?'

'No, the first two, boss sacked 'em. Men was growlin' crook tucker, getting the jimmies, an' all that, they said. But they was makin' it worse than that it was. Geez, I eat anything, but them humps out there, they want the bloody King for breakfast.'

'What about the other two?'

'Well, Jimmy Abbott, he put in a week. Then he told 'em in their gunga. He give 'em some curry. He didn't have to lay down like a sheila to them, he told 'em, not when he could get twenty quid a week in Sydney cookin' for human beans, he says, instead of billygoats like them. Other bloke – forget his name – he just took his apron off one morning and said he was finished. He only lasted a fortnight. But you know what?'

'What?'

'Be all right if they let a man chuck the job and get away. But they don't. Them fellers I mentioned, them cooks, they all got hidin's. Not one of 'em left without gettin' beaten up. I tell you, them humps out there, they want shootin'.'

'Oh, well, some like to have fun.' Macauley hoisted the swag. 'So long.'

'Good luck, mate,' the Abo said. He called after him. 'Thanks for the smoke. You're a gentleman.'

Macauley and Buster camped just a little way out of the town. He was awake first and had the fire going when she woke. The first thing she did was look beside her to see if Gooby was still there. She jumped up immediately, all trace of sleep instantly gone. Macauley, squatting down, holding a broken piece of looking glass in his hand, was scraping off the whiskers with a blunt razor. His face was red when he finished. He used a dab of butter rubbed to grease in his hands as an emollient.

'Remind me to get some razor blades at the shop today,' he told Buster.

He ate slowly and thoughtfully. She fed herself and Gooby and enjoyed the pantomime. Towards nine they strolled back into the town. The shadows on the road were still damp. There was no one about but a man in a red cardigan hosing down the footpath outside the pub.

Macauley sat on his swag in the doorway of the auctioneer's office and watched the town come to life. A girl crossed the street from the bakery. He looked at the swell of her breasts and the swing of her hips and desire stirred in him. He couldn't see her features clearly when she turned her face in his direction, but just the red flash of her mouth on the white skin was enough to whip up his feelings. She was a stranger, an anonymity; he didn't know her and he felt nothing for her, but she was a woman and it was a long time since he touched the flesh of a woman. A long time since he had a wife.

In a little while the girl went back across the street, and Macauley watched her until she disappeared into the bakery.

Buster was sitting on the kerb. He looked at her back that he could span with his hand, the thin stalk of the neck as she bent her head over the toy. And somehow his thoughts seemed foolish and unclean.

A tall blond man came and opened the office. Macauley sauntered in. But he wasn't there long. The man took his name, but he told him he couldn't do anything about interviewing or hiring labour. He would have to see O'Hara, and O'Hara wasn't back yet. They didn't expect him till round about lunchtime.

The man could give him some details: where the camp was, how long the job was likely to last, the rate of pay.

Macauley went down the end of the town, lay back with his head propped against his swag and thought it over.

'Gooby wants to go for a walk, dad.'

'Gooby'll get plenty of walking,' he said.

He could knock up a decent cheque. There was plenty of tucker. It would be a break, a change off the road, a rest in a way. The bank was beginning to sound pretty hollow. And it didn't rain money.

'Gooby said he want to do his job.'

'Okay. Take him over there somewhere.'

Last job he did was a bit of fencing. With one mate. Before that, spud-digging, with two other diggers in the camp. Hard as they were, with the kid burdening him, they were more suitable than other jobs; and he saw them through and salted away the sugar.

'Gooby's finished now, dad.'

'Good. I hope he feels better.'

A man went out to that burr-cutting camp, say. It wasn't a nest of Sunday-school teachers. They were a dirty mob. How could he be a nice feller among a gang of dingos? He wasn't the type. He was a bit like that Jimmy Abbott. No backing and filling with him, either. They'd like it or lump it. He'd throw the bloody stew in their faces, but he wouldn't budge. Unlike Jimmy, he'd stay there. They might sack him, but they'd never wear him down. He'd get respect from them. He'd last the job out all right.

Macauley had no doubt about his confidence in himself. He had been in too many tough spots to fear his inability to handle another one. Always, though, he was on his own, and that made all the difference.

But this time he had a kid, and he couldn't reckon without her. It all came back to the kid – the bloody millstone of a kid. Looking after her and looking after himself at the same time: handling two kinds of trouble. And the two kinds mixing together. She had only to wake up with a nightmare, disturbing the beauties in their sleep, and there'd be trouble. Get under their big hoofs on the job and the ganger would be on his back. Get him in the gun and they'd take it out on her and on him through her, as they thought. A big number nine out of place, a candle knocked over, and she'd be accused of snooping in the huts; something missing and she'd get the blame for stealing it. Be no end to it, and he'd have to bear the weight of it all, the humiliation, the nerve-battle, the shot and shell, the whole damn lot.

Every way he thought of it, it all came back to the kid, and Macauley knew there was no more thinking to be done. It was hopelessly clear. He would not be taking the job at the burr camp.

'Gooby wants to kiss you.'

She held the animal close to his face.

'Ah, get the silly thing away from me.' He knocked it out of her hand.

'Don't!' she shrieked. She raised one hand with the fist bunched. Her eyes were brittle with anger. She relaxed in a moment and picked up the toy. 'Gooby's going to cry now.'

'Come on, and shut your trap. Only for you . . . Ah — ' He gestured helplessly, and started walking back down the street. She followed with soothing words for Gooby.

Macauley took his time. He thought he had made the decision, but as every footstep brought him nearer the main street he began to feel unsettled. The clarity of his judgement became ragged and confused. There was something opposing it, a reluctance to execute his verdict because it was giving in. It was bowing to defeat without having been defeated. It was truckling to a hypothesis, however right it may be. He didn't like the sense of belittlement he felt. He even began to wonder whether he hadn't conjured up the difficulties and formed them into a conviction so as to find a reason to prove that his rejection of the job was not dictated by cowardice.

He thought he would give himself a little longer to resolve the doubt, to make absolutely sure that he was doing the right thing. As he walked down the opposite side of the street he saw two men come out of the auctioneer's office. They stood on the kerb, staring at him. Macauley narrowed his eyes. There was something about them that caught his instinct for danger. He didn't know what it was. He knew when he was being garped at out of idle curiosity, and casually by the town loafers and the post-holders and the women with little to talk about and thirsting for sensation in their dull lives. But these men were not garping at him like that. They were staring silently, there was an air of menacing assessment in their attitudes. They had the aspect of plain-clothes police watching a mark.

Macauley stopped, lowered his swag and stood on the kerb. He pulled out his tobacco and started to make a cigarette. His head was down, but under the brim of his hat his eyes were on them.

The tall one was well-dressed in a bush-dandy way. He wore a brown pencil-stripe suit, and a brown, short-brimmed, high-crowned hat the shape of a hat block. It was tilted to one side of his head. A sponge of curly sorrel hair showed at the temple. His collar-peaks were clutched neatly together by a tie pin under the knot of his tie, and the tie itself was drawn up from the vest to form a semi-hoop. His shoes were black patent-leather pumps with pointed toes. He had square-cut jaws and a gingery look about him, the cold milky-blue complexion of blancmange lightly freckled.

The other was a blocky man, with a dark heavy face. His grey suit was unpressed, with baggy knees and dog-eared lapels. He wore an open-necked white sports shirt. The hat sat on his head like a pork pie.

Macauley leisurely drew on the cigarette and let the smoke curl away from his mouth. He glanced casually up and down the street, not appearing to be particularly interested in them.

He watched them move off, first the tall one, then the short; and they got into line, drifting slowly, not glancing at him again. Macauley followed their progress, the loose, lithe, snaky movement of the tall one, the heavy listing stride of the short. He saw them go into the pub.

He walked on down the street and stood in front of the picture show. Buster looked at the posters. Then he sauntered up again. He walked back down the street. There was something in the air, and he didn't like it much. Like when you woke sometimes at night in the bush, sensing a presence lurking about you; just like a listening nerve in the surrounds of black space, and black space filled with all the faint sounds of the bush, magnified by your blindness and hazarding imagination, and the nerve alert to distinguish the unknown among the familiar.

A truck came chugging down the street, and pulled into the kerb, and young Jim Muldoon hailed him. His light hair was unkempt, his face strained. He looked unslept. He eased himself out of the seat, and walked over to Macauley standing in the sun.

'How's the old man?'

'He's dead,' Muldoon said quietly. 'Conked out just as I got in the door.'

'What, last night?'

'Yeah.'

'Bad luck.'

'Nobody's fault. And it was quick, anyway. Just in the middle of a sentence and — Phut! Didn't know anything about it.'

'A good way to go,' Macauley said.

'Yeah. How'd you get on? Get the cook's job?'

Macauley just shook his head slightly and noncommittally, and Muldoon went on, 'Seems to be a pretty lousy turn-out. Talking to an uncle of mine at the house last night. He tells me they've had trouble there since they started. Old Ned Redshaw that owns the property, he's fed up. He's been giving O'Hara the works proper. Ned's one of his best clients and O'Hara doesn't want to lose him. Ned can make it tough for him with all the other station owners about here, too. O'Hara's in a tight corner. That's why he's running about all over the country looking for a cook.'

'A cook won't mend matters,' Macauley said, 'if that's the way they are.'

'Don't know how O'Hara came to hire them.'

'I don't suppose you're going home yet awhile.'

'No, I'll have to hang around here for a few days now. Fix up things. See what goes. Might have to take the old lady back to live with us. Funeral's tomorrow. That's why I'm in here – to make the arrangements.'

'Yeah, I see. Just thinking I might have got a ride back with you as far as Moree.'

'You're not going to worry about the job, then?'

'No, I've been thinking about it. The rough-and-tumble doesn't worry me. I'm not squibbing the issue. But' – he nodded towards Buster sitting on the kerb – 'I don't think it'd pan out.'

'No,' Muldoon said thoughtfully. 'I see what you mean.'

'A man's crazy to think of it. I don't know why I came here.'

'Well, you didn't know what you know now.'

'I knew I had a kid, that was enough,' Macauley said. He took out the makings and passed the packet to Muldoon. His eye caught sight of the tall man and his mate strolling along the footpath.

'Hey, Jim!' He licked the cigarette paper. 'See these two birds coming up on the other side? Who are they, do you know?'

Muldoon looked. He kept looking, and talked as he looked.

'Yeah, the one in the brown suit, that's Son O'Neill. Gets it easy. Standover man. Comes from down the line, Garah, but gets about, you know, wherever he can swipe a few bob. They reckon he can go the knuckle, too, but I've never seen him fight.'

'Who's the short one?'

'That's his half-brother. Frank Christy. He's a proper bad bastard, that feller.'

'Christy,' Macauley reflected. 'I've heard of him, I think. Didn't he do time for carving some bloke up at Pallamallawa?'

'Yeah, that's him,' Muldoon said. 'Some drunk who was so stewed he didn't know what day it was. Christy got twelve months, but it didn't seem to change him. He's a violent bastard. I don't think he's all there.'

Macauley watched the two men go into the auctioneer's office.

'What about a drink, Mac?' Muldoon invited.

'I could do one, but what about the kid?'

'She'll be all right, won't she? We won't be that long. I don't want to make a session of it. I had a helluva night; I feel bloody half-dead. I'd just like a drink to pick me up.'

'Okay.'

They drove down to the pub, and Macauley told Buster to stay in the truck. He left his swag in the seat beside her. Muldoon waited for him. They went into the bar together. Muldoon ordered a whisky. Macauley had a beer. There were eight or nine drinking beside themselves. The air was cool and clean. Macauley ordered the second round when Christy and O'Neill came in. They ambled slowly down to the centre of the counter, and the barmaid pulled two beers for them.

Macauley noticed the look on Muldoon's face as the men passed. He saw him swallow. There was an impression of subdued agitation and haste about him.

'Come on, Mac, drink it up and let's get out of here.'

'Take your time,' Macauley said. 'Drink it fast, and you can't taste it.'

Muldoon gave a little grin. 'Sure, I know, but it's just that I want to see that undertaker and get it over and done with.'

'I know,' Macauley said, and drained his glass.

Muldoon was ahead of him as they walked casually towards the door, and Muldoon was saying something about there being nothing like a whisky to pull a man up, and then he was through the opening, and Macauley had just reached it when he stopped, arrested by the voice.

'Hey! You!'

He turned in the doorway. O'Neill was walking towards him, with that soft, rolling, cat-footed walk. He looked at the dead white face. The eyes where a pale icy-blue. O'Neill's coat was open, and Macauley observed the slight beer-drinker's paunch.

'You talking to me?'

O'Neill didn't answer. He stood fixedly at Macauley. Macauley's gaze was unswerving. He waited. Christy moved round to the left of his mate. There was a black stony glitter in his eyes, a glare of hostility on his brutal face, dark with stubble. He couldn't keep his lips still. He licked them, bulged them, worked them back in a snarl.

'Want to have a word with you,' O'Neill said. He had a soft drawling voice, not unpleasant on the ear.

Macauley stepped out on to the footpath. The two other men followed. O'Neill stood opposite Macauley. Christy ranged himself again on the left. Macauley saw Jim Muldoon, standing on the edge of the verandah, some six feet away, looking like a friend waiting for another.

'What is it? Macauley said.

'You going to take that job cooking at the burr camp?'

Macauley looked from O'Neill to Christy and back again.

'I might. Why?'

'My mate here's after that job, too.'

'Yeah?' Macauley said.

'Dickson, down in O'Hara's office, says you applied first; you get first preference. There's only two in it, you and my mate here. And as I said, my mate wants that job.'

'We both can't have it, can we?' Macauley said quietly.

'No,' agreed O'Neill. 'That's why you got to forget about it.'

'Come on, Mac,' Jim Muldoon urged helpfully.

'In other words,' O'Neill went on, deliberately placing the words, 'you just don't turn up at O'Hara's office. It's easy that way, and nobody gets hurt. See?'

Macauley felt the palms of his hands sweating. He felt the churning sensation start up in his stomach. He knew there was only one way out of this. Somebody would have to back down, but it wouldn't be him. That went without saying, and if the two men before him knew anything about his character they would have realised it.

'But, I want that job, too.'

O'Neill squinched up his eyes into blue crystals. 'Listen, mug, I'm not playing a game. You'll do what you're told.'

Macauley felt the old familiar sensation of his pride and independence being placed on trial. The wrath in him was swinging on a thread, and the thread was unskeining itself with the strain. He burned with the old contempt and hatred for those who took him cheaply. The fact of these two even considering him for intimidation scorched his self-esteem. Their efforts to daunt him, if they but knew it, only made a gun for his hand, bullets to fit it, cocked it, and wrapped his finger round the trigger.

'You go back to that office,' Christy threatened, 'and I'll tear your guts out.'

'What guts?' O'Neill asked smoothly.

That was as far as Macauley would go. He wanted to set his shoulders and bunch his fists and let the words fly at O'Neill: You can spot the stranger that comes on a visit and mark him down; you can swagger the streets at shearing-time and reap a harvest; but don't lump me in with the weakies and the yellow-bellies busting their cheques over a good time; the curs and the possums who get silly-drunk and fall in fear to your authority. He had seen pigs like Christy powtering in the slops, all grunt and hair. He wanted to tell him to get back in the pen.

But he had to go canny. He couldn't handle two of them together. Aware of the tension, but undismayed by it, he glanced across at Jim Muldoon, standing uncomfortably, chewing a matchstick. He couldn't expect much help from him. He noticed the three or four men watching from the road, and the group inside the pub getting their view through the door. There'd be no help from them, either. This was between him and O'Neill and Christy.

Macauley relaxed. He edged his body casually into position. Then he shrugged.

'I'm not used to being told what I have to do,' he said, 'that's all.'

'Well, what's it going to be?' O'Neill said, already disarmed by Macauley's tone of abjection.

'Maybe you're right,' Macauley said.

And he was perfectly placed, left shoulder thrust out, with the utterance of the last word. In the moment of his victory, in the split second of his laxity, O'Neill was stunned with surprise. Macauley threw his right with the whole tremendous power of his body behind it. He felt O'Neill's belly give like a rubber ball. He felt the expulsion of air in his face. Lightning-like he carried the same fist upwards in a blow that clapped O'Neill's jaws together like the shut of an oven door. Then he danced back, ready for Christy, but Muldoon was wrestling with Christy like a terrier with a baboon.

O'Neill's knees bent outwards. His hands hung slackly at his sides. He was like a girder canting before it drops; a figure collapsing in slow motion. Blood oozed down his chin from his broken mouth. His eyes rolled. But Macauley's eyes glittered with relish. They were eyes of steel. His back arched. He hooked with the left and the right, joggling O'Neill's head this way, then that. And, still, as he was going down, Macauley found time for a hard right that smashed O'Neill's nose. He poised on his knees for a moment, then fell sideways in the dust.

It all happened so quickly the crowd were flabbergasted.

Macauley took in a glance the uneven tussle between Christy and Muldoon. Muldoon was wobbling, his teeth bared like a snarling dog's with exhaustion. A haymaker caught him on the side of the head, dropping him cold. Christy, his chest heaving like a bellows, ran forward and drew back his boot to kick in Muldoon's head, but Macauley knocked him off balance, hit him with a straight left, and sent him stumbling backwards to fall against the pub wall. He sat there, shaking his head, glowering.

The onlookers were coming from everywhere now, making a crude and pliant ring; some calling to stop it; others to fight it out.

'Get up, Christy. You're not licked yet.'

'I got ten bob on the bagman.'

Macauley ripped off his coat and spat on his hands. A feathery smile touched the corners of his mouth, but only a killer gleam flashed in his eyes. This was what he liked: a fight. And better still a fight with a cause for it; a thrashing with a reason to it.

He watched Christy get up, using the wall for support. Macauley wasn't certain whether he was going to come out for more. Then he knew he was. And it stiffened him. For a moment he felt a spasm of fear. Christy grabbed the bottle from the crates of empties stacked against the wall and, gripping the neck, broke off its base against the bricks.

Then he stood there with a different look on his face – an expression of malignant humour. He held the jagged weapon out and slowly turned his wrist in the air with a grinding motion.

'Put it away, Christy, and fight fair.'

'Stop it, someone, or there'll be murder.'

Macauley heard the terrifying shriek of his daughter, but he didn't turn his face. Next second she flung herself at him, trying to drag him away by the hand, looking with terror at Christy.

'Get away!' he cried. 'Get back there. For God's sake, take this kid, someone.'

Two men grabbed her and dragged her back.

Macauley waited coolly now. His nerves were sitting down, trembling with vigour. But there was a darkness on his face like a black light. His eyes were as cold as a shark's.

'Make it good, Christy,' he said. 'Don't miss the first time. Because there won't be a second.'

The words set Christy back, and the expression on his face changed as though he were momentarily unsure of himself against this man. He circled. Macauley watched him tensely. He knew Christy would keep circling, inching closer, till he got him into position. Then he'd rush, bottle out-thrust, grip his antagonist, and twist the jagged glass in his face. It could go on for thirty minutes like this, stalking, circling, waiting for an opening, as though he himself were equally armed.

Macauley had no intention of waiting that long.

'You're a gutless wonder, Christy,' he gibed. 'What's holding you back? Even with that, you're still a dingo. Will I put one arm behind me?'

Some in the crowd laughed. Fury leapt on to Christy's face. Macauley took the initiative. He was ready for the rush. He knew what his strategy would be. Its success depended on perfect timing, split-second action. If he made a slip his face would be prettied up for life. He realised that.

He took a few steps towards Christy, and Christy fell for the feint. He lunged forward. Macauley stood on the spot. He was perfectly still. His eyes were on the frightful weapon. He saw it to within a foot of his face; then precisely at the right moment he flicked his head to one side and the weapon arm slid over his shoulder.

Christy came with it to jerk up short, as Macauley's right hand clutched his throat, the steely fingers digging in and squeezing. In the same instant Macauley gripped Christy's sleeve with his left hand and held it rigidly away from him, partly across his right arm. He didn't know how long he could keep it there, but he had to keep it there, and the only instrument he had to shorten the time was Christy's throat. His hold was like the jaws of a trap.

For a moment Christy was bewildered by the suddenness of the turn that left him victoryless and at a disadvantage. Then he struggled. He tried to jerk his arm free. He swung over his left. He brought up his knees, seeking to disable Macauley. All the time he was staggering backwards, sideways, coughing and choking, dragging the inflexible hand with him. He tried once more for Macauley's groin, but Macauley fended the blows with the side of his thigh.

Then Christy had to drop the bottle. He wrenched his right arm free and fastened his left and right hand on the arm that was squeezing the life out of him, desperately striving to drag it away. But once Macauley knew the danger of the bottle was past he unclenched his fingers and Christy fell away. He clawed at his throat. Everybody in the crowd saw the marks there. They were marks that might have been made by an iron gauntlet.

Macauley went in with his shoulder out. The shirt was tight on his back. The blow struck Christy on the temple and spun him round. But he was tough. He rushed in like a bull, his face distorted with hate and ferocity. Macauley sidestepped, slammed a right into his belly, and let him pitch grunting on to the ground. He staggered up, and the pleasure was all Macauley's. Methodically he chopped his man to pieces. He picked him off, sapping his power, paralysing his muscles, driving him about and around like a frenzied bullock in a corral. He shambled blindly.

But Macauley had no mercy.

'Here I am, Christy. Can't you see me? Look. Here.'

And his huge hands, half closed, would thump on Christy's ribs, his jaw, his chin, hard enough to hurt, but not hard enough to knock him out.

'No more,' Christy gasped. 'No more.'

'No more?' echoed Macauley. 'I haven't started yet. There's a lot more. I've got to get you down. I've got to get the boot in yet. I've got to fillet your ugly phiz for you with your own broken bottle.'

'No! No! No more!'

Jim Muldoon left the crowd and put an arm round Macauley's shoulder. 'Come on, Mac, he's finished. You'll kill him. Turn it in.'

Macauley brushed him aside. Then he looked round at Muldoon's white face and pleading eyes.

'All right, Jim,' he said. 'But this is for you.'

And with that he moved over to Frank Christy, lifted the helpless man's chin and drove a right uppercut underneath it. Christy's feet left the ground and he fell with a thud on his back and lay still.

For almost a minute the crowd stood stunned. Then their ranks buckled and men swarmed. They carried Christy and the still semi-conscious O'Neill into the yard of the pub. Some gathered around Macauley gaping in admiration, congratulating him, telling him Christy had been looking for that for a long time.

'Come on, Mac,' Muldoon urged, taking Macauley's arm, 'we'd better get out of here.'

'I'm going after that job,' Macauley said.

'What?'

'You'd think I'd let that bastard have it? Coming at me with a bottle. Putting the bounce into me.'

Muldoon wasn't going to argue: the battle smoke was still in Macauley's nostrils.

'All right, but have a clean-up first. You're blood from head to hocks. Not here. I know a place.'

'It'll be too late.'

'It won't be too late. Get in.'

He dumped Macauley's swag in the back, and Macauley got in beside Buster. Her face swollen with crying. She was whining like a fan.

'What the hell's the matter with you?' he snapped.

He didn't get an answer, but she stopped whimpering. She looked up at him. 'Look, you're all bleedy.'

'What's a bit of blood?'

He picked up the animal off her knee; dandled it. 'You know what she calls this, Jim?'

Muldoon half smiled. 'Yeah, I know.'

'Gooby,' Macauley said, and he laughed uproariously as though he had just seen the joke.

Muldoon knew a friend of his father. They spruced up there. Macauley put on a clean shirt from his swag. They were only there half an hour. The old people wanted them to have some dinner, but Macauley declined. He was anxious to get away. They gave Buster a biscuit and a glass of milk.

Going back in the truck Muldoon grinned with admiration. 'Just thinking of the way you toppled O'Neill. The way you threw those punches. All in a flash. I've only seen one thing quicker, and that's a cat.'

'It wasn't all that good,' Macauley shrugged. 'I didn't give O'Neill a chance to show what he could do. The other bastard, Christy – he's just a big mug.'

'You certainly can use 'em all right, Mac.'

'I've had my share of hidings,' Macauley said.

The truck drew into the kerb and Macauley shot out quickly and into O'Hara's office. Dickson, the man with the pear-shaped face and short-cropped sharp hair who had taken his name that morning, looked at him with an expression of surprised scrutiny as though the man before him was incapable of earning the reputation that had preceded his appearance.

'Where's O'Hara? Is he back yet?'

'Yes,' Dickson answered. 'But I don't think — '

At that moment O'Hara walked in from the adjoining office. He was a thickset man with a bay window coming along nicely, and a round fat face red and glossy as a wax apple. His plastered black hair was tinged with grey at the sides. He wore a well-kept navy-blue suit. He sat in the chair vacated by Dickson, who moved over to the window and leant on a filing cabinet, still scrutinising.

'So you're Macauley?' O'Hara said, looking up with a faint fixed shrewd smile. 'They tell me you've been livening the town up a bit.'

'What about this job at the burr camp?' Macauley said, impatiently getting down to business. 'I'd like a start.'

'Sorry,' O'Hara said. 'You're a bit late. I've got a man.'

'A bit late?' Macauley said. 'What mullarky is this?' he demanded. 'I come all the way from Millie for this job. I had my name down first thing this morning. Christy was after me.'

The smile stayed fixed on O'Hara's face. 'I didn't say anything about Christy,' he said easily, blunting Macauley's impetuosity. Macauley stared at him, and O'Hara went on, 'I picked up a man at Collarenebri. He's down at the pub now. He'll be on his way to the job this afternoon.'

Macauley was still doubtful. 'But they said when you left Millie you were heading straight back here.'

'That's right,' O'Hara said. 'But I changed my mind. That's why I didn't get back here till just an hour ago.' He opened a tin of cigarettes and held it out. Macauley shook his head and drew the makings out of his pocket.

O'Hara lit the cigarette and looked at the burning match in his. 'I couldn't have given you the job, anyway, Macauley.'

'Why not?'

'I'd have been just asking for more trouble and it would have been signing your death warrant.'

'Ah, break it down,' Macauley said.

'Listen to me,' O'Hara said, beginning to get nettled by Macauley's truculent forthrightness. 'They're twenty-five men out there. At least fifteen of them are Christy's mates. They'd be on to you like a pack of mad dogs. Even if it didn't matter to you, getting your brains bashed out, it matters to me. I don't want any more trouble. I've had enough of it.' He took a hard drag on the cigarette, and the smoke spiralled out of his nostrils as he went on with vehemence. 'Listen, you've knocked about. You know there are bad types of men everywhere. They get into sheds and camps all over the place, but only in ones and twos. And you know what happens. They get sat on straight away. They soon get shown their place. The good fellers won't take any shenanigan from them, and either they toe the line or take the consequences. But, look, out there is the worst mob of bastards ever collected on one job. You wouldn't credit it. There's not one amongst them worth a razoo. When the job's finished they can go to hell. They'll never get a look-in with me again. I'd sack the whole bloody lot now if the shearing wasn't on and it was easier to get men.'

'Well, that seems to sew it up,' Macauley said.

He was ready to go, and O'Hara should have left it at that. But he was a family man, with traditional steadfast ideas about married life and parenthood. And he was curious as well. But he put it this way, 'If it'll make you feel any better I'll tell you this. Even if you hadn't touched Christy and I hadn't engaged another man; even if I wanted a burr cook right now, I still wouldn't have given you the job.'

Macauley looked at him questioningly.

'You have a little girl,' O'Hara said, with an air of virtuous contempt. 'A mere baby. I would no more think of letting her go out there than I would one of my own children. Not only because of the trouble there'd be, but it's no place for a child. The life you lead is no life for a child. What sort of man are you even to entertain the idea of trucking her with you to a job like that?'

'It's like your bloody ignorance to ask,' Macauley flashed. He put his hands on the desk and leant forward. He said succinctly, 'You stay in your own backyard, O'Hara. Your mind's not big enough for anything outside it, and it's not going to grow any more. When you can run your own business efficiently then maybe you'll have reason to tell me how to run mine.'

He walked out. The earth had gone dull. A light wind was blowing from the north, flapping and banging the canvas blind half unfurled between the verandah posts.

'No go?' said Muldoon, reading his face.

'No go,' Macauley said, and Muldoon, curious as he was, could see that Macauley was in no temper to be asked the why and wherefore. He would find out later, he thought.

'Looks like we might get a drop of rain out of this,' he remarked casually, for something to say against the silence of Macauley's cold fury.

Then as he glanced up and down the street his attitude changed, and he said quickly, 'Look out, here comes a dirty big blue thing. Get in the truck. Quick!'

Macauley looked up sharply. 'It's too late,' he said. 'He's seen us.'

The sergeant of police lumbered towards them, pressing the ground as he walked as though one of his missions in life was to flatten the earth. He was chesty and neckless, with jowls like a bulldog.

'You Macauley?'

'That's me.'

'I can run you in.'

'God, what for?' Macauley said, astonished.

'You know what for. Offensive behaviour and a few others in the book.'

Macauley affected a look of mystification. Then his face suddenly brightened. 'Oh, you mean the little — Why, sergeant, it was nothing. Just a little falling out among friends. You know how it is?'

'I know how it is, all right,' said the sergeant. 'You intend to prefer charges?'

'Charges?'

'Didn't Christy attack you with a broken bottle?'

'Not that I noticed, sergeant.' Macauley let him know how he stood about the matter.

'You've got an hour to get out of town.'

'But my friends . . .' Macauley began with pretended concern, wondering if he alone was to be penalised.

'Don't worry, they'll be taken good care of,' the sergeant assured him. He held up one podgy finger. 'An hour.'

'Fair enough,' Macauley said.

They watched him dawdle off, his hands behind his back, his trouser whipping about his legs like tattered sails.

'He's all right,' Macauley said.

'What'll you do now, Mac?'

'Get on my way.'

'You'd better come out home with me,' Muldoon offered. 'For a few days.'

Macauley patted him on the shoulder. 'No,' he said. 'You've got your troubles, Jim. And I wouldn't be much help to you with them. So long.'

They shook hands, and Muldoon had a lonely, sad look on his boyish face.

'I'm hungry, dad.' Buster said.

Muldoon forced a grin as though to ease his departure. 'Well, I better go and see about the funeral.' He pulled the self-starter and the engine jerked into life and gobbled painfully.

Macauley took a few steps forward and placed a hand on Muldoon's arm. 'I forgot to mention, Jim: only for you taking care of that dunhead in the early part it might have been a different story.'

Muldoon made a disclamatory gesture with his hand, but there was great pleasure on his face, and that was the look Macauley remembered as the truck drove away.

'Where's Jim going?' Buster asked, scratching one leg with the other. 'He's a good Jim,' she added.

Macauley looked down the long dull stretch of road running south. He looked at the windy sky and the hastening cloud. There was nothing else for it. The clock was on him.

He pulled back the gauze doors and went into the baker's shop. There was the smell of new bread and clean bags. He tinkled the little hand-bell on the counter. A girl in a white smock came from the back of the shop. It was the girl he had seen cross the road early that morning. He felt a lift in his spirits. Her smile was friendly, but disinterested. It went with the job more than it went with her personality.

'Can you fix me up for a coupla pies and a loaf of bread?' he said.

'Certainly.' She had a soft voice. She turned and bent over a bin. He ran his eye over her figure, round the coastline and up and down the hinterland. He saw the silken shapely legs up to the thighs, and caught the glimpse of lace on her petticoat. They teased the hunger in him. They cajoled his imagination. She turned again, and he fed on her soft, smooth, shapely arms as she rolled up the bread.

In a minute she set the pies down in front of him with the same ready smile. Her eyes were shiny like a dark syrup. Her lips were soft and voluptuous. Her hair was jet and curly. Macauley stared at her with a bold deliberate impassivity, as though she were a figurine on a shelf. She flushed a little and averted her eyes; otherwise her poise seemed unaffected, though he noticed her fluster as she took the money and placed it in the till.

'Wonder if I could get this filled too?' He dumped the empty waterbag on the counter.

Her glance was more interested this time, more part of her personality than a part of the job. It was unsure, but wanted to be probing. She nodded and took the bag. She returned, wiping it with a cloth.

'I'm sorry. It spilled over.'

Macauley kept his eyes on her as he untied the tuckerbag. She seemed glad to find a diversion in Buster. She said impulsively, 'Would the little girl like some cakes? They're a wee bit stale, but quite nice. If you don't mind taking them.'

That's what he liked. That type. They didn't thrust it at you as though you were a down-and-out in need of their charity. They thought of your self-respect. They gave you the benefit of having some.

'Not at all.'

He watched her selecting the cakes from the window, appraising the curves of her hips and buttocks, the tight swell of her breasts as he reached into the corners.

She came back. 'There you are, dear.'

Buster took the bag, instantly opened it, and peered in. She closed it and looked up shyly, hugging the parcel, thrilled with pleasure, but controlling it, just in case to express it before the girl would have made her feel self-consciously foolish.

'Well, we'll be pushing off,' Macauley said.

'Going far?' the girl asked, failing to disguise her more intimate tone of voice.

'Moree.'

'All that way – heavens!'

'Be there in a few days.'

'How're you travelling?'

'Shanks,' he said.

'What?'

'Walking.'

She didn't seem interested in the answers; only in the intrigue of flirtation, the delaying facility of conversation. She looked at him again, meeting his eyes. In hers there was an argument of wavering. She seemed to be daring them to remain fixed against the inflexibility of his brazen-browed gaze. Finally, she lost and looked quickly away. 'It's going to rain, too.'

'Might.'

'I can feel it in my bones. They always ache when it's going to rain.'

'My bones ache, too,' Macauley said. 'But it's not with rain.'

Her gaze swung back to his again. Their eyes clashed. She flushed a deep red.

'And if you want to know what it is,' Macauley said, turning at the door, 'I'll tell you at the dance next year.'

Some twenty yards from the shop, Macauley told Buster to look behind them and see if the girl was watching them. Buster said she was standing on the shop step. Macauley smiled to himself.

Some would have hit him a swipe over the moosh, he thought, if he looked at them the way he had looked at her. But she was the romantic type who played furtively for excitement – the nice quiet type, the quiet waters running deep, the best of the lot. The cheeky ones, the ones that knew all the answers, they split into two kinds: they were barber's cats, all wind and water, or they were town bikes. The first had never been closer to a man than the heat of his eyes and the panting of his breath, and they saw to it they never got any closer. They screamed for help when the game got real. The second, they were so often in the saddling paddock it wasn't natural.

Yet, Macauley realised as he thought of her that the girl meant nothing to him. He didn't know whether her name was Susie or Fanny. He didn't know whether she could read or write; whether she studied the piano, ate meat on Fridays and helped little Oscar with his homework. He didn't know whether she suffered from constipation, took sugar in her tea or squeezed her face before the mirror. He knew nothing about her background and habits, and he didn't care. He wasn't shook on her. She was just a stimulus for his virility and an image on which to sublimate it. She was no more than the embodiment of carnality.

And that way she stayed with him as he trudged on.

The rain came with a helter-skelter brustle at the end of the murky evening. There was no shelter. A light glimmered like a star through the scrub, but it was a long way away. Macauley knew there was a bridge over a dry watercourse ten minutes walk ahead, and he hurried towards it, Buster beside him, neck drawn down.

'Hold my hand,' she screeched, as Macauley picked his way down the gully and came in under the bridge on the higher ground. They found a spot and sat there, Macauley needing to bend forward to keep his head from touching the planks. They said nothing. All was darkness and the slish, the wet tossing of wind. The rain drummed on the bridge and dripped through the chinks of the deck, unseen and unseeing but finding the flesh of their hands and faces, forcing them to shuffle together like dogs in the roost of that bank. The wet wind swirled in. He was cold. He felt the kid beside him shivering. He unstrapped the bluey and threw a blanket over their legs and bodies and the groundsheet over that.

This was no hardship for Macauley. This was apple and pie. In out of the rain and getting warm. A real nook, snug and cosy – comfort could have been improved a bit – but, hell, who'd growl about that. Could have been worse. He could have been out there in the boo-eye, thrusting his body into the wind and rain, getting blown about like an old moll at a plonk party. He expected to hear Buster complain, but no complaint came.

On the contrary, she snuggled against him with pleasure, with impulses of delight.

'I like it here, dad,' she said joyfully. 'It's nice.'

He was reflecting on the day and its happenings. He was thinking of a thousand things, done and going and to come. Sparks of thought that flared and died; pictures that focused and blurred. He saw Christy's face, and he could see it as a baby with the dirty whiskers on it still and the same murderous eyes, and to think that a mother loved it, even though Christy the baby took his milk bottle and smashed the end of it and playfully jabbed it in his mother's face, the dear little thing. The thought made him chuckle.

Buster chuckled, too, infectiously.

And Macauley thought of Jim Muldoon, nervous as a dog with a ghost, shit-scared, and yet coming in to lend a hand: hanging around, not turning tail and finding a hurried excuse to be somewhere else. Muldoon, white to the gills, with the sick nausea of fear in his belly – and yet coming in to lend a hand. That took guts. Real guts.

And he thought of the girl. Minny, Mary or Mable. And he wanted her. And he saw how he wanted her. He wanted her running away from him laughing; and he wanted to catch her and take her and stop the laughing and hear the sweet groaning, the rapture, the last delicious frenzy, and stand up and away from her, the masterful, the vanquisher, leaving her wounded with ecstasy.

Then when he heard the snores at his side it all passed, the whole passionate delusion, and he became aware of the frail weight against him with the straw hat drooping. He looked down. There was a melancholy in the reality of the wind and rain and darkness. He felt as though somebody had been looking into the privacy of his thoughts, and the feeling in turn gave him a sense of wretchedness and abasement.

'Ah, Christ!' he said dully.

He looked again at the sleeping child, and he was incensed, inflamed to a quick malice, spoiling for the release of his guilty anger. He shook her roughly. 'Hey, wake up. Wake up. You'll get a crick in your neck.'

She jerked, and he saw her eyes open in an unconscious stare and nod again, and he felt her slump gently on her return to sleep. His lips tightened, but he went no farther. He eased her back against the hard earth, and she lay there with her head to one side. He twisted his hands with tension, but it was going from him, and he was feeling easier, and in a little while he was all right, quiet and reasoning. He took a look at himself and he stood by what he saw.

I'm a man, he thought. And I want a woman. That's straight. I won't deny it before God himself. If I didn't want one I'd start to think there was something the matter with me. I want a woman all right. Leave it at that. For all the good it is thinking about it, I might as well be docked. Leave that as it is, too. I don't have to go on like a pimply-faced whore-chaser, do I?

The rain didn't look like diminishing, though the wind was sweeping about in a twist of currents, and blowing now against the side of the bridge. He drew his feet up, put his arms round his legs and rested his chin on his knees. He saw the faint glisten of water below his boots. There was nothing else to do but stay where he was. He had no regrets. He knew what he would have done if he had had the choice. He wouldn't have left Boomi. He would have hung round there until the weather declared itself. Nobody but a bunny with his brains bashed out would venture a black-soil road with a sky ready to leak at any tick of the clock.

But Boomi was no good. Not when a copper put a time limit on a man. It never paid to cross a john. They had memories like elephants and they could be as vindictive as a tossed-out mother-in-law. They had the weight and they could throw it about; if they were a bit nasty from birth let alone from other reasons the uniform gave authority to the dirt in their natures. Defy an order, get tough, and you might as well wipe off a town for good. They never let you stay in it on your return. A few hours, and they had smelled you out and were giving you the push: We're moving you on; we don't want your type here. Get going. They could do more than that. They could throw you in the peter stone-cold sober, mess up your good looks, take your clothes and fling them back at you next morning with your roll missing and only a few bob left in your pockets to help you heed the advice they dished out: Get out of here, you drunken hooer.

And once they gave you the prod to get out of town it was a good idea to do it without delay. The sergeant back there – he wasn't a bad bloke. But he would have picked him all right, and if he wasn't the type to put the boot in later, to hold a grudge in perpetuity, he wouldn't have spared him when it came to the magistrate hearing about the trouble in the town. And what a fool a man would have been to put that trouble on his back when it could be avoided. Without delay – that was always the ticket. Because sometimes they changed their minds. Even though the sergeant back there that wasn't a bad bloke looked the other way, became a lamb of the law for a moment, instead of a limb about it, it was quite on the cards for him to come back five minutes later and pinch a man.

So he left the town, and in leaving it he knew what might lie ahead. But the risk had to be taken. There was always the chance of striking a farmhouse, a camp, an old shack with an old man living in it alone since the wife died; or the other way about. And there was always a chance that the change in the weather wouldn't come to anything.

But tomorrow is the worry. Plodding along on that sticky road. They wouldn't make much headway. And there wouldn't be much chance of a lift. Traffic would be held up. Still, no use thinking about that now; time enough later. But he wished he was on his own. On his own he would have tackled it without a thought and kept going, slow and all as the going might be. With the kid it was doubly hard; more than that – a failure from the start.

Macauley passed a hand over his eyes. He felt the ache of weariness behind them and the drag of sleep. He reshuffled himself so that he could lay his head back. He wriggled the stones more comfortably under his back. He slipped his hat over his face to keep off the spray, dug his heels into the dirt to keep his propped position and dozed.

Suddenly he pricked up his ears. There was a new sound in the wind and the rain and it belonged to neither. Macauley sat up. He strained his hearing, the sound was irregular, a beat, then a vague elusive note. It was distant and whiffling, but a reality. He scrambled carefully from under the bridge and peered round the pitchy, blown countryside. Far down the road, but approaching, he saw two blurry orbs of yellow light.

He scuttled back and shook Buster awake, and he let her sit up and rub and yawn the sleep away as he quickly heaped the swag into a convenient roll, which was all he could do in the circumstances. He strapped it tightly.

'What's the matter, dad?'

He didn't answer. He lurched away, and looked down the road again. The orbs were bigger. He waited. He heard the sound coming up stronger – *chukkachukkachukkachukka*. It was like a winch running out the cable. What sort of maniac was this he wondered. But he wasn't worrying. Didn't matter if it was the Devil himself so long as he could help them.

'Come on,' he said to Buster. She clutched his trouser leg as he clambered up the slope and squelched on to the roadway. He stood in the middle, waving his hands. Buster took the lead and waved hers. The rain beat in their faces. They saw the lidless eyes coming up bigger, glaring in the seethe of rain, and, unsure that he was seen, Macauley stepped to the side of the road, still waving, shouting. He heard the sound of the engine change to a *chud-chud* of dying power. The truck stopped.

'How far are you going?' Macauley cupped his hands to his mouth, walking round to the driver's side.

A nose and eyes between hat and coat collar was all he saw pressed against the window.

'Right through – Moree.'

'You got room for a couple more?'

The answer came from the back of the truck. 'Yeah, come on, mate, hop on.'

Another voice said, 'Hurry up, for the luvva Mike, and let's get moving.'

Macauley looked at the window and the nose was motioning him to climb aboard. He dumped his swag in willy-nilly and heard the yelp of a dog. He lifted Buster and willing hands grabbed her. The truck had started off, clugging madly, as Macauley hauled himself over the sideboards. His legs and arms touched men and dogs: if they didn't touch them in one direction they touched them in another.

'Up here, mate, there's a possy, if you can work yourself in.'

Macauley found there were five men altogether. Three were in the tray. Their mate, an old man, they let sit under cover with the tin lizzie's owner and driver, Slippery Dick. Now with him and Buster added, that made twelve of a kind in the back of the little truck – seven sheepdogs, four men and a child, and all their gear. The only covering they had was a couple of station-tweed blankets, or woolpacks.

The dogs were tied up short, three on one side and four on the other. The truck slithered sharply, zigzagged, then righted itself again.

'Seems to be in a hurry,' Macauley said.

'Ah, the bastard's mad; he'll have us all killed before he's finished.'

'Can't wait to get home to mum.'

'He won't be on no bloody nest if he keeps that up.'

Macauley knew this Slippery Dick by name, repute, and to look at, but he had never had any personal truck with him. He was tall and lean with melancholy eyes. He had some ginger hair on his head – that was if you could find it – and some more on his top lip. His face was like a withered passionfruit. He was a drover and burr-cutters' cook, and possessed very little regard for his personal appearance.

As the truck went for another snaky slide, men and beasts were all thrown together, rolling from one side to the other.

'By hell, Slippery Dick's right,' someone called out.

'I heard his name was Dirty Dick,' another man said. 'In the burr camps as a cook. But he changed it a bit to Slippery.'

'What's the flamin' difference? I'll bet he was still slippery with dirt and grease in the cookhouse, and you couldn't look at him there without slippin' your eyes.'

The night seemed to get even darker and the continual rain swept and swamped them as they sat and kneeled in all positions amongst the dogs, all fighting in the little congested area for cover under the station nap. The old boneshaker didn't improve their hearing. It seemed to become frantic – chugging, coughing, spluttering, backfiring – as though it were about to come down with a bad turn. Macauley said he didn't think it could swim. It was slipping and sliding everywhere now and churning the mud into their midst.

They whirled sometimes through space, it seemed to them, and not with the greatest of ease, either: sometimes the truck would nearly turn round as though to go back the way it had come. But the worst was to come. They had been traversing the best part of the road, it appeared to them, when they saw what they were up against now.

The truck began to drag, stick, skid, pull away, and crawl on again. But not for long. It staggered on lumpy wheels. It clawed the mud out of its face. It tried hard, but it was on its tyres. It signified defeat with a whine and a flutter. When everybody had thought that life had gone, it fooled them by giving a last fizzy burp, leaping forward and collapsing with a jerk.

Slippery Dick got out.

One of the men cried cheerfully, 'What have we stopped for, Slippery – tea and scones?'

Slippery Dick was moving around the vehicle, his boots clogging and squelching, the rain drumming on his hat. 'She's broken down – and if that wasn't enough we're flamin' well bogged as well.'

'Give it away, Slippery. Let's stick it out here till the mornin'.'

'Mornin', be buggered,' said Slippery Dick. 'You want us to get bogged proper, dumped here for a week. I want to get home before the road gets too bad.'

The men laughed heartily. 'How is he?'

'Come on, you pack of lazy cows,' Slippery Dick said. 'While there's life there's hope, my mother always said.'

'If your mother was like you,' came the retort, 'she'd tell you anything.'

For all their badinage the men were glad of the change from their cramped quarters, and the dogs were pleased, too, to feel they had more room and station-tweed. Macauley told Buster to stay where she was in the corner and he jumped down with the rest. They rolled their trousers up to the knees, ready for any emergency while Slippery repaired the disordered truck. It was only a minor trouble, according to him, and he muttered about spark plugs and distributors. They felt the babble was all designed to keep them good-tempered.

Finally, he got the engine started, and with all hands pushing hell-on-wheels, as Macauley christened the truck, struggled to get free. She roared in low gear, grinding fruitlessly, jerking, spinning her wheels hysterically. The men joked and chaffed Slippery Dick. He wanted to be careful the engine didn't drop out of her, they told him. It didn't matter about the mudguards falling off. They were no use anyway. Was a safety pin any good to him, they wanted to know.

'Righto,' squealed Slippery Dick with the strain. 'This time.'

'Okay. Let her go.'

They put all their weight behind hell-on-wheels. With demented screeching and rapturous straining she made a terrific effort, clearing herself.

'Good on yer, Slippery.'

'Keep pushing, for God's sake,' bleated Slippery. 'I don't want her to cut out again.'

He kept her going slowly for about two miles with the men pushing from the ground, skidding in mud and slush. One man lost his footing and down he went bodily into the sticky spew. Slowly as they were moving, he had to move quickly to catch up, twisting and slithering like a drunk on a dance floor, and not without having several more falls. When he grabbed the tailboard he was laughing. It was he they ought to call Slippery Dick after that, he reckoned.

'All right,' Slippery Dick shouted back. 'I think we can get along good enough now if you get into the truck.'

They clambered in, just a mass of mud, glued and dried to their legs and arms and faces, and while the old rattletrap, giving out noises to terrify the countryside, dragged itself doubtfully along the road in the drizzling darkness, a fight went on for the survival of the fittest between men and dogs.

The dogs were more hostile than they had been during the first part of the journey, for while the truck was being pushed they had had the relief of more room and the comfort of the woolpacks, but now the interlopers were back – and they were rougher and bigger men with the stickfast black soil padding their bodies: and the lot of them were terribly in each other's way: slipping, sliding, bumping and rocking among themselves, dogs and all clashing in a tangled-up mass. And no matter how much they tried to keep out some of the cold chill and rain, or protect themselves, they couldn't fail to miss a dog, mostly his backside which collided with their faces, brushed their faces, swacked their faces and bunted their faces.

'Poow!' exploded a man. 'Get out of this, you rotten mongrel!'

'Hell, I'd sooner smell the kitchen gas than go through this ordeal again.'

'Next time I hope I have nasal catarrh. Or at least that

they ain't shearing-shed dogs, anyway.'

'Thank Christ they're tied up short; if their heads had as much freedom as their fannies a man wouldn't be in the race.'

'Well, you can't say you haven't kissed a dog's backside, that's one thing,' Macauley said. 'Neither can I.'

The three men went on enjoying their castigation, all agreeing that the damn dogs spoilt the trip for them.

They slid and slipped their way with further pushing until they came within sight of Moree. Then they started to sing, loudly and exuberantly:

'Strike up the band,
Here comes Slippery Dick the drover,
Dogs on his hands,
Every inch a rover;
Stand in the rain,
Don't give him pain,
He's every inch a dro–o–ver.'

It was six o'clock in the morning when the truck pulled up at the hotel. And what men they looked! The first round the pub were the cook and the yardman, and when they got over their fright, Macauley, who knew the ropes, took the initiative and got busy with the yardman, putting the acid on him to help him clean up a bit. Macauley knew the shearers were well heeled. They had just finished a short shearing yesterday afternoon and were fresh from the cut-out: in between pay-off, after which they piled in with Slippery Dick, and their arrival here, there had been no time for them to do more than cash their cheques and down a few drinks in Boomi.

Macauley intimated all this to the yardman, handed him a ten-shilling note. When they saw this the shearers dipped into their pockets and followed suit. They were generous. They handed out a greenskin all round, and told the yardman to keep the change. He was a sick-looking little man with spaniel eyes and a scraggy neck. He stuttered excitedly, pleased with his good day's pay before the day had even started.

He led them to a bathroom. They took all their baggage. Macauley had to wake Buster. She was stupefied with fatigue; her face was dirty and unusually pale. She tottered beside him, head askew, eyes closed. In the bathroom the naked men with warm water, an old blunt table knife, and a scrubbing brush were removing the corroded, hard-caked black soil from their flesh. One of them, the one they called Darky, was a very hairy-legged fellow: he was grimacing with pain as he tenderly set about removing the tucked-up folds of his trousers. The trousers when unfolding pulled the soil from his legs abruptly and all the hairs on his calves were pulled at the one time, causing him to show his teeth and wince with anguish.

Buster looked at him with big-eyed pity, unconsciously baring her own teeth.

Macauley undressed her and scrubbed her and told her to take over while he went to work on himself. She looked peaky and worn, and it worried him a bit, and the worry annoyed him. He told her not to fiddle about; to hurry up. She wasn't curious. She went on lathering herself. Everybody was doing the same.

Having cleaned themselves the men set about cleaning the outsides of their suitcases. They made a separate bundle of their muddy clothes, tied it up in paper and packed it away in their ports. With Macauley, it was different. His swag was wet. He unstrapped it and raked out a new change of clothes for himself and Buster – dungarees for him and a khaki shirt and clean socks and his best sports-coat; for her fresh socks, a pair of sandals, blue drill overalls, a grey linen shirt and a pullover. They were all damp, for the moisture had penetrated even to the centre of the swag. But there was nothing he could do about it.

It was an hour before the bath house was clear. There was dirty water, scummy water, mud and silt everywhere, and when the yardman saw it he seemed to doubt his good sense, but he put on a brave front and told them with a gesture of good-fellowship to leave it to him.

Their clean-up completed, the men chyacked each other and dragged in the pure air in great lungfuls; it was wonderful now to be brand-new again and feel so well and none the worse for their night's ordeal, although Darky demurred, saying he still smelt a bit of dog about him.

Slippery Dick was still hanging about the pub near his truck, and although quite at home in his dirty state he looked a bit sheepish when he saw his charges standing there clean and well dressed. His hat was so encrusted with mud it looked a beehive with a brim. He took it off, and in a habit peculiar to himself brought it round the group asking them if they would kindly settle their debts as he was anxious to get on his way. He knocked a shilling off each man's fare for the help they had given him along the road. When he came to Macauley he took the money out of his hat, replaced it on his head and shook it. 'You wasn't a passenger. You didn't hire me. I give you a lift. Get me?'

'I get you,' Macauley said, knowing that Slippery Dick was

making the concession of one battler to another. 'But, here, buy yourself a drink anyway.' He flicked a coin, and Slippery snatched it out of the air like a bird closing its beak on a gnat.

They watched him get into his mud-trap. He leant out as hell-on-wheels shook all over and the miserable covey of dogs vibrated with the rumpus. His face was a plaster cast between hat and drawn-up coat collar; only the eyes were alive. He pulled his lips back over his discoloured teeth in a stiff grin, and said, 'You blokes look as if youse see the silver lining. I seen it all night,' he said. And he rattled away.

The men were going to sink a brandy or two and then have breakfast in the pub. Macauley let them drift off. He didn't need the brandy. And he didn't want to give the impression of being a hanger-on. But he thought breakfast was a good idea. It was time he lined his tubes again.

He ordered steak and eggs, and a smaller version of the same for Buster. But she only picked at the food.

'Eat up,' he said.

'I'm not hungry.'

'You've got to get something into you.'

He relished the meal and pushed his plate away, feeling he could do it again. He turned to Buster. Her food was growing glazy with cold. He looked round him briefly. The shearers from Boomi were in a far corner. A thin, prim spinsterly woman manoeuvred an artistic fork three tables away. There was no one else as yet in the cool dining room.

Macauley took up Buster's fork, speared a piece of meat and held it to her mouth. She shook her head. He transferred the morsel to Gooby's stitchy lips. 'Look, he'll eat.'

But Gooby shook his head, too, and turned his face haughtily aside.

'Gooby's sick, too,' Buster said.

'Sick – you're not sick. Don't go getting sick on a man, for God's sake.'

He looked at her pinched face and the faint warm colour in the cheeks; at the eyes, dull, watery and heavy-lidded. It looked like a cold coming on. She probably needed a good sleep more than anything. That would put the sting back in her. But he felt a weariness in his spirit.

Outside on the kerb he stood thinking, trying to sort himself out. Where to from here? What next?

It was fine but dull now. Life was drifting into the town. A fresh-faced baker jogged by in a painted cart. Two blackfellows hunched up with their hands in their coat pockets dawdled along the street. With them was a dog with a visible backbone and ribs like a tin shed. A cherry-faced butcher in a striped apron came round the corner with a tray of meat on his shoulder and went into the pub.

Macauley rubbed his stubbled chin, looked down at his boots, caught Buster sitting on the kerb silently bent forward with her chin cupped in her hands. He looked away again in thought. He had friends in this town and he thought of them: his mind turned them over as the plough turns over the furrow: there was Arch Morley out there on the highway near Telleraga; old Mrs Crouse, who used to run the tearooms at Pilliga, down the other end of the town; Chuck Piercey, the broken-down publican from Come-by-Chance, living over on the east side; Miss Towsey, who played the church organ and had a brother in the priesthood, on her own out there towards the blacks' camp; and Beauty Kelly, the best mate a man ever had, in the same direction.

Of them all his pick was Kelly, but it was unlikely he would still be there. It was two years since Macaulay had seen him, and he could remember the day: Kelly with his grand ideas for getting into the grape country round Mildura and Swan Hill and pegging out a claim. He could start from a tent and go to a house, maybe with burlap walls and a flat-iron chimney, but still a house; and in time, with the grace of God and a bloody lot of sweat, he'd have a mansion with rugs on the floor and a built-in nightcart, and a great window of quartz glass so you could look out over the spreading vineyards and go green with envy or cock your hat on your head according to who you were and how you felt about a friend of yours that made good off his own bat. That was Kelly, and that was his talk with the big day coming up. He had the money saved then for the new start. And he was putting things in order. He would be gone now.

So Macauley settled for Miss Towsey, the next best by reason of human type and geographical distance.

'Come on,' he said to Buster. 'We're going for a stroll.'

Buster stood up obediently. There was a faint excitement in her hazel eyes. 'Where to?'

'Not far. If you walk fast you'll walk that cold off.'

'All right,' she said.

'How do you feel?'

'Not very good.'

'Walk as fast as you can.'

'All right.'

Macauley went up by the park, walking round the puddles in the footpath, and out past the post office. There was no lift in the grey gloom. Children passed on their way to school. He heard the sound of their voices long after they had passed. He heard the high whine of a circular saw. The noise carried a long way in that still air.

He was thinking of Miss Towsey. Funny, he had never known her as anything else. Just Miss Towsey. Even Barney never let on. He called her Sis. Maybe it was Eileen, or Adela, or Theresa, or Monica, one of these by the look of her; and maybe she took it off like a pair of beads and put it away in mothballs with the trousseau and all the little knick-knacks she had been getting together for her wedding day and after. Not that she went all cross-grained and lantern-jawed when the fellow jilted her. What was his name – that bloke with the bubble eyes and the manners of a curate and the Vaseline on his hair and the topaz watch-fob. Walter something. He got in tow with some rich bitch from the States, and it was all over for Miss Towsey. No, it didn't put her off balance. She accepted it as the will of God and nursed it as a secret sorrow, keeping it to enjoy on rainy days by the fire and when the cold lamb looked forlorn on Mondays.

He could see clearly: a bright horsy-faced woman, with a quick sweet voice and kind brown eyes; always giving a little tilt of the head and saying, 'Oh!' in a sympathetic way. Even her figure, in some way, displayed benevolence. She walked with quick short steps, clasping her handbag in front of her, and she wore hats that could pass for cut-down sewing baskets.

Barney Towsey was shearing sheep at twenty. At twenty-one he was prowling round with a Bible in a seminary. Then he was ordained. He got the call to China, and that was where he was now, pushing Chows around or the other way about.

Macauley stopped by the side of the road. Fifty yards through the trees in a clearing stood Kelly's old house. It didn't look a scrap different. Still the same old weatherboard with the high-pitched roof and its verandah roof pulled down over its eyes: still the same galvanised-iron tank beside the lone orange tree in the yard: with a few fence posts that stood leaning in all directions and the wire stands looped and broken.

But there was a bike against one of the posts, and it looked familiar. He squinted his eyes thoughtfully, and looked down the road, sighting the brown-painted roof of Miss Towsey's house ten chains farther on. He seemed to be tossing up a decision. It came down heads. He sauntered across the flat towards the bike, turned down the path bordered with up-ended jam tins and a few shamrocks, and knocked on the snail-grey door.

A man opened it and filled the doorway. Neither man spoke. Their eyes were locked, poised in stares of dawning recognition. Then the expressions changed. Kelly's mouth fell open. Macauley's face squinched and cracked.

'God strike me fat! Look who's here!'

'Beauty!'

'You old bastard! Where'd you spring — '

'Hell, I didn't expect — '

They were all over each other like jubilant dogs: wringing hands and pats on the back, arms round shoulders, laughing, pushing faces, slapping, giving out backhanders on chests and stomachs, shaping up and feinting and falling together and laughing and stumbling through the doorway and into the house.

Kelly stood back grinning joyfully. 'Aah, Mac, it's good to see you again.'

'Good to see you, too, boy.'

'And who might this little fairy be?' Kelly cried, bouncing down to his knees before Buster and spanning her waist with his big hands. 'Where'd you blow in from, Snooker?'

'I'm not Snooker,' Buster said gravely. 'I'm Buster.' She tried to wriggle free. Kelly gave a roar of delighted laughter.

'Okay, Buster!' he chuckled and gave her a smacking kiss on the cheek. 'God love me, Mac, I can't get over it. Fancy you turning up.' He was exuberant. 'I'll swing the billy. Had your breakfast?'

Macauley told him they had, but he said he'd be in a mug of tea just to celebrate the occasion. Kelly said he had something better than that, and produced a bottle of gin. Macauley shook his head with a smile. It was too early in the morning for him. He'd stick to the tea.

'Well, take off your hat. Put your feet up. Make yourself at home. What's mine is yours. You know that.'

Kelly was humming gaily as he filled the kettle and stoked the dying fire in the stove.

Macauley found it hard to credit the change in the man. He remembered the Beauty Kelly of fifteen years ago. And he remembered him through the years. He remembered him the last time he had seen him. And there hadn't been much difference: he was still Beauty Kelly and worthy of the name. And men were not looking at just one aspect of him when they labelled him with that name. They were looking at him all over. He was a man six feet tall and built in proportion. He had the shoulders of a Peter

Jackson, broad and powerful, tapering down to a slim waist. In his clothes he was arresting; stripped he was a spectacle. His hair was black as tar with a blue sheen on it like the sheen on a wild duck. His face was clean-cut and flawless. The features were perfectly symmetrical. He had a complexion that would have been the pride, the vanity, the joy of any woman. The skin was as soft as a doeskin glove; the flesh creamy with a bloom of rose on the cheeks. His mouth with its full lips had a carven appearance; the large warm brown eyes glowed and flashed. The eyelashes were long and clotted like a doll's. And with all these attributes he was blessed with the stamp of ruggedness and virility. He was a marvel of masculinity, and wherever he was he excited gasps of wonder and admiration and envy.

Two years ago, Macauley remembered, he had lost almost none of it, though time was at work but in a process of slow-fading, as slow as the growth of a tree.

'And what have you been doing with yourself, Mac? What's new?'

'Ah, just poking about. What about you? I'd thought you'd have a wine distillery going by this time.'

'The grapes. No, I gave that away. I'm down at Warner's, you know, the skin buyer's.' He brought the teapot over to the small table. 'It would be my bloody luck, too, to have to go to work today of all days, but — '

'Hell, you go through . . . ' Macauley gestured.

'You can put the time in here, do what you like; you've got the run of the place, and we'll have a good old get-together tonight.'

'I'll be right,' Macauley said. 'Got a few things to dry out, kid needs a sleep, and a rest won't hurt me either.' He broke off suddenly, the import of Kelly's words just striking him, and looked across the table. 'Where's Ruby? Out, is she?'

'Ruby's dead, Mac.'

'What!'

'Yeah.'

'No! God! When?'

'She's been dead a year.'

'God Almighty!'

Macauley frowned in disbelief. She had been so alive: there was so much laughter in her. He watched in stunned silence while Kelly keeping his head down lifted the hot mug of tea to his lips and sipped. He set the mug down and pulled out a tin of tobacco and started to roll a smoke.

'Seems funny, don't it?' he said quietly, looking up.

Macauley nodded. 'How? What happened?'

'Well, you know when you were here last?' He drew hard on the cigarette. 'She seemed as good as gold, didn't she? Three weeks later she blacked out. Doing the washing, she was. We didn't think anything of it, just passed it off. In fact she made a joke about it. Said she was going to throw a joey at last. But it happened not long after, and this time I took her to the quack. He told her to go to bed for a month. It didn't do much good. She went back to him, and came home laughing, saying if she did all the things he wanted her to do she'd be living the life of an invalid. Well, you knew Ruby. She had all the go in the world in her, and she kept things quiet. She was sick off and on, and sometimes she couldn't hide it. But I don't suppose I'll ever know how crook she really was.' He drew again on the cigarette and looked across the room in objective reflection. 'Anyway, I'm just having my tea one night when suddenly she keels over. Just fell sideways off the chair without a sound. When I picked her up she was dead.'

His eyes glittered. His teeth were tight together. He grimaced, but caught the grimace and straightened his threatening face. Macauley didn't say anything. He thought it better not to. Kelly didn't have to be told how sorry he was.

'Well, look at that,' Kelly grinned, pointing to Buster curled up in the folds of his unmade bed, hugging her fetish.

Macauley swung himself out of his chair. 'Hullo, she's out to it already.' He covered her over with a blanket.

'Bonzer kid, Mac.'

'She's a bit heavy with the cold. Sleep'll do her good.'

'Struth, she would have gone nap on her, Ruby. She couldn't have any, you know.'

Macauley said nothing. He settled back in his chair and put the mug to his lips. Kelly rolled another cigarette. Suddenly he threw himself back with a laugh. 'You'll never guess who I bumped into the other day.'

'Who?'

'Lucky.'

'You didn't!'

'Lucky bloody Regan!' Kelly thumped the table in gleeful delight. 'The same old Lucky. Full as a boot and happy as Larry. What a pity you didn't get here sooner, Mac.'

'Well, it's a small world,' Macauley said, 'and smaller still when you're hoofing it, but I haven't struck Lucky for . . . must be eight years now. Where's he been, did he say?'

'Up in the bloody Hartz Range scratching for mica with a bunch of Italians.' Kelly gave a laugh. 'He's the colour of a sizzled-up steak and tosses the dago language round like it was his own.'

'Is he going back there?'

'No, he's back in New South Wales for good, so he reckons.' Kelly pushed his mug aside and leant his elbows on the table. 'He's got a shed at Pokataroo. You going that way?'

'I might.'

'You might even land a pen there. It's old Wigley's place. Eucla. You know.'

'Yeah, I know.'

'And listen.' Kelly was becoming exuberant again. 'Half the old gang'll be there, from what I hear. Mick and Ted Bennett, remember them?'

'Mick and Ted, yeah,' Macauley said.

'Stepper Mackenzie?'

'Yeah.'

'They'll all be there. Bluey Green?'

'Bluey, too?'

'The whole bloody lot.' Kelly grinned excitedly. 'God, Mac, it'd be like old times again. Why don't you be in it?'

Macauley smiled thoughtfully, feeling the warmth of Kelly's pleasure in wanting him to have the enjoyment of the experience.

'I don't think I can, Beauty.' He glanced towards the sleeping child, and Kelly followed his look.

'I don't want to be quizzy, Mac, but, if it's a fair question what's the drum?'

Macauley told him how he had Buster for six months: he sketched in the whole story quickly and briefly. At the end of it he found Kelly peering at him.

'God, man, you believe in making it tough for yourself, don't you?'

'It just happened.'

'Why didn't you put her in a home, or something?'

'I think it's come to that,' Macauley said.

'Why'd you take her in the first place, Mac?'

Macauley reached for the teapot and filled his mug. He held the spout over Kelly's pint, above the cold scum that was settling on the tea. Kelly shook his head. Instead, he reached behind him into a cupboard made of two kerosene boxes and pulled out the half bottle of gin and a glass with it.

'Like a drop of this now?'

'Not for me.'

Kelly half filled the glass. He drank it straight and half filled the glass again. 'You don't have to tell me, Mac, if you don't want to.'

'I'll tell you,' Macauley said, looking squarely at his mate. 'There's not much to it. I came home one night and found her in bed with a bloke. I took the kid and left and I never went back.'

'That's bad, Mac.'

'Don't get me wrong, son. I didn't take that kid for goody-goody reasons. I took it to spite her, to hurt her. But I made a mistake.'

'Mistake?'

'It was me that come the gutser.'

'How?'

'Because she didn't want the kid. I did her a favour. I took the kid off her hands. And it was like giving her a present. I take it off her hands and put it on my own back. Laugh that off.'

'You haven't had a kick from her?'

'Not so much as a kiss-me-foot.'

'But, Mac.' Kelly was casting round for a way to put it gently. 'Six months you said. It didn't take you all that time, did it, to wake up to what you've just told me? I mean – it's crazy, lugging that nipper round the countryside. Not fair on you and not fair on her. Would have been better if you'd settled down somewhere if you were going to keep her with you?'

'Settle down? Me?'

'Well, what did you intend to do with her when you took her?'

'I thought I'd work that all right when the time came.'

'Why didn't you put her in a home, or give her over to the care of someone? Why didn't you do that?'

'I don't know. You get caught up before you're ready. Things don't pan out. You drift along, half dragged, half pushed, and the time goes by. Maybe I didn't want her to get her hands on Buster. Maybe I was still waiting for a crying letter. I don't know.'

'Yeah, I think I know how you feel,' Kelly said. And the way he said it made Macauley look at him more discerningly: at the creeping grey on the temples, the scraggy ruckles under the chin, the puffs of flesh under the eyes and the faint puce tinge coming into the skin. He noticed again the quick fidgety movement, the nervous, slightly unfocused shift of the eyes, and suddenly all the vague perceptions he had been feeling since he came into the house crystallised. He knew that what was shadowing that lined face was a sickness of dissipation. He was looking at a drunk. Not a drunk that wobbled and twisted his features and talked with a thick whine. And rolled home and went to bed in his hat. But a controlled, disciplined drunk, a chronic drunk whose system was saturated like a sponge, and who when he felt the sponge drying out even a little bit had to wet it again. And he knew what happened when the sponge was given more than it could absorb, how it spilled over, and carried the man in abandonment to the heights or dropped him to the depths, both of them a madness.

'You've got a problem, Mac,' Kelly was pondering, sincere. 'I wish I could help. I don't know what to suggest except a home.' He turned suddenly. 'Could she stay here with me? Hell, I'd only be happy — '

'It's my pigeon.' Macauley shook his head. 'Let me worry about it. Say, what time have you got to be on the job?'

Kelly looked at his wristwatch. 'I'll have to shove off now.' He gulped down the last of the drink. 'I hope you don't mind. I'll see you tonight.'

'I might duck along and see Miss Towsey for a while,' Macauley said, standing in the doorway with his hands on the frames.

'She's not there now,' Kelly said, straddling his bike. She's down at the presbytery. Housekeeping. Okay – don't do anything I wouldn't do,' he said with a grin.

'What do you want me to do, lead a dull life?' Macauley called with a chuckle. He watched the pedalling figure out of sight, and he watched the way he had gone for minutes afterwards. Then he turned back into the room and moved about it in thoughtful inspection.

It had an arsy-versy look about it to him as though it had come under the influence or taken on some of the characteristics of its occupant. The floor was dirty, stained with maps of dried liquid and spotted with cigarette butts put out underfoot and trodden flat. The table stood with its legs in four jam-tin boots, all filled with mildewy water. The tabletop needed a scrub. The shelf above the stove was piled to the ceiling with oddments, including old hats, old gumboots, and a woman's green umbrella. Some of the canisters that belonged there stood on top of the meat safe, which stood on a three-ply tea case beside the window. The stove itself was slightly tilted where the brick alcove had apparently subsided. The hob was dusted with grey ash. The bed was probably made up once or twice a week. Even the alarm clock on the floor beside the bed leant drunkenly on one leg and gave out with a muzzy chick-chock.

Macauley shook his head. He wandered down the little hall to the back door. He looked in the rooms either side of the hall. There was a double bed in one, with dust on the counterpane, a cheap chest of drawers and a frail cream-painted dressing table. The mirror was furry with dust. The other room was filled with junk.

He went back into the room where Kelly did all his living, and took off his coat. He built up the fire, unstrapped his swag, and arranged his blankets and garments about the stove to dry. He swept the floor clean, splashing water on it and driving the suds out the door with a millet broom. He changed the water in the jam tins and scrubbed the tabletop. He straightened a calendar on the wall and brought its leaves up to date.

Then he sat down and rolled a cigarette. There was a furious sadness in his eyes.

Buster woke up and reared aloft, hot, heavy and mussy-haired. She called her father immediately. Where was he? When he didn't answer she raised her voice and there was a trace of panic in it.

'I'm here,' he said, looking at her from the junction of the hallway and the room.

She looked at him sheepishly; then dangled her legs over the bed, clasping Gooby and rocking herself, humming drearily. She sneezed, hawked, and took up the humming again.

'You better go out there and wash your face,' Macauley said. 'It'll freshen you up.'

'All right.'

He heard her sneezing outside, spluttering and spitting. When she returned her movements were sprightlier and she went into a spasm of chatter. Both faded away quickly, and she sat listlessly on a chair, nursing Gooby, while Macaulay shaved.

'Gimme a hanky, dad.'

'What for?'

'I got a runny nose.'

He tore off part of an old shirt that he kept for nose-rags and told her to look after it as the handkerchief supply was getting pretty low. She was always losing them. He found bread in a box and meat in the safe and made a meal. Buster asked for a sandwich in a spontaneous access of false hunger, and only nibbled away half of it. Macauley told her he was going down the town; if she didn't feel like coming she could get back into bed and stay in the house until he returned. It would do her cold better, but she was adamant about coming.

Macauley thought he might run into someone he knew. He wanted to put out some feelers about work, and get some lead on the future. Mainly, he didn't want to sit round the house. He was seriously turning over the possibilities of trying for a job at Eucla. It had a lot of appeal. What a picnic to meet up with some of the old gang again – Lucky, Stepper, Bluey, the Bennetts: the yarns, the laughs – hell, what a picnic. Another thing, too: it wouldn't be hard to get through there with the kid. Be easy, in fact. He could coast along. There'd be no bellyaches with that mob. The big point was – money. The chips were fizzling out fast. He'd have to take on a job, and soon, whether it was Eucla or not. And if he didn't crack it there it would have to be some other shed. And that meant deciding on the big problem once and for all – whether to take his two-legged handicap with him and carry on the battle or lodge her somewhere in safe custody. That decision was already made. The time had come to end the predicament. Wherever he went he knew that soon she would not be going with him.

He strode into the office of Grazcos and a smiling fat amiable man dressed in a brown suit and with a face like a chunk of soap came up and put his hand across the counter. 'How are you, Macauley?'

Macauley's hand engulfed the other and squeezed it: it was like a small, damp, flabby fish. 'Not bad, Stan. What's doing?'

'Nothing at the moment, I'm afraid. How long'll you be here?'

'I don't know. Not long.'

'Might be able to place you in a few days if you're about.'

'What about Eucla?'

'Eucla?' The little mouth closed and pursed for a moment. 'That's Wigley's place.'

'That's right,' Macauley said.

'We've got nothing to do with that.'

'Since when? I thought it was a Graziers' shed.'

'We haven't had it on the books for a couple of years – that's last year and this.'

'Who's got it?'

'Nobody. Wigley got some bee in his bonnet – he's a fussy old goat, you know – and reckoned he could do a better job than the contractors. He's doing all the hiring. So if you want a job there you'll have to see him.'

'Long way to go on spec. When's he start?'

'Next week sometime, I think. I imagine he'd have all his men by now, but why don't you give him a call on the phone and find out?'

'Okay. I might do that.' He half turned to go. 'If I'm still here in a few days I'll get in touch with you.' Suddenly he half raised his hand as the fat man was about to leave the counter. Macauley thought he might get a line on his friend. 'Beauty Kelly – is he still around?'

He saw a sharp look come into the fat man's eyes. The fat man looked to each side of him, then he leant his bulk on the counter and said in a sad confidential voice, 'You wouldn't know him, Mac. They reckon he's psycho.' He paused. 'Got a job at Warner's. He's a good worker, never misses a day, but works for only one thing – to get the money for grog. He must have a constitution like an animal.'

'Just works to drink, eh?'

'Take a tip, Mac – don't get in a pub with him, don't go on a bender. He's sudden death. And I know you two are great cobbers.'

Macauley nodded. He understood.

Suddenly the fat man stood back, and his face creased in a smiling imitation of shrewdness. 'And who's chasing you, the tax commissioner?'

Macauley jerked his head up. 'What do you mean?'

The fat man chuckled. 'Why don't you pick up your mail these days?'

'Mail?' Macauley was puzzled. 'What mail?'

'Don't you see *The Worker*?'

Macauley continued to look puzzled. The fat man pivoted slowly and went back to his desk. He picked up sheaves of papers, and pulled out drawers. He bent over, holding his stomach with one hand and he retrieved a newspaper from the floor. He fumbled for the right page as he walked back to the counter. Then he found it and laid the copy down in front of Macauley, pointing with a finger at a little panel in small type.

Macauley read, 'There are letters at this office addressed to the following men.' He mumbled away the names until he came to J. Macauley. And he kept looking at the nine letters.

'That's you, isn't it?' the fat man said. 'It's been lying there for three months to my knowledge. You ought to collect it. Who knows – your rich uncle might have died and left you a lot of money.'

'Do you want the paper?' Macauley said.

'Take it with you,' said the fat man. 'I'm glad I thought to tell you.'

Outside Macauley stood and read the notice again. Who was the writer of the letter? There were two major sources by which correspondents could contact him – the *Worker* office which held and forwarded mail and the Graziers' Co-operative Shearing Company. *The Worker,* official organ of the Australian Workers' Union, publicised the advice in its pages which had a wide distribution among workers in the pastoral industry, whether they were employed on farms, stations, or in shearing sheds. With the Graziers', letters were only forwarded when the addressee's location was known, usually in one of the company's run of sheds. It was highly probable that whoever had written the letter was familiar with Macauley's itinerant life and knew that he did not confine his occupations to the shearing industry. On the other hand it could have been an ignorant shot in the dark. His name could have got among the prospects in an advertising department in the mysterious way that names have of doing such a thing. It was always happening – a circular detailing the merits of So-and-so's combs and cutters; a pamphlet on rotary hoes; an art union brochure. Once he received a fat packet of oozing sales-talk on sweetmaking at home for profit. The literature kept coming, chasing him all over the country. In the end he wrote to the firm telling them what to do with their paper and wishing them happy boiled lollies.

He folded the newspaper and shoved it in the back pocket of his trousers. In his calm way he was curious and a little excited. There was no harm in writing after the letter, anyway.

But he needed an address, and that necessity helped him to resolve his next move. He would push out west. If he pushed out west he could put in an appearance at Eucla and try for a job there. If it didn't come off nothing was lost since it was on his way. He knew the ropes better than the fat man in the Graziers' office. A phone call was all right, but not a patch on being on the spot. A voice talking to a voice over a crackling wire was unsatisfactory: often the tones gave a wrong impression of a man and the impression was often enough to make all the difference between success and failure. The idea was to get before a man, let him see all of you, let him size you up.

But how to get to Pokataroo? He glanced at the smooth overcast sky. It looked unpromising. The road would be bad enough already without any more rain. It would take three or four days at least to walk it in even good weather. He'd had enough of black soil to do him for another twelve months. The chances of a lift? It was most unlikely there'd be anything going through, none of the big stuff, anyway, the trucks and freighters, the best choices for a ride. A light car could make it, but the chances of finding one were pretty remote; and when a man did find one it was odds on he'd be knocked back. The only way was the train, south to Narrabri, west to Burren Junction, change there, then north to Pokataroo – a triangle, a helluva roundabout way.

Buster was fumbling at his trouser pocket.

'What do you want?'

'Hanky.'

'Where's the one I gave you?'

She held it aloft. It was a sodden rag. He told her to put it in her pocket and he gave her his piece of shirt. He took her hand and led her across the street. They went into a chemist's shop. Macauley asked for a bottle of eucalyptus. The chemist was a lanky man with mild blue eyes and golden hair, fluffed out on either side of a centre parting so that the top of his head was quite flat. He had a sympathetic, affectionate voice and feminine mannerisms. As he delicately reclined the bottle on its mauve wrapping paper Buster gave a volley of sneezes, arresting the chemist's movement. He looked at her feelingly and then at Macauley.

'This for the little girl?' he asked.

'That's right.'

'Poor little thing – she doesn't look well at all, does she? So frail, so skinny.'

'You should have seen her before I brought her out in the bush,' Macauley found himself saying in bridling defence. 'Had a cough even. A bad cough. That's gone now.' Then he wondered why he had bothered to speak at all.

'I would suspect her of malnutrition, poor little dear. Do you keep the milk up to her?'

Macauley looked into the bravely inquiring eyes.

'She's got her own Jersey,' he said, not without some truth.

'Oh, that's splendid. Milk is so nourishing. So much the child's food. And a little cod-liver oil emulsion with it, too, is a good thing. An excellent body-builder. Calcium and malt, too, for good teeth and strong bones. A child must get off to a good start in life. Now we have some very fine patent — '

'Never mind,' Macauley interrupted. 'Just wrap that up.'

The chemist bent to his task. He hesitated. He looked up with his head cocked to one side. 'I could give you something very much better than this, you know. To be candid, sir, I would put it right at the bottom of the list. It has practically no medicinal value. Its reputation is a leftover from the old horse-and-buggy days when — '

'Listen,' Macauley said, a little heatedly. 'I've seen that stuff do things for a man that no chemist or doctor could do. All they could do was take his money and string him a line of heifer dust as long as your arm. You're talking to the wrong man. Wrap it up.'

The chemist acquiesced agreeably but looked a little hurt. He recovered his equanimity when Macauley asked for a packet of aspirin. As he handed over the change he exhorted considerately, 'She has a very nasty cold, and you must watch it. You must keep her in bed, keep her warm. You must see that she doesn't get a chill. You must ply her with lemon drinks and liquid nourishment. Don't forget now. Goodbye. Goodbye, little girl.'

'Hooroo,' Macauley said. 'Keep up the milk.'

He bought chops, potatoes, beans and lemons and they went back to Kelly's house. He gave Buster a few drops of eucalyptus in a spoonful of sugar, and had to carry out the pretence of giving Gooby the same. He made up a bed on the floor, gave her an aspirin and a warm lemon drink, and tucked her in. The quicker he lightened the burden the better. He pulled out a dog-eared pad and envelopes and while he drank a mug of tea wrote a note to the *Worker* office. He asked for the letter in their possession to be readdressed to him care of the post office, Collarenebri.

He addressed the envelope in pencil, sealed it and put it in his coat pocket on the wall.

Then he set about getting tea ready – beans, potatoes and chops. He found flour and baking powder, but no sultanas, and made a plain brownie. It rose in a hump at one end, typical of the stove. He laid newspapers on the table and set it for two. He expected Kelly home between five-thirty and six.

He had the food in the oven, keeping it hot, when six o'clock came and went. At six-thirty he went to the door and looked out. It was dark and a light rain was falling. A wind was rising. There was no wavering bulb of light on the road. He shut the door. At seven he put a feed on his plate and started to eat. He ate slowly and thoughtfully, listening for sounds, wondering what had happened to his mate, and whether he oughtn't to go down the town looking for him. He finished his tea and rolled a cigarette. He washed his dishes and pannikin. He made a fresh cigarette. He sat smoking. It was eight o'clock.

The wind strengthened, beating the rain against the windows, soughing in the trees. At fifteen minutes past eight he heard a sound like the jangle of a falling bicycle. He looked towards the door expectantly, feeling an unaccustomed tension. Five minutes went by and nothing happened. Then he heard the sound of a man's voice, half strangled.

He strode to the door and pulled it open. A triangle of light hit the ground. The rain hung in it like a misty curtain. Macauley peered into the wet outer darkness. He saw nothing. He stepped out onto the edge of the verandah. He heard the voice before he saw the man. The voice was calling, 'Ruby.' And after a pause, 'Rube, where are you?'

The man came round the side of the house, and it was Beauty Kelly. He kept on going. His walk was half between a lope and a shamble. He was bent forward, his shoulders drooping if such shoulders could ever droop. He was twining his hands in front of him. He kept calling the woman's name. Macauley saw him disappear like a phantom into the darkness and like a phantom come back from another point in the circle, the shirt-front a smear of white, the face paler and the bare head a wet glistening darkness.

'Hey!' Macauley shouted.

Kelly stopped for a moment, then quickened his gait, walking directly towards Macauley. He had a wild appearance. His eyes were staring, fixed like marbles. Rain ran down his face. His mouth was half open. He was panting. He gazed at Macauley like a stranger.

'What's the matter, old-timer?' Macauley said softly.

'Where's Ruby?' Kelly cried harshly.

Macauley took his arm and Kelly submitted with a stunned docility. But at the door he wrenched himself free and flung himself inside, lurching down the hall gasping and croaking the woman's name in a way that gave Macauley the jitters to hear it.

He stumbled back, one hand raised, dragging along the wall. His head wobbled. His jaw hung slackly. His face was a distorted fury of dejection and incomprehension. The bottle swinging in his coat pocket made the pocket look like a pannier. He'd had so many drinks, Macauley thought, if he bent over he'd tip one out. He must have been in the pub for hours; God alone knew how long. Macauley braced himself.

He stood back as Kelly swaggered towards the table, pulling out the bottle of gin. He tore the cork from it with his teeth, and put the bottle to his lips. He saw Macauley looking at him. He slammed the bottle down on the table, and in the same movement reached out and grabbed Macauley's shirt and dragged himself up close.

'Who are you?' he demanded. 'Where'd you come from?'

Macauley put his left hand out against Kelly's neck, applying no pressure, just leaving it there. 'I'm your mate.'

Kelly shook him, his face twisting berserkly. A hard light came into Macauley's eyes. 'Beauty, it's me, Mac.'

He edged himself in, thrusting his face close to Kelly's, and he repeated the words, but realised the futility of doing so. They made no impact. They fell against a shut brain and died before they could penetrate it. There was no recognition in Kelly's face. His eyes were flaring, unfocused, unseeing.

'Where is she?'

He grabbed Macauley by the throat, shrieking the invective of a madman, and tried to force him back against the wall. Above the unnerving violence Macauley heard the terrifying screams of Buster. He twisted round, walked backwards a few steps, and joining his hands brought up the arms like a hoop of iron breaking the grip on his throat.

Kelly lunged forward, throwing a vicious straight left. Macauley easily evaded it, and as the big man swung into him he clipped him hard on the chin and caught him under the armpits and lowered him to the floor. Buster's thin, hoarse, reedy wailing came up loud in the sudden uncanny silence. Macauley's chest was rising and falling as though he had just run a long way. He looked over at her propped up on one elbow in the corner.

'Quit it,' he said.

'Ol' bugger man,' he heard her snuffle to herself. 'Killing my father.'

She got up and looked down at the prostrate figure; there was a mingled expression of curiosity and pleasure on her face. She looked up at Macauley. 'Will he go to the boneyard now?'

'Get back to bed,' Macauley said. 'You shouldn't be out of it. Go on, do what I tell you, and cover yourself up.'

'All right.'

Macauley dragged Kelly to the bed, pulled off his shoes and coat, and rubbed his head with a towel. He covered him up. He walked about the room for ten minutes, letting the tension ease down in him. The warrigal wind shouldered the door in, swooped under the papers on the table, and upset the gin bottle. The fluid ran out with a sound of a big dog lapping against his thirst. Macauley was slow in setting it upright again. He shut the door first. He blew out the light, kicked off his boots and got under the blanket.

He lay on his back, hands cradling his head. He wasn't tired. He could feel Buster's warm backside against his hip. She was passing off again into a snuffling sleep.

In a little while he heard Kelly stir, saw the figure twist over and lie still again.

Macauley had only darkness to look into. He had only the wind and the rain to listen to. He had the future to think about and the past to remember. And he remembered the past.

In the city, before he went to the rivers, before Lily Harper, before sweet Lily – right back to the beginning of memory.

The city, it had a hold of him from the time he was born. It pounced on him in darkness, gripping his feet. It smacked his arse and said, Wake up. Look around. See what you've got for a present. It said to him at the age of five, Run away with me. Get going. And he ran away, and they didn't find him for hours. He sat on a policeman's knee, and the city spun past and around him like a slow hurdy-gurdy. His mother flung him against the wall with her hand to his throat and fumed viciously at him. His father beat him and he bawled to himself up in the smelly bed, and in the darkness he pitied his hunger and loneliness and the city winked at him in a medley of colours through the dirty window.

It pushed him round, the city, and brought him up. It fed him in cheap restaurants. It rushed him down the grimy stairs of the residential and belted his heart in his ribs as he rushed for the tram stop. It jogged him into work. It put him at a machine in a factory full of windows, petty spites and intrigues. It had a use for him.

Get tough, it told him. I'm doing this for my own good. I'll make you and you'll make me. Millions work for me. They set me up and I have a name. You start a crusade and I cop the credit. Develop an art, a science, and the fame is mine. The big wheels and the little wheels, they work for me.

'*Boom-boom-boom-boom-boom*,' Kelly bawled.

But he saw it for what it was worth and he had the answer. He saw the world ended as the world must end for each man. He saw the city slacken its hold of him at last. It threw him aside, discarded him as useless to its welfare and a drain on its economics. And he knew, he saw he had been working for a dictator. But he had the answer.

No, he said, I won't truckle to you. Upya for the rent. I'm as tough as the next one and I'll go out where the world is wide. There the world has something to give me. And I don't need a penny for the slot and a key for the door. I can get a bed on the earth. I can get fire from the forests. I can get a drink from the rivers and a feed out of a hat. I can get freedom. I won't be stood over by you or anyone else because nobody stands over me. And you can shove that up your chuff and take another swipe: I'll put you on your back before you'll put me, big and all as you bloody well are.

'Who'll take a glove now? Who'll take a glove?'

And yet after a spell he went back to the city and it was just as though the city had it in for him; it hit him like a novelty, licked him all over with smarm and gave him a good time. He dropped his guard, and he didn't see the punch coming until it was too late. It caught him with its treachery. It blinded him. It left him with half of his brain working. He saw her at Callahan's party, the same Tubby Callahan they put away in the black sod of the plains at Millie: he saw her and met her there.

'You'll have a go, will you, friend? What, you'll take the lad in the green trunks? You'll take Macauley. Haha, you must be the town joker.'

And he saw her all the time when he was away from her and he met her again and again. All about him was persuasion. The persuasion of wanting to give her love and pleasure and do all that was right for her. The persuasion of her talk and the talk of her parents: the good a man could do for himself, the future he could carve out for himself in a big city full of opportunities.

'Why, this boy's only a middle. By the look of you you're sixteen stone if you're a day. You want it easy, don't you son! I'll give you Kelly here. How'll that do you?'

And it made the years before him seem like an abyss, like the waste of a stony desert. What had he been doing? Where had he been running? Nowhere but round in a treadmill, squandering those years that were gone for ever; tipping out those precious years like water. It put a panic in him, and he rushed desperately after jobs and he found one and seized it with joy and relief as though it were a lifesaver.

'Listen, junket-brain, it's either Kelly or nothing. Stop wasting my time.'

A sawyer in a timberyard. Good money. Good conditions. All of this, all in a little time, all in a month – his brain still groggy from the punch. Only Callahan said it wouldn't work out. Only Callahan told him to call it off before it was too late. And he said to Callahan it was like his hide, and he told him to go to hell and mind his own business and keep his insulting tongue where it belonged, inside his big gob. Fancy saying that to Callahan. Fancy not taking any notice and seeing the light when Callahan talked. A man like Callahan.

'So you'll take Kelly, will you? You've got the pricker properly, eh? You'll knock him into next week, willya? All right, we'll see about that.'

And he woke up in the morning, in the filtering dawn, and she was beside him; she was well branded and there was no question of whom she belonged to; but he still didn't come to his senses. He didn't come to his senses till three weeks later; the effects of the blow wore off and left him alone and discontented. He wanted the woman, but he didn't want the life. He paced up and down the captivity of the job. The city roared in his ears with a terrible pandemonious laughter. He couldn't get away from its grimy fingers jabbing him in the chest. He walked over its great belly, rolling and rumbling with noise, and the jar went through him and stayed in him like quivering chords. It blew its smoke and grit and soot in his eyes with a nonchalant contempt.

'You hear that, friends. The local boy here says he'll massacre my boy. See it on the inside. Get your tickets on the right.'

He walked a hill to his room, but it was a wooden hill. The smell of the city was in his nostrils, and in his mouth. He opened the door and the flavour changed. He shut the door, and shut it in and shut it out. It was all round him. He lay on the bed, and the sky was a stride away pressing down, pressing the polluted air into his lungs, and it was a wooden sky that never knew a star. He looked to the compass points, and he saw no trees and no horizons. He saw dank walls of stone. On the wooden earth nothing grew, no flowers, not a blade of grass.

Some men can live in a box; some men are like a wheel.

And he knew which one he was. But it wasn't a matter of knowing that he couldn't stand it any more. It was a matter of stripping off and putting up his fists and fighting back. He gave in to nothing and nobody. He might get beaten in the end, but he wouldn't give in. So he split his life two ways – one for her and him and one for him, and he was happy enough. Now there was none for her and him. Only the one for him.

'Roll up! Roll up! Boom-boom-boom-boom! Step inside and see the boys in action. The best money's worth on the showground today.'

Macauley sat up, found the makings and rolled a cigarette. In the flare of the match he peered across at Kelly, tossing and turning, flinging out his arms, babbling away in his drunken nightmare. The windows rattled. Rain drummed on the iron roof. The wind hoyed in the chimney. He lay back again, the cigarette end glowing and dying and glowing in the intervals of thought.

He remembered the night, the last big laugh of the city, the sign of the big thumb erect, and the sickness was in his guts. He usually let her know when he was coming home. But he didn't this time. It was just an accident of circumstances, not an oversight, not a deliberate omission. Where was the reason for that? It wasn't an intended surprise but it would be accepted as that.

There was no light under the door. He turned the knob. He pulled the switch and walked into the bedroom and switched on the light there. All he remembered was his wife jerking up and blinking in a stupor of startled sleep, her hair mussy, her breasts hanging out of the nightgown. And the man beside her lifting a face of sudden fright and flinging the bedclothes back and tumbling out of the bed all in the one action and sitting there staring.

In a cot in the corner the child lay asleep.

The woman covered herself. Her face was white. Her lips moved; she gulped and swallowed. But she couldn't say anything. Then the fright went out of her face, and the guilty confusion, and she looked at him with defiance and something of the waiting viciousness of the taipan. And he looked at the man, and the man was calm and inquiring with a smirk of bravado on his surly face.

He could remember the man shrugging and then speaking; telling him, well, now he knew how it was what was he going to do about it – the cheeky koala-headed bastard.

And the slut, in a savage mood now, ready to start in on the roasting; telling him it was no use backing and filling; they were finished; it was all over between them.

But he didn't go out on the tail of that. There was no lock to the door, so he jammed a tilted chair under the knob. He pulled down the kitchen window. He took off his coat. He looked at them. The woman held a hand to her face in a gesture of alarm. Her eyes were wide with fear. The man stood with the slinking look of a cur dog.

Macauley told him he was going to take him apart.

The man put his hands out and his head down and rushed. He stopped in his tracks and arched back with a groan of agony as though his stomach had struck a ramrod. He was fat and jelly. He bullocked his way in, head down. He flung his arms like a swimmer. Then he fell back against the wall. He put out his hands, placating, squealing harshly. He wanted to be left alone. He had enough. There was no need for two sane men to go on like savages. Couldn't they talk it over like civilised people?

Fists thudded into ribs.

He left the wall doubled, grunting for breath, spitting blood.

The woman was shrieking, 'Don't! Don't! You'll kill him!'

For another five minutes the butchery went on. Macauley

pulled the man's head back, held him upright by his hair. The last hit put him across the bed, and Macauley remembered him there with his head in her lap, with all his nakedness under her horrified eyes.

He's all yours.

Macauley said nothing more. He looked about the room, hating it, clenching his fists with the violence left in him and nothing to loose it on. He disregarded the tapping on the door. He took one last look at the woman, sobbing bitterly, and looked from her to the child who had slept through it all half doped with aspirin.

He grabbed her up and took her as she was in her pyjamas. Her head fell on the pillow of his shoulder. He wrenched the door open and the group of nightclad tenants on the landing gaped and shuffled and made way; and he tramped on ragefully down the stairs out of the residential for ever.

And he went on remembering, his brain stepping and catapulting itself from one thing to another up and down the years until he saw himself on the floor in Beauty Kelly's house, the present heavy on him, the future waiting to be unpicked, and his mind rambling out to explore it.

Kelly was chanting the count, banging the big drum, lining the fighters up on the board again, spruiking to the crowd: chuckling and gibbering and muttering. Then, in a little while, he stopped. Macauley heard him reaching down automatically for the clock, and then winding it twice – for time and alarm. And he realised that all along he had not been unconscious; he had been awake, plotting the past, enjoying a delusion. In a few minutes he heard Kelly snoring.

Macauley felt for tomorrow, but his mind faltered, fainted, caught in the drift of sleep.

He was awake early and moving quietly about. He lit the fire and put the kettle on. While he waited he got most of his gear together, and went over his finances. He kept his money, the folding kind, in a travelling branch of the Colonial Sugar Refining Company – an empty golden-syrup tin. With what was in that and loose in his pockets he had £4 17s. 6d. That wasn't bad. He wasn't on the rocks yet.

He heard Buster stirring. He crept over to her, rousing her and telling her to be quiet and not wake the man up. Her face was scarlet and burning, her eyes sick and cloudy, the lids dropping heavily. She stood up and struggled into her clothes. Macauley did up the buttons, He threw a towel on her shoulder and she dawdled outside to wash her face.

When she came back he had his swag rolled and strapped. She wasn't hungry but he made her eat a piece of toast slathered with butter. She enjoyed the hot lemon drink, holding her hands round the mug and sipping silently. Macauley crunched into the toast and washed it down with tea. Then he gave her more eucalyptus and sugar, and sprinkled eucalyptus on her handkerchief and told her to snuff it up every so often.

Suddenly the alarm shrilled, momentarily startling them. On the bed Kelly twisted, then turned quickly over, stifled the clock and fell back. He shook his head and opened his eyes. He sat up covering his face with his hands and letting the hands drag down the flesh and fall away. He smiled and nodded when he saw them.

'Well, good morning,' he cried, stretching and yawning. 'How'd you sleep?'

'Stay there,' Macauley said. 'I've got the tea made.'

He poured out a mug, and brought it over to Kelly. Kelly laughed. 'Well, how's that for a pal? Thanks, Mac.'

There was no sign of a hangover about him. He looked fresh and spirited. But Macauley noticed the same subtle mien he had detected yesterday morning. Kelly was still in the holts of sousy well-being.

'You remember winding that clock last night?'

Kelly darted a glance at him, looked amused. 'Matter of fact, I don't, but I'm not surprised. It's a funny thing, that.' He laughed. 'Don't matter whether I come home pickled, dog-tired, out on my feet, somehow that clock always gets wound. I always leave her set for seven-thirty. She gets me up everytime. Never fails.'

And Macauley understood why: the habit that was an extra organ in Kelly: the habit that was his offsider and bodyguard. It never let him down. He had trained it to understand that it couldn't afford to. It had to stir him. He had to be up for the day and ready for the job. Ready for the job, for to miss work meant the dread of being without money. And the dread of being without money meant the terrible despair of being without drink. He needed all he was getting. He had to make certain there would be no change.

Kelly suddenly leant forward with a look of dawning apprehension: 'Say, Mac, I was okay last night wasn't I?' he asked with a certain anxiety.

Macauley handed him the cigarette he had just rolled for himself and began to roll another.

'Well, wasn't I?'

'I managed you all right,' Macauley said dryly, 'but it would have been easier with a straitjacket.'

Kelly relapsed on the pillow, an expression of sheepishness and concern on his face. 'God, a man's a mug,' he said sincerely but without sincerity. There was no condemnation in the words. They were only a cover for his humiliation and an apology for his guilt.

He saw Macauley get up, move round the bed, and hoist his swag.

'Strike me pink, Mac, you're not leaving?'

'Yes, I'm on my way, Beauty.'

'Hell, I thought you were going to put in a few days. I — '

'I'm going to give Eucla a burl. Want to get there as soon as I can.'

Kelly leapt out of bed, looking worried and licking his lips; gesturing, not knowing what to say.

'Spare me days, Mac, you've only just come. I mightn't see you again for bloody years.'

'Sure you will. Good luck.'

He held out his hand, and Kelly took it in both of his, shaking it warmly and with an iron grip. He lost his subdued mood for a moment and, in a spasm of affability, bent down, clasped Buster's shoulders and made to kiss her on the cheek. She turned her face away quickly with a light of fear and scorn in her eyes.

'Go away. I don't like you,' she said.

Kelly straightened up, giving a wry smile to hide his embarrassment. He saw the half-full bottle of gin on the table, and started towards it. 'Mac, before you go.'

Macauley shook his head. 'It's still too early for me,' he said.

He watched Kelly pour out a nip, his hands trembling slightly. Here it was again, the resumption of yesterday, the repeat performance. And maybe it would end with the same big climax. 'How many bottles have you got of that stuff?' Macauley asked.

'Why?' Kelly said unsuspectingly. 'Just what's in this, and I think another half-bottle here.' He withdrew a bottle from the kerosene-box cupboard, and now there was an expression of slight dismay on his face as though he was expected to offer Macauley a drink to take with him.

'Show me,' Macauley said.

He picked up the two bottles and walked quickly outside. He smashed them to smithereens on a stone. Kelly leapt to the door and the consternation was still on his face, but resolving itself now into a grief-struck rage. Macauley stopped him before he could do a thing or say a word.

'If they were a mob at you, I'd do the same,' Macauley said. 'I'm not Barney Towsey talking, but I'm telling you to give it away. Take a pull on yourself. Get on your feet. I'll be back again, and I want to see you right. I'm still your mate – but I'm leaving here bloody shocked that a man like you could come to this. You're too good.'

Kelly's face was crumpled in pained astonishment. But Macauley lashed out ruthlessly, 'I've met strangers and they've said to me: "Did you ever hear of a man named Beauty Kelly?" they've said. If they didn't know you, if they never met you, they'd all heard of you. There wasn't a man alive that didn't look up to you once. The tailors fought for you to wear their clothes. The gutter wouldn't look up to you now.'

He shouldered his swag.

'These tins. I was here the day she put them down in that border. Take a look at 'em some time as you pass by. Maybe you'll see her kneeling there looking at you. It might help.'

He drew in his breath and let it out in a slow sigh. His eyes stayed squarely on the man at the door, standing there with a dumb and stricken look, stony with anguish. Macauley softened his voice for the sake of entreaty.

'Pick up your guts, Beauty,' he said, and turned away.

They arrived at Pokataroo in the mid-afternoon. It was the end of the line and it looked like the end of the world. The tracks stopped at the two stout buffers, and beyond them the grass took over. Cars pulled out from the terminus with their passengers for Collarenebri ten miles west. The laughter and chatter of friends and relatives died. The few people drifted away. An Abo sat humped on an oil drum, arms folded across his incurved chest, hands dug into the armpits.

Macauley said to a fettler standing on the platform. 'How does old Wigley rate these days – gorgonzola or otherwise?'

A faint smile came on the weathered brown face. 'Aw, take him right and you'll get on.'

He had three miles to go, south. He filled his tuckerbag, bought tobacco, and set off. The weather had been fine for a day there, with brief flashes of a watery sun, enough to dry out the ground a bit. Yet it wasn't easy. After trudging for a mile Buster told him she felt dizzy. She looked pinched, and her breath came quickly in short reedy gasps. He picked her up and carried her the rest of the way.

Macauley felt pretty good himself. The snooze in the train

had refreshed him. He liked the confident feeling he had. This might be home on the pig's back. The chance of getting a few quid together, a reunion with the old mates, a spell of work to break the monotony, good tucker, and plenty of it.

Be extra good if it panned out.

He heard the station dogs before he saw the homestead. It was a squat cream bungalow with a verandah all round and a high-pitched dull-red iron roof. A chain-wire fence enclosed it. It was laid out in paths and optimistic gardens. Macauley walked under a pergola and knocked on the side door. It was open but the secondary gauze door was closed to. The smell of warmth and food came out to him.

A slim quarter-caste girl answered his knock. A good-looker: Macauley appraised her straight away. She didn't miss his up and down look. And she didn't turn her head away shyly. When he came back to her face her eyes were levelled at him and burning like black rubies. He changed the subject.

Wigley wasn't in, but Mr Drayton, the manager, was. Macauley told her to send out Drayton.

The brooding sky was hastening the twilight, and he could smell the rain. Buster stood slumped beside him like a sick bird.

Drayton came, a tall, spare elderly man with frosty hair and a white moustache. He had a habit of listening with his body slightly bent and his hands joined behind his back. His head moved from side to side like the head of a mantis. Macauley said his piece in a few words.

'Well, I don't know,' Drayton said, in the crackling voice of a much older man and clearing his throat every few seconds.

'You see, Mr Wigley's away; he's gone to do some judging at a sheep show at Dubbo, and we don't expect him back for a few more days. But I know he's got all his men.'

'There's a chance one or two of them mightn't turn up,' Macauley pointed out.

'Of course,' the voice cracked on the notes again, 'there's always that chance, as you say.' The head moved, eyes blinking in self-conference. Drayton was obviously a kind and conscientious man; and he was obviously pondering what decision Wigley himself would make in the circumstances. 'Well,' he said at long last, 'there's no harm in hanging round and seeing, I suppose, if you feel like doing that.'

'I don't mind.'

Drayton looked up. 'A bit of a wait, you know. We don't start for another six days.'

'That's all right with me. Any objection to a man camping in the huts?'

Drayton had to ponder again. 'Oh, I don't think so,' he said slowly. 'You might as well be comfortable if you're going to stay, mightn't you? I certainly don't mind, and I don't think Mr Wigley would.'

'Good.' Macauley said.

'I'll get the key for you. Come round here.'

Macauley and Buster followed him round to a small shed-like building full of stores and provisions. Drayton took a bunch of keys from the wall and gave him one off the ring.

'You'd better take a lamp, too, to see your way around.'

'Might be handy.' Macauley nodded as he took the hurricane lantern.

'Tucker?'

'We're right for that,' Macauley said.

'No wood down there yet,' Drayton said in a considering pose. 'What you'd find'd be wet anyway. You don't want to be messing around lighting fires and cooking. I'll get the cook to give you something to keep you going tonight.'

Outside, he stood and pointed to the east. 'Shed's about half a mile straight through there. You'll find straw in the wool room for your tick. The loading-stage door's not locked. Just give it a push.'

Buster sneezed again, and Drayton appeared to notice her for the first time. 'She doesn't say much, does she?'

'She's a bit off-colour with the cold, that's all,' Macauley said. 'Otherwise she's the greatest ear-basher ever God put breath in.' He said it pleasantly. Drayton laughed. He took Macauley's billy, and told him to wait at the side door.

Ten minutes later the dark girl came out with a billy of hot tea, and a white oatmeal bag full of tinned foodstuffs. She handed them silently to Macauley. He accepted them silently. But as he took the billy she let her warm hand slide back over his fingers. It brought his eyes up to hers again. They were the eyes of a calf. But they were full of sin. She was smiling. She turned quickly and let the door slam after her.

Macauley had to try seven doors before he found one the key would fit. It was a small room with a window. There were two beds with mattresses of meshed steel standing lengthways against each wall. Between them at the far end was a kerosene case propped on its side by four battens to form a table. The air was warm and dry.

It would do him, Macauley thought. He put the lantern on the table, dumped his swag on the bed, and unrolled it. He emptied the oatmeal bag. There were tins of sausages, ham and chicken, corn beef, condensed milk; there was a jam tart wrapped in tissue paper. They had even thought to put in a tin-opener. Maybe they never heard of a man opening a tin with a sheath knife. He took tin plates, knives and forks, and the mugs and set them on the floor. He was as hungry as hell. He could eat a horse, tail and all.

Suddenly he thought of Buster, and looked round. She was lying curled up on the bed, with her cheek pressed into the wire. Her eyes were closed.

'Hey, don't you want some tea?'

There was no answer. Gently he shook her shoulder. The little body rolled unconsciously. Macauley stood back, thinking. Perhaps she was sicker than he thought. But she hadn't complained. Not much. Not much at all. Kids soon let you know when their big toe aches. But maybe not all kids, it occurred to him. He was aware of the rebellion in his understanding, aware of his anxiety and his feelings about the damnable nuisance it was.

He lifted her head and placed a folded towel under it. He covered her with a blanket. Then he took two striped ticks and went across to the shed fifty yards away and filled them with straw. He hauled them back one on each shoulder like bloated carcasses. He put a knot in the end of one. He'd run his together later with needle and cotton.

In five minutes he had her lying on the warm stack, covered to the neck with a blanket, and the light shaded from her eyes.

She had submitted to the change with a few irritable whimpers, her eyes all the time fastened in heavy sleep.

Macauley felt the cold currents of air on his face. He saw the flame waver in the lamp. He heard the sudden seizure in the trees – they mopped air. Already the lilt of the storm was in them. At the door he stood thrust against the blow, watching the darkness coming, hearing the blatter of tin on the cookhouse roof, seeing the lone bird wallowing in the murky sky. There was the toowomba, the low deep toowomba of thunder.

Rain, bloody rain; was there no end to it? Get down on your knees and cry your heart out for it and the sun blazed in your eyes. Weep for the sun and the heavens poured. In the cruelty of the drought men poured corn into the sapling troughs, running along the ground for hundreds of yards, and the starved sheep came when they saw the men, came like fowls running to the hand that spreads them grain: came at their stiff-legged trot, wobbly, their sides sunken in. The strongest ran in the lead but the others could not keep his pace. Their forelegs buckled and they fell, threshing and staggering up, struggling along with heaving ribs. The lambs did not rise. Only their eyes moved when you got near them, and spasmodically, their hind legs. Kill them before they died of weakness. The tree-loppers went up the trees and the emaciated creatures waited below for the boughs to fall. As they fell the animals attacked them, chewing in a frenzy. It was easier to give them the faces and the forms of men. It was easy to hate and be bitter. No rain.

They floundered in the bogs. They were caught in the washways. They floated down the swollen creeks like kapok bundles. They dotted the paddocks like hummocks of snow, chilled by the wet and the cold, dead and dying. Too much rain.

No rain at the right time, too much at the wrong.

Macauley forced the door shut. He ate a meal out of a tin with bread and butter. He drank the lukewarm tea. He made up his bed and lay on it. He wished the tick were filled with gumleaves. There was nothing better. Straw had a stink, and it broke up and the fluff irritated your nose. It made you spit grey phlegm. It was only a personal distaste, a molehill, but he seemed to be magnifying it into a mountain. He caught himself in a guilty apperception. What the hell was the matter with him? Doing all this grouching and bitching: for God's sake what was he running in – the old maid's handicap? That feeling he had to grumble, that faint temptation to lose heart and spirit – they annoyed him. He never grumbled. He never lost heart.

It had all started when he had taken on the kid: since the big act that had revolutionised his life.

He glanced across at her, and his eye fell on the monstrosity she called Gooby, lying on the floor under the bed. He looked at it for five minutes. Testily he got out and jammed it down under the blanket with her, only its head sticking out in a google-eyed stare. He eased the nap away from her face so that she might breathe more freely. He blew out the lamp and tried hard to go to sleep. The wind howled round the building, determined to wrench it from its foundations. Then it dropped and the rain sprinkled like pebbles on the roof.

The next day Macauley had a look round, glad to get out of the room and stretch his legs. The rain fell gently. He walked over to the cookhouse. The cook room was locked, but the kitchen door was only secured by a slip bolt. He walked round on the wooden floor, casting his eye over the long bench, the brick oven, the open fireplace with the beards of soot on the black hooks hanging from the rail. He went into the mess-room, with its long table, white as soap, and the forms against its sides. There was a notice on the wall from last year; it was scribbled in pencil and headed up: Craphouse Duties. It gave a list of men's names and their rostered days. It ended up with the injunction in snaggled capitals: Kangarooing it Not Allowed. And in smaller letters: Remember others have to sit where you shat. The notice was signed by the shearers' rep.

Chalked on a weatherboard slab at the far end of the room was an inscription: Fang Davis shore here in '37. Underneath it was a postscript added by some other hand: Yes, the moaning bastard.

Macauley knew Fang Davis. He was never done grizzling. If it wasn't the weather it was the sheep. If it wasn't the sheep it was the tucker, if not the tucker the accommodation. He had a mean, pinched-up, achy face, and went about with his hat brim cocked up at the back and a hand to his stomach as though he never felt too good. His day was an ordeal of jealousy and frustration. He was never satisfied with his tally. He would have done better only, he whinged, his back ached, he jinked his wrist, or his corns gave him gyp.

The recollection made Macauley laugh impulsively.

He went outside and surveyed the scene. Everything was nice and compact. A small two-room dwelling twenty yards from the cookhouse was the classer's and expert's quarters. The shed itself stood on a slight rise. He inspected it inside, the long board, the wool room, the empty bins, the slatted tables, the Ferrier press. The empty pens smelled of ammonia. Grass grew in the chutes. Soon the earth there would be trampled bare. Everything was ready to go.

He walked down the slope. The first huts were the usual barrack-like building, three rooms adjoining and a door to each. They were walled, roofed, and, he guessed, partitioned with corrugated iron. They were comparatively new. The second huts were only an improvisation. The building was an old house, probably once the cottage of a boundary rider; it stood four-square like a box and was divided into four separate rooms. Macauley walked right round it, peering through the dusty, cobwebbed windows. In the room diagonally opposite the one he was occupying the old fireplace still stood in what once must have been the dining room: or the kitchen, most likely, he thought. The brick chimney stood intact except where it had crumbled away at the lip.

Macauley went back into his room. Buster was still asleep the way he had left her. Her face was scarlet. From time to time a cough bubbled in her chest, racking her body for the few moments it lasted. He roused her gently, raised her on his arm and dosed her with eucalyptus. He rubbed her back and chest, massaging the medicament well into the flesh. She seemed to breathe more easily, quickly resuming the stuporous sleep.

In the afternoon Macauley went up to the station. The cook was a large woman with a blobby face and a pile of rufous hair going pink instead of grey. She listened indifferently, caught in the act of holding up the ends of her apron. All Macauley wanted, he said, was a bit of gravy beef; whatever she could spare. She dawdled off, and returned with a small newspaper parcel. She handed it to him without a word and turned away.

Macauley saw the quarter-caste girl coming out of the hen-house with a bowl of eggs. He walked down there. She appeared not to notice him as she picked her way through the sludgy churn of the fowlyard to the gate. She was wearing a green cape with a hood thrown over her shoulders.

'Hey, how about a chook for tea?'

'You see Mr Drayton 'bout that,' she answered without looking up.

Macauley stood at the gate, watching her come up, watching her unlatch it. The hood had fallen back and the raindrops were caught in her jet hair. They spotted the velvet texture of her skin like tiny beads of perspiration. As Abos went, Macauley thought, she was a beautiful girl.

He pulled the gate back for her.

'I like chicken,' he said.

She darted him a swift look from her piercing black eyes – a wicked and challenging look. Then she giggled and ran towards the house, and he looked after her spindly legs. No matter what else they had or where they had it, they never got away from those pipey shanks.

Macauley cut the meat up fine into the billycan, added enough water to cover it and sat it on the hob to soak for an hour. He raked up enough wood here and there to make a fire and keep it going. He mixed in several small stones to absorb the heat and complement the coals. Then he put the soup on to simmer. On the rich extract he fed Buster for that day and the next, spooning it into her mouth while she sat propped up, glazy-eyed, and interested in nothing.

By the middle of that second day Macauley was beginning to feel the monotony. The strain of watching vainly for some improvement in the child only added to the pall. The drifting rain, the gloom, the wet world and the smell of damp about everything – he was sick to death of it all. The growth was black on his face; his eyes had a stormy look.

He felt the restlessness ease in him when he saw Drayton riding down from the shed. He reined in his horse at the door. He wore a black glistening oilskin. His face was pink and healthy.

'How're you putting it in?'

Macauley nodded that all was well. He shifted his shoulder against the other side of the doorway.

'Wigley not back yet?'

'Day after tomorrow. He rang up this morning. I told him you were here.'

'What's he say?'

'He thought it was worthwhile.'

'Good.'

Buster coughed, a cough that seemed to be catching chokingly at her breath. It ended with a querulous whimpering that faded away. Drayton leant forward over the horse's head and peered inside the hut, concern on his face.

'Is she down to it?'

'She'll be all right,' Macauley said. He didn't like Drayton's pondering expression.

'It takes it out of them, doesn't it?' the elderly man said with a mixture of sympathy and worry. 'Is there anything you want? Medicine? Tucker?'

'I might pick up a bit more scran tomorrow if it's okay. Something with blood in it. Some of the cookhouse pots would be handy too, if you'll let me have the pantry key. I'll look after it.'

Drayton nodded. 'I'll probably be back this way later. If not, in the morning.'

'Okay. I could do with something to read, too.'

Drayton came back about half past four, with a bundle of papers and magazines and a chunk of freshly killed beef. He left the key and told Macauley he could have the run of the cookhouse. Then he was gone. Macauley promised himself he would remember Drayton in his will, and moodily set about preparing another meal: first going through the ritual of feeding and rubbing Buster and then eating, himself.

He lay on his bunk flipping the pages of the magazines. But for some reason he couldn't concentrate. There was a seemingly causeless distraction in him. He sat up and rolled a cigarette. He took up a paper. Put it down. He stretched out. He got up and went to the door. His nerves were on edge. He felt keyed up, in a wrath of boredom, indecision and vindictiveness.

He went over to the cookhouse. The fire glowed slowly under the bubbling camp oven. He turned the meat over and replaced the lid. He threw a few more chips on, boiled the billy, and made a mug of tea. The rain was still falling, the wind blowing in swishing gusts. He sat on the box by the hob, holding the palms of his hands outwards against the trembling fire. He sat in a silence of brooding.

He was like that when the knock came on the open door. He looked sideways sharply, half rising, and he saw the dark girl there, still in the green cape and hood, the lantern at her side. He walked over to the door, surprised and suspicious. He looked down at her face. He could smell a fragrance about her he hadn't smelled before.

'I brought these,' she said quickly. 'Mr Drayton told me.'

He took the magazines and glanced up to meet the enticing question in her eyes. It was not on her face. Her face was sober and virtuous. He felt his senses tangling with hers like barbs in a net. They quietened his voice.

'Drayton didn't send you,' he said.

'Yes, he did.'

She touched the hood and it fell back. There was a poppy-red ribbon tied in her hair. He felt the ravening hunger eating through his control.

'Drayton was here today. He brought me enough reading to last a year. He wouldn't send you with more. You came off your own bat.'

There was no deceit on her face now: the expression accorded with that in her eyes.

'Why did you come?' Macauley teased the passion surging in him.

'You don't like me,' she said. 'I go away.'

'Was it for this?'

He threw his arms about her, crushing her against his desperate body, twisting his lips on her mouth, dragging her back with him into the room. He sank down with her, and her lithe nimbleness excited him still more: he felt her strength repelling him, and in the fury of his craving it only tantalised the power he wanted to spend on her; he had a momentary fear that she was opposing him, that there was antagonism. And then it was gone. It was gone with the softness and pliancy that came in her; she relaxed like a kitten with her claws in him; he saw the goading glee on her face in the firelight, the parted lips, the glittering eyes. All the rage of his yearning and resentment was dynamite.

He crawled away, and sat on the box with his head in his hands. When he felt fingers caressing his hair he didn't look up.

'Am I nice?' she asked.

He didn't answer.

'All the men say I'm nice. White men, nice men like you. I don't let black trash touch me. I spit on them.' She added with venom, 'They don't belong to me.'

She uttered a soft trill of laughter. 'Men are strong like bullocks, and rough; then they are like little lambs. It's funny.'

'Better go home,' Macauley said.

'I like you. You like me?'

'Go home now.'

'Not yet,' she said.

'Now!'

'No!' She said it petulantly.

He lifted his head with a violent motion. 'You black bastard, do what I tell you! Get home. Get to hell out of here.' He hauled her up, and pushed her stumbling to the door. 'Get away and leave me alone.'

She picked up the lantern and ran away without a word, frightened of the menace in him.

Macauley went down on his haunches. Absently, he fluffed

the ashes over the coals until there was only a grey heap, a core of life for the morning. He sauntered over to the room. He didn't light the lantern. He put his face close to that of the sleeping child. He could feel the heat from the flesh, like a glow on his cheek. She didn't seem to be any hotter. Her breathing was no more irregular.

He lay on his back, staring into the darkness, fuming with the abjection in him; bristling to meet the arguments and accusations of conscience, but finding them unanswerable and incontestable. He hated the weakness that had let him down. He hated the ignominy of capitulating to a harlot, and a black one at that. Macauley, the gin jockey, they could say. The black velvet for Macauley; he can't get the white satin, poor sod. He hated the rebuking contrasts: this going on here and that going on over there.

'Christ Almighty,' he said aloud.

The next day, in the afternoon, Macauley was standing at the cookhouse door when he saw a little figure of a man coming across the paddock from the north. Macauley squinted to see if he knew him, but he didn't. He couldn't place the busy little waddle of a walk. He waited.

'Good day,' he said as the stranger came up.

'How's she going?'

Macauley noticed the little roll, the coat pulled together with three odd buttons, the white-spotted blue cravat twisted round the neck and filling the space between the lapels. He also noticed that the tuckerbag was as long and narrow as a folded umbrella.

'Cripes, this floggin' rain'd make you cry, wouldn't it? Can't the duddy weather office give us a bit of a change?'

'Think it's on its way out now,' Macauley said, scanning the light drizzle. 'Feel like a mug of brew? I've got her swinging.'

The little man took off his pork-pie hat and slapped it against his knee. His face was as small as a child's, pale and wrinkled like a withered apple. The eyes looked like currants.

'Come far?'

'Caidmurra.'

'On your pat?'

'I had a mate, but he got himself pinched. And just quietly I been a box o' birds ever since.'

'Booze?'

'No, the silly cow, makin' up to the tabbies and that. He'd go round to the kitchen for a handout, and if there was no blokes about, he'd come the smoodge to the women for a bit of a love-up. Mad bee. It was gettin' me down. I tell you.'

'He was looking for trouble,' Macauley said.

'I always knew he was up to his capers when he was a long time away. When he come back I'd dress him down something woeful. And he'd eat me, you know. Big enough to hold an elephant out, he was. But he'd only hang his head and look unhappy. And it used to make me feel like a real low heel, the way he looked, and that. You know?'

Macauley drank his tea, not interested, but listening, glad of someone's company.

'I wanted like billy-o to shake him off, but I didn't know how. Anyway, he gets up to his tricks again, after promisin' me he won't, and this time he draws a heavyweight. She clocks him with a fryin' pan or something, raisin' a lump on his scone like an egg. And she puts him in. A week later a john-hop picks us up on the road and takes him off me. And you know what he does when they take him off me? He cries. Just like a big boob.'

'What'd he get?' Macauley asked.

'I dunno. The case hasn't come up yet. But he'll do a stretch, poor silly bee. Seven years me and him were together, and I often think to meself how I stuck it out. Dinkum. That tea's all right. I think I'll double up. What's your line?'

Macauley told him who he was and what he was doing there. They talked. The little man's name was McCausland, but he was better known as Polka Dot, a title probably inspired by the cravat round his neck which had been there so long it would have required a surgical operation to remove it. Polka Dot never swore. He said that a man could express himself without swear words: the continual use of them only showed that a man had no education. He found that he could get all the emphasis he needed with euphemisms. He thought he might as well wait, too, for the shearing to start, but he wasn't particular whether he got a job. Still, it was a chance to loaf and fatten up, he said, and shouldn't be thrown away.

'I'll go down and see the head serang,' he said. 'I'll put it on him to let me bunk up in one of the huts like you. I got to get some tucker, too. I got a bit o' meat there, but she's gone funny.'

'Listen,' Macauley said, the thought just occurring to him. 'While you're down there find out if there's anybody going into Colly. If there is ask 'em if they'd call in at the post office and see if there's any mail there for me.'

'Righto, mate,' Polka chirruped. He turned at the door. 'What's this Drayton like? I know Wigley, and he might have a bit of the boss about him, but he's all right. I don't know Drayton.'

'He'll put you in mind of your mother,' Macauley told him with a faint smile.

'Silver hair and a heart of gold, eh?' Polka laughed. 'I get it.' He went off with the empty sugar bag under his arm.

It was an hour before he returned. He was whistling. Macauley had just finished attending to Buster when he poked his head round the door. He stepped inside, his eyes twinkling as he held up a key in one hand, and the tuckerbag, like a fat rabbit, in the other. He stepped across to the bed, and said, 'Is this the little titter?'

Macauley hadn't told him about Buster. He looked at Polka. But Polka was still looking down at Buster and touching her nose with an amiable wiggling finger. His next words explained the source of his knowledge.

'I told Drayton I'd already met you, but I didn't know what he was talking about when he said how is the little girl. I thought he musta mistook me for a mother of ten, or something.' He chuckled.

'How'd he say it?' Macauley said.

'Just asked.' Polka pulled a face at Buster. Buster looked at him gravely with eyes as big as saucers in the thin, burning face. Polka tried again, tipping his hat forward and giving it a life of its own on his crawling scalp. He saw a faint tremulous smile creep into the lips and melt away. He chuckled with pleasure.

Macauley idly rolled a cigarette, sensitive to a vague premonitory feeling.

'Not like that narrow-gutted mate of mine, Hinchey,' Polka

said. 'When he got crook and that way you couldn't get a smile out of him for love or money. Wet-nurse him all the time. Polka, where are you? Where's me strides? Hand me that mug. Help me up. I want this. I want that – all the duddy time. Struth, I was wore out.' Even the memory seemed to give him a momentary look of exhaustion. Then he added with an emphatic cry, 'And he was a grown man, not a bit of a kid.'

'What about the mail?'

'Aw, yeah. Drayton's going in himself tomorrow,' he said. 'In the mornin'.'

Macauley put the cork back in the eucalyptus bottle, and picked up the pint still with a little broth left in it. He glanced at Buster. Her eyelids were drooping. She turned over on her side and dropped off, embracing Gooby.

Polka lowered his voice. 'Don't look too good, does she?'

'She hasn't got any worse,' Macauley said. He said it with a slight truculence that he couldn't help. Polka lifted his eyebrows wonderingly, but instinct told him to say no more.

They went outside.

'That's where I am,' Polka said, pointing to the first row of huts. 'Last room this end.'

'Among the silvertails, eh?' Macauley bantered.

Polka didn't catch on for a moment. Then he saw the contrast between the new and the old building where Macauley was camped, and he laughed. 'Somebody thinks I'm a bit of all right, anyway,' he followed up the jocose theme. 'That boong piece at the station – you had your peepers on her yet?'

Macauley looked at the twinkling currant eyes without a flicker in his own. 'I've seen her,' he remarked.

'Should have seen the way she looked at me,' Polka grinned. 'Made me feel goosey all over. The real come-on, it was if' – and the grin widened – 'me memory serves me right. Strike me pink, I thought to meself, what have I got she can't get elsewhere.' He laughed.

'Ah, you're a dirty old man,' Macauley said, affecting a casual humour to hide his real feelings.

'Well, I'll go and dress for dinner, m'lord.' Polka bowed and walked off.

Macauley didn't go to sleep for a long time that night. At daylight Buster's coughing woke him. He looked across with a fagged bleariness at the small lump under the blankets bouncing with the hacking violence exploding within her body. He sprang out of bed, and for a moment watched the agitation, the face bursting and shuddering with the choking paroxysms, the throat gulping, the nostrils flaring and snorting, the tongue protruding from the mouth. Then he turned the child on her side, and waited for the coughing to ease itself away in panting spasms and a thin, sick lugubrious whine. He touched the hot brow. He listened and he heard the purring chest, the wheezy breathing.

He sat on the bed, twisting his hands, running them through his hair. He felt a fury for the growing helplessness in him. The strengthening suspicion of defeat maddened him. Oppression tried to settle over him but his ferocious nerves jarred at its touch and repelled it.

He got through the morning. At dinnertime the rain drifted away, and it was good to feel the sun again – but there was no warmth in it, only colour. The sky was dark blue, and clean as a new billycan.

Towards evening, with the chill already in the air, Wigley and Drayton rode down from the station. Macauley watched them dismount and go into the shed. He waited for them to come out. They rode casually down to the first huts, veered and came round by the cookhouse. Macauley stayed at the door of his hut, leaning against the frame, smoking, until they approached him. He nodded.

'Everything all right?' Wigley asked peremptorily. He was a stocky man in riding breeches, fawn sports coat, and grey tweed hat with a drooping brim. He had a hawky face with a high colour and eyes like slits of blue crystal, set in a web of fine lines. They were hard but not unkind. Macauley did not fail to notice the subdued appearance of Drayton.

Wigley glanced in the room, then at Macaulay. 'I understand you've got a sick kiddy there. How is she?'

'Not the best,' Macauley said, feeling his way. 'But I'll get her right.'

'What is it?'

'I don't know – just a helluva cold.'

'Sounds like 'flu to me from what Drayton says.' The sternness of Wigley's gaze made the words seem stern, as much as did the officious and bumptious manner. 'You know we start shearing here next week, and I don't want any hold-up?'

'What hold-up could there be?'

'Sickness.' Wigley shot the word out. 'I don't want men going down with 'flu. Off work. Short-handed. All the rest of it. I don't want the trouble.'

'I'll have her over it before then.' Macauley duelled.

'I'm sorry,' Wigley said shaking his head firmly, 'but I can't let you stay here. I don't even want the risk of it. Why, you know what shearers are. They've only got to know there's sickness here and they'd make a stink about it and refuse to come. And you couldn't blame them. It's not a fair thing to ask a man to subject himself to the risk, to come to a place where he knows a sick person to be. You'd think twice about it yourself.'

'She'll be right by then,' Macauley insisted.

'Right or not right, there's still a danger of infection. I don't want it. You'll have to go.' He swung off the horse. 'Where is the child?'

Macauley stood back as Wigley stepped into the room. He stayed at the door, watching Wigley inspect the child. He turned as Drayton called his name, and saw the letter in his outstretched hand.

'I just remembered I had it,' Drayton said, with his look of pondering sympathy.

Macauley took the letter and his eyes snapped open and narrowed. The old address was in the handwriting of his wife. That was all he had time for. Wigley's feet clattered on the floorboards. His face, six inches from Macauley's, was like a beetroot. 'You should have had that child in hospital days ago!' he rapped. 'I'll make arrangements to have her taken there straight away.'

He grabbed the reins of his horse from Drayton's hands.

'You'll do nothing of the bloody kind,' Macauley said, and the way he said it arrested Wigley in the act of putting one foot in the stirrup-iron. He stood poised, scrutinising the glaring eyes, full of quick heat, and the bearded face and the shaggy head. He was not used to being spoken to that way, but he was a man who knew something of men, and he thought he understood

Macauley. He mounted his horse, and leant forward over the animal's neck.

'What are you getting tough about?'

'Nobody's getting tough,' Macauley said, the eyes softening in their fiery intensity, but not shifting from Wigley's face.

'I think you'd be wise to do what Mr Wigley says,' Drayton put in nervously, nodding his head with a kindly persuasiveness.

'Why not, man?' Wigley followed up. 'That child is sicker than you think. What's your objection?'

'Look, Wigley,' Macauley said, 'you've told me to get out.'

'I've told you I can't have you here.'

'Same thing.'

Wigley galloped ahead. 'And if you were a reasonable man you'd see my point.'

'You want to send my kid to hospital.'

'Good God, man, where's your complaint there? It won't cost you anything. I'll bear all the expense. I can't be any fairer than that, can I?'

'It's an offer you ought to accept with gratitude,' Drayton encouraged with a pleading expression.

Macauley ignored him, still looking at Wigley.

'You know how I'm placed,' he said quietly. 'Yet you tell me to get out. You're doing me a bad turn. Well, let it stay at that.'

'You don't think I like doing it, do you?' Wigley demanded.

'Let it stay at that,' Macauley said. 'Don't try to buy it back with a favour.'

'What on earth — '

'Just so you can square off. Just so you can be a good feller with me and a good feller with yourself.'

'You're a bloody fool!' exploded Wigley. 'What chance have you got of getting away from here with that child? I'm trying to help you.'

'So the favour's all for you, then? It's not for me after all. Look, Wigley, the only one you're helping,' Macauley told him bluntly, 'is yourself. You can't wait to get rid of us. The quicker the better. You've got the shivery-shakes. You're away ahead of yourself, with a shedful of sick men and the pens full of jumbucks waiting to be shorn, and thousands to come, and you losing dough by the minute; down to your last ten thousand, and wondering where the next feed's coming from. It hasn't happened. But the panic you're in has made it happen already.'

Wigley was fuming, his lips compressed and quivering, his face a choleric red.

'I ought to get off this horse and thrash you for that. You're an insulting ungrateful swine. You haven't got the breeding of a dog.'

Macauley's eyes glinted, but he was perfectly composed.

'The sheep, the sheds, the men, the dough, even the 'flu germs – they'll all be here, Wigley, when you and me are dead and gone.'

Wigley sprang off his horse. Macauley didn't move from the doorway. Easily, he blocked the two wild haymakers, and caught Wigley's arms by the wrists. 'Don't do anything you might be ashamed of later, Mr Wigley.' He took his big hands off the other's wrists, and Wigley jerked himself away.

'If you're not off this place by tomorrow I'll get the police to shift you.'

'Never mind the threats,' Macauley said. 'I'll be gone. I bear you no hard feelings. I know your form. I just wanted you to know that I know it.'

Drayton, white and trembling, shaking his head with regret of the whole unpleasant incident and obviously feeling some guilt for his own part in it, told Macauley in a quavering voice that he ought to be ashamed of himself for his insolence and stupidity. He leant over to help Wigley onto his horse, but Wigley brushed his arm aside, mounted, and cantered away, with Drayton following anxiously in a jog-trot.

Polka Dot edged round the side of the house and waddled up. He looked at Macauley as though he were seeing him in a new light. 'I heard the whole show from lights out to God Save The King. Cripes you tossed him, didn't you? Neat as sixpence.'

'How's the time?' Macauley said.

'She must be gettin' onto six. Can you do a feed?'

'I can eat.'

'Yeah, no doubt about you, you made him look meaner than catcrap. Well, I'll go and get her ready.'

'Okay. I'll be over soon.'

Macauley sat on his bunk and pulled the letter from his pocket. He looked at it for a minute, breathing hard; then he opened it. He felt the ends of his fingers tingle as he read. It started off without any preliminaries.

> I hope this finds you, because I want you to know a few things. You thought I'd come crawling after you for the kid, didn't you? You thought I couldn't get along without her. Fat lot you knew, you bastard. The laugh might have

> been on your face that night, but it's on mine now. You have a turn with her and see how you get on. See how she gets on your nerves for a change. Don't come back here. I don't want to see either of you again. You ruined my life, but thank God a good man has come into it now. You hurt Donny, you broke his jaw and smashed his ribs and he could go you through the court, but he's too big a man for that. He's a gentleman compared to you. He's kind and thoughtful, not like you. You're nothing but a selfish brute, and you always will be. I wasn't right in the head when I married you. Donny and me will be married just as soon as the divorce is through. I can nail you for desertion, and that's what I'm going to do. But don't think I'm finished with you yet. I'm not. One day I'm going to get you if it's the last thing I do. You mongrel. I hope you die.
>
> M.

That was the only signature. Macauley read the letter through again, feeling the impact of loathing and vindictiveness in the words. He looked at the postmark on the envelope. The letter had been posted four months ago, two months after he had taken Buster. But it may have been written sooner, written to relieve a heart flooded with hatred and humiliation, set aside in a drawer for its acrimony to mature, nursed in a handbag like a malevolent vial. Until it was finally sent to its victim.

Slowly he crumpled the paper and rolled it into a ball between his palms. He felt the cold creep round his ankles and into his fingers. He heard the slight querulous whimpering of the child in fugitive sleep. The dark came down, sifting into the room.

'Hey, Mac!' Polka called from the cookhouse. 'Come on, mate, and feed your face.'

Macauley went over. He flipped the paper ball into the fire with a grimace of bitter contempt. There was a storm in his head. Polka was all for talking about the set-to, but Macauley told him tersely to put a sock in it. Polka looked taken aback for a moment, but affably agreed, saying he knew a lot more tunes. He chattered away, aware of Macauley's inner turmoil, and doing his best to crust it over with levity. But even his good humour was blunted by Macauley's moody silence and laconic replies; and in a little while his enthusiastic crusade dwindled to a few simple platitudes about rain and wool and the state of the country.

He went outside, and came back five minutes later, rubbing his hands and scrooging his shoulders. 'By cripes,' he remarked with a shiver in his voice, 'a man'll want all the feathers on the bed tonight.'

He stood on the hob with his back to the fire, watching Macauley rolling a cigarette.

'Are you fair dinkum about pushin' off tomorrow, Mac?'

'You heard me tell him,' Macauley said, without looking up.

'Yeah, I know – but I mean, with the kid and that . . .' Macauley seemed to be reflecting and Polka went on, 'I reckon you ought to stick it out. What could Wigley do? He's not that hard, anyway, not underneath.'

'I'll eat grass first,' Macauley said.

Polka looked glum. He rolled himself a match-thin cigarette, a racehorse, and tucked the ends in thoughtfully.

'Well, it's tough luck, that's all I can say. But nobody's fault.'

'It's somebody's fault,' Macauley said.

'Aw, crimey, Mac, nobody can help gettin' crook. I know how you feel, but what can you do? Like that mate of mine, Hinchey. He was always doin' somethin' or gettin' crook at the wrong time and that. I coulda kicked him in the ask-no-questions a dozen times a day, but it wouldn't have done any good.'

Macauley stood up. 'I need wood. All I can get. See what you can rake together for me, will you, Polka?'

He walked back to the hut in a ferment of antagonism. He took a tomahawk from his swag, stuck the handle through his belt, and carried the kerosene-box table round to the room with the fireplace. He rammed his shoulder against the door. The lock tore away from the splintered woodwork and the door crashed open. He threw the box into the room.

He walked away into the freezing darkness. The cold wind cut into his bones. It seemed to come off the ice of the stars, glinting frostily in the cold remoteness of space. Macauley couldn't help feeling that matters were getting to a stage where they were becoming comical. Fate was certainly laying in the boot; piling it on. It was the last straw when a man had to go searching for fuel, when in a few days there would be a woodstack outside the door that a pole vaulter couldn't jump over.

But he was a crafty man who knew where to look without wasting time. He cut away the dry bark from the leaning sides of trees and the underparts of logs. He split the dry wood away. Splintered wood he got in plenty from the openings of hollow rotten logs. In an old green tree, hollow from the ground for some distance up there was a thick debris of leaves and twigs that had blown in there and accumulated with time. He took it all. He armed himself with a few solid wet stumps and thick junks and carried all back to the hut in two trips. Polka had collected half a tubful of chips, wet and dry from the woodheap, several scantlings from round the shed, and had thrown in a couple of kerosene cases from his room.

'By cripes, she's cold, ain't she?' Polka shivered.

Macauley built the fire carefully with the wet and dry wood and plenty of old newspapers and magazines screwed into wads. He poured some kerosene over the pyre from the hurricane lantern. He set it alight and fanned it. The flames crept up, tasting the wet wood and retreating into thick crawling smoke. He worked over it, hearing the struggling crackle, the spitting, sizzling, and hissing of the drenched sticks.

Then he had the fire established, and when it had warmed the room, driving out the chill, he went back to his room. He placed Buster on his bunk while he carried the bedding round and threw it on a mattress along the wall opposite the fireplace. He went back and wrapped her up and brought her out. She was dreeing mournfully. The night air caught at her throat and brought on an attack of coughing. He felt the humid heat of her head against his cheek, the steamy warmth of her body.

'You think it'll work?' Polka asked.

'There's a chance,' Macauley said, not pausing for a minute. 'If I can knock that fever and congestion it'll help.'

He poured eucalyptus into his palm and rubbed Buster's back, chest, and throat. Her flesh was a burning pink, laced with blue veins. It was tight on her chest and the chest was like a frail ridgy basket. Her shoulder blades stuck up like the bones of a trussed fowl. Her spine was a rod of blunt discs.

Macauley rolled the thick pads of his hands up and down. She cried out and twisted. He used the whole bottle of eucalyptus. He rubbed his hands dry with each application. Buster burst into moaning screeching sobs with the agony. Her squalling was nerve-racking. Polka stood with a look of suffering on his face. Macauley didn't falter. His face was set like stone. He rubbed the flesh raw. Then he was finished. He wrapped up the tortured bundle like a parcel and left her to whimper herself to sleep.

'Why don't you hit the sack, mate?' He said to Polka. 'I'll be up all night, and I don't feel like talking.'

Polka took the hint, tucked his neck into his coat collar, and braved the frigid air.

Macauley stoked the fire and threw on more wood. It was the length of the fireplace and two feet high, a great roaring shock of flame that tore up the chimney and sat like the red wick of a giant candle on the top, sparks flying from it as from the streaming tail of a comet. It was so bright it lit up every corner with a furious glow that scarcely cast a shadow. The temperature mounted. In a little while Macauley couldn't get near the fire without shielding his eyes with his hands and smelling the scorch of his clothes.

The room was an oven. Inside the blankets the child cooked. He watched the sweat break on her face and run down it in rills. The towel that pillowed her head became a sodden pulp. His own clothes hung like a dishcloth. He stripped down to his underpants. When he went to the door and stood on the step the night air hit him like a douche of icy water. He left the door ajar and rammed open the window a little.

He sat at the end of Buster's bed while she tossed and turned.

Thoughts came unbidden, mulling round in his mind. If she dies, I'll be free. It's a way out. His mind seized easily on the temptations of freedom – the freedom he used to know. Able to say yes or no like that. None of this dithering about. Off the mark in a tick; a hundred roads to choose from and a hundred towns to put the finger on. Jobs to take on or turn down at the drop of a hat.

What would be said if she died? Nothing. But how would he feel? All right. He could turn round and say to himself: I did what I could. Still, why should a man say anything. Was it just an effort to bluff conscience, satisfy integrity? All that nursing, all this bush doctoring – was it done just to appease something in him; all the time he was doing it did he half hope that his efforts would be unsuccessful? He couldn't be sure whether he did or didn't.

In the morning, in a trickle of dawn, he came out of his stupid doze and he saw the face on the pillow, frail, peaked, white as a wood grub, smeared with a faint pearlescent sheen of sweat. He felt the pulse in the thin wrist. Like the leg of a chook, he thought. Against the puny chest he heard the clear unreeded bump of life. He looked at the ashes of the fire. There wasn't a chip unburned. Everything had been consumed.

When after a while he saw Buster's eyes open his face was expressionless.

'You feel okay now?'

All he got was a faint smile and a nod. The lips were burned with fever, dry, cracked, covered with a film of brown skin. The teeth gleamed, prominent like a rabbit's.

'I'm thirsty.'

He turned away. 'I'll get you a drink.'

He went outside. The dew hung in loops on the fence wire. The grass sparkled. What was the matter with him? He didn't have to light that fire. Swaddle that brat in a cocoon of clothes. He could have stayed in the other room, in the biting acid of the cold. No doubt about her, though, the way she had pulled through. He felt irritated by the unvolitional feeling of admiration oozing through his confused thoughts.

When he went back she sat up and guzzled the water.

'Where's Gooby gone?'

He went round to the other room and got Gooby. He saw her eyes sparkle as he gave it to her. She hugged it and tucked it in beside her with a great show of finicky adoration.

'I'm hungry.'

'You only think you are.'

'No.'

'I'll see what I can get for you,' he said.

He buttered her a hunk of bread, and when he returned with it, Buster was sitting up. Now that she was better and looked like getting well he could afford to be aloof and resentful. He sat on the bed, thoughtfully rolling a smoke while she opened her mouth wide to accommodate the size of the bread. She translated her sudden access of well-being into exuberant loquacity. Macauley let her babble on as though he didn't hear.

'I was awful sick, wasn't I?'

Could have let it happen.

'I'm not sick now. Gooby's not sick either.'

You didn't know I thought about it.

'Is the fire all out?'

Only me to think about you, and me thinking about you like that.

'You made me better, didn't you, dad?'

Could have been dead now; you wouldn't have known.

'Why don't you talk? Dad!'

God, I don't know what's the matter with a man.

'Dad, talk to me. Haven't you got any tongue or something?'

He looked round. 'Shut up,' he said. 'And don't give me any lip. You mag too much.'

'Where's our other room gone?' she asked.

Of a sudden she found that she couldn't finish the rest of the bread. She gave it to him and lay back weak and exhausted. Macauley told her to rest. He went over to the cookhouse. Polka was there, looking every inch a swagman. He was hunched up to the coals, drawing on a thin cigarette.

'How's the kid?'

'Okay. I think she'll be right now,' Macauley said.

'Aw, yeah, the fire. You was lucky.' He nodded, then shuddered. 'Strike me dead, I curl up inside a woolpack, overcoat on, all the nap I got, and yet duggar me if I can sleep.' He looked up, dropping his misery for a bright smile. 'And the titter's all right, you say.'

Macauley nodded. 'I don't know,' he said, with a note of pleasure in his voice, 'she's the toughest little bastard I've ever struck. If she was a celluloid dog she'd run through hell and make it.'

'Not like him,' Polka sighed.

'Who?'

'Hinchey, that mate of mine. And it wasn't like he didn't have any savvy or that, you know. He had plenty. That's what I can't understand.'

Macauley put a hand on Polka's shoulder. 'Listen,' he said softly, 'stop fretting about your mate. He's feeling it more than you.'

Polka jumped up, expostulating. 'Frettin' about him! I'm not frettin' about the silly bee. I'm just sayin', like. I'm — '

His eyes met Macauley's perspicacious gaze, and his words faltered, and he turned his head.

'Dammit,' he said angrily. 'Look at that duddy blackfeller's fire. I could kick its guts in.'

'Why don't you put some wood on it?'

'Wood!' squeaked Polka. 'Don't you think I would if we had any? We're skinned out. Unless we go knock on the kitchen table.'

'Take it easy,' Macauley said with a bit of a grin. 'It's not that bad. Come on, we'll rake some up.'

Macauley wanted to get away as soon as he could. It would take him all day to walk to Collarenebri, and he didn't want to be coming into the town in the dark. Yet he wanted to give Buster a chance to get a little strength into her body. She would have to be nursed along steadily, and he knew what he was going to do about that. What he had in mind was Walgett and Bella Sweeney. He could bank on a ride through from Collarenebri to Walgett, and there he could park Buster with Bella until he found a job, and maybe Bella wouldn't mind even keeping the kid with her.

He managed to get Buster to eat some meat. Then he dressed her warmly. She wobbled weakly outside in the sun and sat on Macauley's swag. Macauley saw that the two rooms were left as clean as when he went into them, and that nothing was left behind, and then he was ready for the track.

Polka waddled up to him, looking glum. 'Sorry to see you go,' he said.

Macauley shook his hand.

'I've took a real shine to you, Mac,' Polka went on. 'You'd be a good mate to knock round with.'

'You'd kill me with kindness.'

Polka grinned. 'Not me? I can be a hard bee when I like. Trouble is, I don't very often like. How are you off for lettuce?'

'I'll be right.'

'What I mean is I can dook you a caser if it's any good.'

Macauley patted him on the shoulder in a gesture of thanks and refusal. 'You'll be here when the boys come. If a bloke called Lucky Regan is among them tell him I said what big eyes he's got. Stepper Mackenzie, Bluey Green, Mick and Ted Bennett. Tell 'em I was asking after them and they can still pull up a log to my fire any time they like.'

'I'll do that, mate.'

Macauley lifted the swag onto one shoulder and hoisted Buster into his arms on the other. He was surprised at her lightness and realised how much weight she must have shed.

'Look after yourselves,' Polka called. 'Send me a message stick some time.'

'What address?' Macauley turned for a moment.

'Aw, just care of the wide open spaces, Australia,' Polka waved.

Macauley had a little matter to tidy up at the station first. It didn't take long. When the dark girl came out from the kitchen in answer to his knock he thrust a pound note into her hand. She looked at him bashfully, half frightened.

'Take it,' Macauley said. 'It's yours. I owe you nothing now. We're quits.'

He said no more. He was gone with her looking after him, he knew, and he felt better. He felt better because he no longer felt beholden; he had put the concupiscent happening with her in its proper place and given it its proper name. She had nothing on him now and he had nothing on himself. He had cleaned up a debt.

He had walked a mile before he lowered his two swags and had a spell. He smoked a cigarette while the sweat dried on his face.

'Do you like carrying me, dad?'

'Sure,' Macauley said satirically, 'I love it. Come on.'

He hadn't got a half mile before a utility truck came along behind him and stopped alongside. Macauley recognised it as Wigley's; the one he had driven home from his sheep-judging visit to Dubbo.

A ruddy-faced man with a cap and buck teeth called to him, 'Come on, hop in.'

Macauley threw his swag in the back and got in beside the driver. He took Buster off his knee and sat her in the middle. When the truck was under way Macaulay looked the station hand up and down discreetly, noticed his workaday clothes and the muddy boots.

'You're not going to Colly?' he said.

'Hell, no.' The driver jerked his head round as though he were surprised about something. 'I don't have to. Wigley told me to pick you up and take you there.'

Macauley sat back with a faint, gratified smile.

He was walking down the street in the last of the sunshine when he saw Luke Sweeney ahead of him. He recognised the humped back, the hands in the pockets lifting the flaps of the coat, the slight limp in one leg that still carried shrapnel from Armentieres, the bent head as though the man was stiff-necked when all he was doing was being pensive.

Macauley hastened his walk and called from three yards behind, 'Hey, you old bag of bones, what are you looking for now?'

Luke Sweeney turned as though expecting to see a small cheeky boy with a man's voice. The instant he saw his mistake the fight went out of his eyes, and surprise jumped into them. He shook Macauley's hand with delight and all the vigour he could muster.

'Blow me down, wonders'll never cease. Me and the Cow was only talking about you the other night. We thought you musta been pushing up daisies, it's been so long since you were here.'

Luke Sweeney was an introduction to Bella Sweeney long before you saw her. He used to say, 'She's one of them women, you know.' And if you didn't know, Macauley reckoned, you did when you saw her.

Her figure was a continent. Her great chest curved like the

Bight. Her buttocks were the hump of southern Victoria. Her legs were Ayers Rock, twice. She engulfed him, fed from his pathetic frailty, so that the dissipated juices and living fluids left him a desiccated being to mark their going, atrophied the struggling flesh on his bones and built hollows in his face and filled him with shadows. He was a frame of bones scraggy and gaunt as dead timber; a wildling pressed between the gluttony of her passion and the dangers of her tremendous vitality. Yet he thought the world of her; glorified in the deluge of her love; relished her with pride, pleasure, and mischief.

'When'd you get here?'

'Just a while ago,' Macauley said. 'We struck a lift with a cocky from Colly, right through. Soft seats, too. How's Bella?'

'Who, the Cow? Bigger than ever, and still loves me like mad. You know, she'd drink rat poison if I kicked the bucket. I wouldn't want that. But I tell you, boy, I'm finding it a helluva job to go on staying alive.' Luke Sweeney's eyes twinkled waggishly. 'I'm gonna get overlaid any day now.' He laughed with good humour. 'Another thing. I'm having nightmares. I think I'm sleeping on the side of a mountain. I think I'm a bear. I climb the mountain. Then I get the shivers. I start screaming. I find I'm not alone. There's a great big bare behind.'

He burst into uproarious laughter, slapping one hand with the other. 'Ah,' he broke off, 'a man's got to have his little joke. Say, where'd you get that?' He pointed at Buster.

As they walked along, Macauley told him the story of what had happened and why he was there.

'I didn't want to be any bother, Luke, and I wouldn't ask your help if I didn't need it.'

'Ah, rubbish, what are friends for?'

'I've come to the stage,' Macauley said, 'where I've even got to touch you for a quid.'

Luke Sweeney raised his eyebrows. 'Well, that just about breaks my bloody heart,' he quavered in a miserly voice. Then he laughed and slapped Macauley on the shoulder. 'You're such a proud, independent cow I wonder how you got the words out even.'

Macauley half wondered himself. He couldn't imagine himself saying them. But he wanted to be sure that Sweeney didn't misunderstand him. 'On my own I wouldn't be in this fix. And I'm not asking for charity, don't think that. Just a little help on appro. I'll settle with you when I come good.'

'No bloody fear you won't. I don't forget the time you stuck to me out at the Ridge when I was just scratching.'

'You owe me nothing,' Macauley said.

'I owe you everything, what are you talking about? Only for you, me and her would have chucked it in long before. We wouldn't have stayed there in that god-forsaken hole gouging our guts out for sweet damn-all. It was you who talked us into staying, and you who put me on to that duffer and told me to give it a go. Remember?'

'I remember.'

'And what do I do?' Sweeney said. 'I come up with a stone worth five hundred quid. I come up with the Black Beauty, and from then on I never look back. Tin-bum, they call me. I get on to opal all over the place wherever I sink a shaft and put up a windlass.' He chuckled. Then his eyes narrowed shrewdly. 'You know, I often suspect you put that stone there for me to find.'

'Don't kid yourself. Me dum five hundred smackers when all I'm doing is making wages myself!'

'It was too pat; it was too easy even though I know the luck of the game, the way it can be under your nose all the time and you can't see it.'

'You're talking through your hat,' Macauley said. 'You've had too much of the sun.'

'I'll believe it if I like,' Sweeney told him. 'Anyway, it was the makings of us. It got us a lot of things we never had before. It set us up on easy street. It got us this boarding house and a lot of other things.'

'You worked for it,' Macauley said.

The boarding house was an extensive old timber building two storeys high and with a verandah running round the top storey. It had been a hotel in the days when horses had a big say in the affairs of men, and the fact that it stood on a corner was not the major evidence. There was a big backyard with the stables still standing. There was nothing shabby about any of it. It was painted buff and green with maroon pipings.

Macauley and Sweeney went through the gate in the fence and walked across the yard rutted and cobbled with hard black mud. They stopped on the flagstones of the back verandah, and Sweeney put his face to the gauze door of the kitchen.

'Hey, Bel,' he called, 'come and see what I found.'

The door opened and the doorway was plugged with a gargantuan female. This was the woman Sweeney called the Cow. She had a casky bosom, as if stuffed, an uddery bulge against the garish print dress covered with yellow and vermilion flowers. An amber scarf was tied round her head and tucked in, giving her a poly look. Her face was a massive blob of radiant flesh, with the features a long way in from the perimeter as though they had been superimposed, forming a face within a face. There was a vague, elusive doll-like prettiness about it.

She gaped at Macauley, blinked and burst into a sunshower of tears. She threw her two arms like the weekend joints round him, Buster and all, and the touch of her face on Macauley's tough skin was like the touch of a powder puff: What had he been doing, the big lump, and where had he been and how was he feeling, and who was the piccaninny? – she flung the questions with shrieks of joy, slapping, pummelling and pushing him with the hilarity of an elephant at its mother's homecoming. Then she stood off, her blue eyes sparkling with laughter and happiness, and as if she hadn't made her rapture clear she hurled a pudgy arm round Sweeney's head, pulled him off balance and squashed his face against hers so that one eye was twisted skew-whiff and the lips pouted like a cod's.

'And what do you think of my Lukey?' she shouted lovingly, giving him a resounding kiss on the nose. 'Isn't he looking well?'

He struggled like a cat with its head in a fish tin, and she only released him so that she could give her overwhelming attention to Buster, who was standing beside Macauley and looking up as though at some strange horror in the sky. Sweeney twitched his face into shape and picked up his cap, breathing heavily from his exhausting ordeal.

Bella Sweeney astonished Buster with her terrible affection. She lavished her with darlings and sweethearts and poor little dears. She gripped her under the armpits and hauled the unwilling child into the air, kissing and hugging her. Buster grunted, and held herself away, arching, not knowing whether to be distressed or paralytic and so settling for both. Bella carried her inside protesting, but when Buster was satisfied no harm was going to come to her she sat still in a caution of wonder and timidity.

In the private lounge room Sweeney explained the situation, and Macauley was grateful. He didn't relish the idea of going over the same ground again.

'Of course,' Bella boomed, 'you can stay here as long as you like. And we'll soon get this little cherub strong and healthy again, won't we, love? You poor little baby, you must have been sick.'

She fondled Buster to her and Buster sniffed virtuously.

'Hey, you be careful of that kid, Bel,' Sweeney warned her. 'She'll break. She's not like me you know – rubber bones and no nerves.'

Bella gave a hoot of delighted laughter. 'Isn't he a funny old bugger, my Lukey?' she chortled. Caught in the direct rays of her wifely adulation he put his hands up protectively, and said, 'Now, Bel, now, you've had enough of me for one day.'

She rocked with mirth, and Sweeney grinned to see her. That was the way it was with them.

Macauley and Buster were given a balcony room. It was clean and neat. Bella told him any dirty duds he had to sling them out; the black girl would be round in the morning to do the washing.

Buster said as she bounced on the bed, 'I like this place.'

'Well, don't smash the mattress.'

'Are we going to live here now?'

'For a little while.'

He looked at her: pale and emaciated as she was, and still with the cough, it was hard to believe that it was the same child who looked like death only the night before. He had a sense of gratified pleasure in his success, not so much because he had put her on her feet as because he had bested his anxiety and overthrown what had seemed like certain defeat. And from that feeling he drew much confidence and hope: whether illusory or not, he could sense a turn in his fortunes, a run of good luck for a change. Striking the ride through from Collarenebri so quickly portended to it; so did the welcome he had received here and the cushy prospect of staying for a few weeks, which he told himself truthfully was for the sole purpose of getting Buster completely well and giving him the opportunity to plan his future – and hers. He had resolved that they should split up. What he would do with her he had yet to work out.

He felt even more certain that he was right about his lucky streak coming right way up when he walked down the town next morning and chanced on a job as a builder's labourer. He had done the work before among the many other odds and sods in his catalogue of toil. The contractor's name was Varley, an easygoing man who had a good name as a boss. He took a fancy to Macauley, especially after he saw the way he worked on the job. He was a laconic man who didn't pay compliments every day of the week but he said to Macauley, 'What I like about you is your conscientiousness.'

'It's your money. You want to see something for it. I'm not doing any more than I'm being paid for.'

'That's not it. You're doing as much as you're being paid for.'

Macauley shrugged. 'The boss who doesn't stand over a man like a gyppo taskmaster gets more out of me,' he said.

'I wish others felt the same way,' answered Varley, with a sigh.

This great institution of labour could be a tough proposition sometimes, Macaulay thought. Hammer one nail in a piece of timber and the boss thought you were a slacker. Hammer two, and your mates slurred you as a crawler. But it depended on the mates. Safest way out was to work for yourself, and not everybody could do that. Even then a man had his troubles. He liked the mates on the job, and they liked him. What Varley thought about them was his own business.

That first day Macauley had a job getting Buster to stay behind. Bella had to use her impressive authority of blandishment and affection with the child. She told her she had to stay in bed and she insisted on keeping her there. When Macauley returned in the evening Buster greeted him with joyful enthusiasm that wouldn't be quelled. He learned that she had been asking all day for him, asking where he was and when he was coming back; getting out of bed from time to time and looking up and down the street from the balcony.

'You were away a long time,' she chided him.

'I was working,' Macauley said.

Luke Sweeney knocked and came in. He nodded in Buster's direction. 'I suppose Bel told you.'

'Yeah, going on like a fretful pup.'

'No, about the quack?'

'Quack? What quack?'

'Bel got old Doc Elliott in to have a look at the sprat there. He reckons she'll be okay with a bit of convalescence. He nutted out some jollop for her cough. Bel's been giving her the invalid treatment all day.'

'Good of Bella to do that,' was all Macauley could think of saying.

On the second and third days Buster reacted to his absence in the same way, but as the week went on she became used to it. Either she adapted herself to missing him, or she didn't worry, knowing that he proved himself able to keep faith.

'That child loves you,' Bella told Macauley.

Macauley coloured with embarrassment, the unexpectedness of the remark confusing him.

'What about a few records on the gramophone, Bella?' he said.

Bella continued to stare intently at him, touched by her admiration for Buster's feelings, scarcely aware of Macauley's awkward glances.

'She loves you with every ounce of love in her body, the precious little darling.'

Macauley coughed and looked for his tobacco. 'The gramophone. Tell me where it is and I'll get it.'

'I've been giving her milk, custards, broth, and she laps them up. Eats them like an angel. Even the rice puddings. And you know how kiddies detest rice pudding?'

'Yeah,' Sweeney chipped in, 'you'll have her as fat as you before you're finished. Then you'll have competition. With me, I mean.'

She gave a squawk of laughter. 'Isn't he a funny old bugger, my Lukey?'

At the end of the second week Macauley was sitting in his room brushing his boots when Luke Sweeney came in with a great auctioneer's bell in his hand.

'Where are you off to?' Macauley said. 'To get the cows?'

Sweeney sat down beside him with an impish look on his face. He winked mischievously.

'Where's the sale?' Macauley persisted, but Sweeney wouldn't be tempted to tell his secret.

'You noticed that nipper of yours lately, Mac?' he said. 'She's so happy it's coming out of her ears.'

'She's not getting in your hair during the day?'

'Hair?' piped Sweeney, lifting his cap off his bald dome. 'What hair?' He suddenly flipped his fingers. 'Say, I didn't tell you, did I? I'm getting myself a couple of coursing dogs.'

'Coursing dogs?'

'Yeah,' laughed Sweeney. 'To chase the hairs off my chest on to my head.' He slapped Macauley on the knee. 'Ah, a man's got to have his little joke,' he said, wiping his eyes.

'Where's Buster now?' Macauley said.

'Where do you think she is?' Sweeney gestured. 'Three guesses.'

'With Bella.'

Sweeney nodded: 'They're as thick as thieves, the pair of them. The Cow's taken to her like she was her own, and the little 'un's really attached. She hasn't made up to me anything like the way she has to Bella, but I get on all right with her. Listen! There she goes!'

From below Macauley could hear the loud rhapsodic notes of a woman singing. He could have heard them with his head under a pillow. They had all the vociferation of an untrained Wagnerian soprano.

Sweeney crept to the door, held up a finger commanding Macauley to pay attention, and jangled the bell for all he was worth. The singing ceased abruptly. Sweeney giggled. It started up again, rather hesitantly. Then when it was in full stride, Sweeney rang the bell again. The singing stopped. He tittered.

'Terrible, isn't it? On the nose.' He held his nostrils together.

Macauley didn't commit himself.

'Every morning it goes on. Caruso and the waterworks all rolled into one.'

Macauley nodded.

'This is the only way I can stop it,' Sweeney explained. 'And the poor thing loves to sing, you know.' He made a gesture of lenience. 'Not that I do it every time. Some days my constitution don't feel like it's been shot to pieces.'

Bella started again with caution and defiance. She sang a bar. The bell rang. She screeched four notes. The bell jangled shrilly. It went on for five minutes – Bella sneaking out furtive arpeggios, the bell answering; then both voice and metal dinning in unison. Sometimes, so great was his expectancy, Sweeney was a little early with his answers, sometimes a little late.

Finally, satisfied that the dragon was dead, he shut the door and sat down beside Macauley again. 'Funny part about it, she doesn't know who's doing it. She doesn't know where the sound comes from. She's never picked me. She rampages through the house trying to locate the culprit. When I come on the scene she says, kinda peculiar, "That bell was ringing again, Luke." I say, "What bell, dear?" "Didn't you hear it?" she says. "I've been lying down all the time and I never heard any bell," I say. She's beginning to think it's in her head.'

'She'll know when I blow the gaff on you,' Macauley said.

Alarm hit Luke Sweeney's face as if it had suddenly been switched on. 'God Almighty, don't you ever do that, Mac. You wouldn't. You couldn't be so cruel to a man. I'd shake to pieces and fall down in bits.'

He thought he had better go and put his bell back in its hiding place, and crept out.

Macauley walked down into the dining room. There was nobody there. Then a voice said to him, 'Look, daddy.'

He turned instantly and stared. He hardly knew Buster. She was wearing a little girl's frock, pink with white trimmings, pink socks and black patent shoes. Her hair was tied with a broad pink ribbon. She was holding the dress out at the sides, and smiling, a little shyly. Bella melted into view behind her, her face one big silent smile.

'Well, what do you think of your little daughter now? Isn't she sweet?'

'Why — ' Macauley gulped. 'I — it's — it seems so long since I saw her in an outfit like that. Well, in a dress, I mean. I'd forgotten.'

He felt somewhat awkward. He didn't know what other acknowledgement he could make. The way Bella looked at him she seemed to be expecting him to make a fuss.

'I hope she remembered to thank you,' he said tritely.

He saw the let-down look on the woman's face, and he went out vexed with himself.

Macauley's job was to finish on the Friday of the third week. Varley had nothing else to offer him immediately, but he told Macauley he was set for a job any time with him, and he voluntarily gave him a reference. He also gave him a letter of recommendation to a building contractor he knew in Coonamble, and another to a sawmill owner in the same town.

When Macauley asked Bella what the damage was she told him to go and jump in the lake. He knew it was useless to argue and try to press the money on to her. And he knew they were not being patronisingly generous in refusing to take it. They were genuinely pleased, both of them, to have been able to help a friend. He appreciated that, but he wanted to let them see that he hadn't lost any of his principle. He told them he would send it to them; and if they didn't mind keeping Buster for a while he would square that account, too, when he got a little sugar together.

When he looked at himself he wanted to be able to say, I owe nothing to no man.

Bella Sweeney collapsed her huge bulk in a rickety chair that went *eeek* every time she moved her body. 'Mind,' she said. Why, she had been feeling sick all the week whenever she thought of the prospective parting. Imagining the loneliness after Buster had gone.

'I would have missed her something dreadful,' she said, sadness finding its way even on to the natural jollity of her face. 'I've got so fond of her. I don't let things get me down, as my Lukey can tell you, but that would have been something hard to have got over.' She beamed. 'She can stay here as long as you like, Mac. She can stay here forever. I'll keep her if you'll sell her.'

'It'll give me a chance to put some work behind me, get flush again, and work out what's the best thing to do with her. I was thinking a boarding school might be the shot.'

'Oh, Mac, she's too young.'

'Anyway,' he said, 'I'll get her off your hands as soon as I can.'

'You'll have a hard job,' Bella chyacked him with a great laugh. She rose, twisted round and flumped back in the chair. 'Even though I know the position, Mac, I still don't know how you can bear to part with her.'

'Well . . .' Macauley blustered. He could think of nothing to say one way or the other. He drummed his fingers on the table.

'It mightn't be easy,' she said.

'Easy? What do you mean?'

'She mightn't want to stay with me.'

'Hell,' Macauley said, 'there shouldn't be any trouble about that, should there, the way you two hit it off.'

Bella lowered her voice. 'Will you tell her?'

Macauley sighed, and started to roll a cigarette. 'Suppose I'll have to, yes. But I'll leave it till the last minute.'

'When'll you leave?'

'Around about dark, Saturday, I thought. When she's gone to bed.'

Macauley looked up. Bella was laughing at him silently: her eyes smiling, but full of penetrative intentness. He felt uncomfortable.

'Well, what's the matter?' he demanded, a little testily. 'Don't you think that's a good idea?'

She exploded with laughter, rocking and shaking in the chair. Macauley stared at her mystified, watching the jiggling jowls, the eyes crinkled into blue slivers, the blubber bouncing under her dress; hearing the staccato peals of hilarity pounding from the open mouth. He frowned as though he thought she had gone crazy.

She floundered in the chair and swelled to her feet. She gestured hectically. 'You poor man,' she gurgled. 'You kill me.' She rolled away in an upheaval of mirth.

Macauley looked after her, disconcerted, stroking his jaw.

On Saturday morning he took Buster for a walk. She was dressed in the outfit Bella had bought her and seemed to feel very pleased with herself. She was intent on looking in every shop window they passed. Macauley let her have her way, quelling his exasperation, out of consideration for the fact that this was the last walk they would have together for a long time.

It was while he was lingering outside one of these shops, waiting for Buster to finish discussing the contents of a shop window with Gooby, that Macauley saw the woman coming along the street. And when he saw her, merely taking her in as just another pedestrian in the arc of his glance, he swung back and looked at her twice. He couldn't quite believe it, but in the back of his mind he was conscious of her appearance being all part and parcel of the good-luck feeling he had been having ever since he came to Walgett. It was just as if she, too, had stepped right out of the barrel after the marbles had been whirled.

He halted her with a smile, and touched his hat. 'Mrs Callahan.'

She knew him almost instantly. She was a stout little woman with a chubby face and glasses. Her hat was black straw with a sprig of red cherries on it. She waved her hands and clicked her teeth. Macauley grinned. He knew the gestures so well. She was like a dago, Callahan used to say. Tie her hands behind her back and she'd be dumb.

'No, I don't believe it,' she exclaimed, staring at him. 'I just don't believe it. How are you, Mac?'

'Never better. And you – by God, you're looking well. How do you keep so young?'

She laughed, flattered. 'Take my Kruschen every morning. Just enough to cover a sixpence. Well, fancy meeting you,' she clicked. Her greenish-grey eyes alighted on Buster, who had just come up, and was nudging her father's side. 'Is this your little girl? Mac, don't tell me.'

Macauley nodded.

'Doesn't she look like you, though!'

'Reckon.'

'The dead image. Same mouth. Same eyes. Mac, she's you to a T. Prettier, of course.' She laughed. 'And tell me, how's Marge?'

Macauley looked at the ground for a moment before replying. 'More than I can say. We've split up.'

Mrs Callahan's eyes turned cloudy. 'Oh dear, I am sorry to hear that.'

He shrugged. He didn't want to elaborate.

'Is she still in Sydney?'

'Far as I know she is.' He didn't want her to pursue the

subject. 'And what are you doing in these parts? They told me in Millie you were living in Tamworth.'

'So I am,' she said. 'I've been here nursing my sister. I've got to take her down below for an operation. You were in Millie, were you?'

'Yeah.'

'You heard about Tub, of course?'

He nodded. 'I cleaned up his grave.'

'Oh, that was kind of you, Mac.' She looked away. 'Poor Tub. He was cheerful right to the end, you know, though the pain must have been awful. I don't know why he had to die. When I think of all the rotten people in the world doing frightful things and going on living I often wonder why a good man like that had to go the way he did.'

'Yeah, it's hard to work out,' Macauley said. 'But I suppose there's a reason.'

'Only God knows it,' she said. 'Ah, well.' She cast off the shadow and brightened. 'You been here long?'

'Three weeks.'

'What a pity I didn't see you before. And what a wonder we've missed each other. I've been here nearly a week now.'

'Still, I'm glad to have run into you again.'

'So am I. And I'd like to have a real good chinwag. I'd ask you round, but you know how it is. It's not my house, and Amy is not well and I've got my hands full with her.'

'I couldn't make it anyway,' Macauley said. 'I'm off to — ' He stopped and glanced down at Buster who was preoccupied with gawking round her. But Macauley lowered his voice. 'I'm off to Coonamble tonight.'

'We're leaving Monday,' she told him. 'Isn't it funny?' She laughed. 'But you must drop in when you're in Tamworth.'

'I'd like nothing better. What's your address?'

She told him, and described how to get there, and he told her to look for him towards the end of the year. She said the welcome sign was out all the year round to him, so it didn't matter when he turned up. They parted, both happier for having met.

About three o'clock that afternoon Macauley was getting his things together and rolling his swag while Buster was absent with Bella. Suddenly the door opened and she came skipping in. She drew up short, and looked all round the room frowning. He kept on being guiltily active.

'Are we going?' she asked.

'We're not,' he said, truthfully.

'What are you doing that for then?'

'What?'

'All that.' She made an all-encompassing gesture. Suspiciously she walked to the chest of drawers and pulled out the bottom drawer. She looked up at him with her head on one side. 'What about my clothes?' she demanded in a tone chiding him for his oversight.

'Look,' Macauley said, 'I'm just doing a bit of sorting out. Run down and talk to Mrs Sweeney. I'm busy.'

He pushed her out the door and shut it. He sat on the bed and shook his head. Then a decisive, stern expression settled on his face, and he continued with his packing. He strapped his swag and threw it on the bed. He opened the door, and saw Buster slouched against the wall, looking like a puzzled dog.

He ignored her and walked on down the verandah. She

followed him. She never let him out of her sight for the rest of the afternoon. It began to get on his nerves. Putting off the moment of telling her didn't help any. He wondered why the hell he couldn't come out with it and be done with it. He was never a man to fiddle about. What was the matter with him now?

The four of them, as usual, ate together when the rest of the boarders had finished, and at the tea table Macauley tried to appear unconcerned, giving the impression that he would be there for years to come. To some extent he seemed to allay Buster's suspicions. She ate her food hungrily and with relish, her head down. Now and then she looked up under her eyebrows to see if he was still there. Macauley continued to strengthen her gullibility without being blatant about it. Luke Sweeney didn't help him. Neither did Bella. When he looked at her he got the impression that she was enjoying herself.

While Sweeney washed the dishes and Macauley dried up, Bella took Buster upstairs and put her to bed. Buster didn't demur. She went quietly. This was her usual bedtime and every night Bella tucked her in.

Macauley left it for an hour. Then he went up, stealthily entered the room, and took his swag off the bed. He held it in one hand, standing still for a moment. Then he bent over her bed to see if she was asleep. She was on her back, calm. He came down to within three inches of her face before he saw her eyes, big and accusing. It was as though she had been waiting to catch him red-handed.

'Where are you going?' she cried in a tone of censure and uncertainty.

He felt a surge of anger. 'You should be asleep.'

She propped herself on one elbow. 'You going away?'

'Listen,' he said, impulsively seizing the opportunity, 'it'll only be for a little while — '

'No!'

'Just a little while.' He hurried out the words against his panic to persuade her before she had a chance to get worked up. 'I'll come back later for you.'

'I'm coming, too,' she cried.

'Mrs Sweeney — '

'No!'

'. . . will look after you. You — '

'No, I want to go!'

'. . . like Mrs Sweeney.'

She was crying with alarm and consternation and desperate imploration, drowning his wheedling words in a torrent of mumbling and hurling sounds of opposition. He was surprised at the definiteness of her antagonism. Her demented unreasonableness enraged him.

He stood up. 'Listen,' he shouted. 'I don't want any shindy about this. You'll stay here, and do what you're told.'

He moved to the door with the swag on his shoulder. She sprang out of bed and tried to drag him back. He dropped the swag, and in a burst of temper took her up and smacked her backside hard. He put her roughly back into the bed and ripped the blankets up over her head.

'Now stay there,' he said.

He whipped the door open, and slammed it hard after him, and walked on with the rage still high in him.

Half a mile along the road he began to feel remorseful.

He felt churned up as though his guts had been puddled and put through a mangle. His hand still tingled. He argued with himself. He didn't have to hit that hard. He didn't want to leave her like that, anyway. But there was no help for it. It had to be done. There was no other way out. Yet it was a sneak's way out, and when the hell had he started being a sneak? He was never a sneak in his life. If he wanted something he took it no matter who was looking. If he wanted to do a thing he did it, and damn everything else. He had intended to tell her. Well, why didn't he? Skulking out like that, deceiving her, leaving her to wake in the morning and find him gone and throwing the onus on others to explain and pacify. She knew he had intended to go that way, too, or did she? Could a kid fathom that? The hurt, the disbelief of knowing it seemed to be in her voice. Or was he only imagining that? Sneaking out. What did he have to sneak out for? If he had to sneak out there must be a reason, there must be something he was ashamed of. And if there was something he was ashamed of . . . ?

Still, it was the only way to handle a kid like that. And it didn't kill, it didn't maim her. It was for her own good. She couldn't be expected to understand. But she would. And she'd get over it.

He hadn't gone much farther when he heard her calling him. For a moment he thought it was in his mind. Then he looked back along the dark road towards the lights of the town. He fancied he could see a spectral figure, darkness shaped of darkness, moving towards him. He heard the scuff of feet – the slap-slap-slap of walking and the skip-skip-skip of running.

He sat down on his swag just off the road behind a tree.

He heard the panicky feet. He saw the child come into view and pass him. She slowed down, stopped, listened. He saw her run. He picked up his swag and started off. He heard her ahead of him crying a sort of rhythmic daddy, daddy.

He caught up with her a half a mile farther on. She was sitting in a huddle on the road. She launched herself at the fortress of his strength and protection, refusing to be spurned, trying to convince him that she would never be cast out from the citadel where she belonged and was safe.

She thrust herself up against his solidity and silence. He saw that she had Gooby snuggled under one arm and a bundle of her clothes under the other. She dropped them and clasped his legs.

'For God's sake!' he said. The unnatural noise in the stillness was unnerving. He shook her away. She clasped his legs tighter.

'What the hell are you doing here? Didn't I tell you to stay with Mrs Sweeney?'

'I want to come with you.'

The tears of shock and hysteria were vanishing; relief and pleading were taking their place.

'Listen to me, stop that bawling. You hear?' He waited for a minute.

'Stop it!' he shouted.

'All right.'

His voice frightened her. She feared a hiding. But she thought if she cried hard enough it would be a weapon against that. Now she sensed the annoyance and rage in him and realised that further crying would only provoke him to hit her.

He felt helpless.

'Didn't Mrs Sweeney feed you?'

'Yes, all right.'

'Didn't you have a good bed to lie in?' He was talking to her as a grown-up. 'Didn't you have a cat to play with?'

'Yes.'

'She treated you like you've never been treated in your life before. You had the best of everything. Well, didn't you?'

'Yes.'

'Well, what more do you want? What more can I give you?'

'I want to come with you.'

He sighed, beaten, angry at his impotence. He softened his voice. 'Listen, don't you understand? I'm not leaving you. I'm only going to get a job, and when I start work I'll send for you.'

'No!'

'You'll only be with Mrs Sweeney for a little while.'

'No, no, no, no, no, no!' she raged implacably.

He gave up. 'Strike me dead, I don't know. I ought to wring your little neck and chuck you in the bushes there.'

She started to cry again. He listened for a while, letting his anger burn itself out. 'All right, all right,' he snapped, exasperated. 'Shut up your snivelling.'

He watched her gouging her eyes dry with the backs of her hands. Her convulsive sniffles jerked her body like an attack of hiccups. He had to decide what to do: whether to return and tell the Sweeneys what had happened or rely on their savvy to realise what had happened. He had decided to go back when he saw the lights of a car coming along the road from the town.

He stood on the side of the road to let it pass, but it stopped as it reached him. It was a utility, and a man who seemed to be all hat was driving it. Then a body leaned across him and Luke Sweeney called, 'Hey, Mac, have you got the kid?'

As soon as she recognised the voice Buster ran behind Macauley and clutched the seat of his pants like a crab. From this rampart of defence she shouted, 'Go away, funny old bugger. Go away, my Lukey.' She said it as though it was one word or else the name of a Chinaman.

Macauley walked over to the truck, and Buster went with him like a parasitic body.

'Bel saw her going down the street like a bat out of hell. I had to go and get hold of Andy here, and then he couldn't get his jalopy started. We scoured the town.'

'I don't want to go with you,' Buster screeched.

'Shut up!' Macauley said.

He walked round to the off side of the truck. 'Looks like it won't work out, Luke,' he said.

'We can take her back,' Luke Sweeney said. 'She'll tame down after a few days.'

'I'll run away again,' Buster threatened savagely.

'Well, what's it to be, Mac?'

Macauley thought for a moment, appearing to be undecided, but actually not wishing to show the weakness of backing down too quickly. Then he said, 'I reckon I'll have to make out somehow. Sorry you've had all this bother.'

'Aw, no bother,' Sweeney said. He chuckled. Macauley could see the devilment on his gaunt face. 'Told you a lie, Mac. We didn't scour the town. Bel said she knew where Buster was making. She only sent me along to see if the kid reached you all right.' He gave a yelp of laughter. 'Okay, Andy.' He nudged his mate and gave Macauley a tap on the cheek. 'So long, you big softy. Come and see us again before I fill me coffin. Don't let the undertaker be the last to let me down.'

Macauley watched the red tail dwindling, and he could see Sweeney in the truck wiping his eyes and saying the bit about a man must have his little joke: Sweeney the dead man full of live men's bones, the satellite of a great sun who piped off his energy and consumed him and who yet, if he was lost to her, would burn to an ember and go out.

'He's gone now,' Buster said irrelevantly.

Macauley looked down at her. 'God, you make a man wild.' He heaved a great sigh. 'I don't know what I'm going to do with you, dinkum.'

Her eyes were full of malevolent reproof. She said with the utmost indignation, 'You shouldn't have left me.'

They walked on for another two miles, neither of them speaking. Macauley because he was thinking, Buster because she wasn't quite certain what her fate was to be: should he suddenly turn round and decide to go back to Walgett she was ready to rebel.

Then Macaulay told himself there was not much point in walking farther. They might as well wait for the daylight and a lift through. It was the easiest way with her.

He made the bed, one blanket under, one over. It was only an overnight doss. Buster seemed more assured. She snuggled into him.

'Dad?'

'Don't talk to me,' he said. 'I'm disgusted with you.'

'What would happen if the sky fell on you?'

'Who cares?'

'All the stars would go bang, wouldn't they, and there'd be big bonfires and the fire brigade would come.'

'Shut up and get to sleep.'

She was like a warm dog against his back. She started to hum a little tune to herself, a tune full of broken bars. Then she muttered the words, getting them right, but flat here and there on the melody.

'With a swing of the left foot
A swing of the right . . .
Oh, what a dancer,
Oh, what a skite . . .
Oh, what a dancer, oh, what a skite.'

It was an old bush ballad Bella Sweeney must have taught her.

'Stop that racket,' Macauley said, and she obeyed.

In the morning when he woke he turned over. She was asleep, her face streaked with dirty tears. For a long time he looked at the tangled silky hair, the lay of the eyelids on the cheeks, the sooty eyelashes, the small pink mouth: and there was great sense of her tininess, loyalty, and defencelessness in him. And he was moved. He felt disturbed and hostile against unknown threats.

Along the road Buster let it be understood that she still hadn't quite forgiven him for his treachery. That he could actually go off and leave her to fend for herself against the world – when he was her father, the very centre of her existence, and beloved of her – passed her comprehension. It shocked her to the soul.

Prompted by the hurt, she suddenly glared at him and told him he was a mean old nasty old father.

'That's what you think,' he said.

Her look was fiercely reproachful. 'Don't you do that any more. See!'

Her savage resoluteness amused him. He was tempted to hedge with her.

'What? What'll you do?'

'I'll run away.'

'You mightn't find me.'

She thought for a moment. Then she said quickly, slurring the words, 'I'll walk along the road, and all the roads, and keep going on the roads 'cos I know you always walk on the roads and I'd find you.'

'I heard you say something last night I didn't like.'

'What?'

'You called Mr Sweeney a bugger. You mustn't say that.'

'Why?'

'It's — just don't say it, that's all.'

'Mrs Sweeney says it. You say it, too.'

'Yes, but I'm big.'

'Can only big people say it?'

'Girls don't say it,' Macauley explained, sorry he had mentioned the subject. 'It's not a nice word.'

'Why?'

'I don't know. It just isn't.'

'Can I say it when I'm big?'

If you ever get to be big, he answered tolerantly to himself. She skipped ahead of him, happy. She was back in the overalls again, and he couldn't help noticing how much plumper they were in the behind, and how much more of her stuck out in front. She had really put on weight, and it was flesh, not fat, and firm wiry flesh at that. He thought he'd have to see that she didn't slip back. It was a good foundation to build on, and he could easily improve on it with a bit better attention and care. Even if he only kept her at that . . . He suddenly caught his thoughts in mid-hop, and wondered.

Towards high noon a semi-trailer came along and they got a lift through to Coonamble. The town was full of Sunday. Macauley didn't stay there long. He just looked. He just looked it over, standing in one place, and then went out a little way and set up camp on the banks of the Castlereagh.

At sunset a contraption comprised of a man and a pushbike passed them by, veered off the road, pulled up on the river bank forty yards away and came apart. Macauley was interested to see it was in two pieces. The bike was so stacked and saddled with gear it looked like a rubbish dump on castors. The human half of the machine Macauley couldn't observe too well with the failing light, but he saw that he was shaggy, saggy and baggy, wearing an eyeshade pulled down to his eyebrows, and the legs of his trousers tucked inside his socks.

As he prepared tea he noticed the stranger busily doing the same. He had a quick jerky walk, almost a short-stepped run as he buzzed about his demesne. Macauley recognised him for what he was, and hoped he wasn't too ratty. If he was too far gone he'd come along in a while and tell Macauley he was trespassing on his property and order him off under pain of imprisonment: he'd probably add that he was a personal friend of the police commissioner and the governors of every state. If he was another type he'd charge Macauley with spying on his thoughts, or of finding and keeping the packet of tobacco he lost. And if still another type, the bad and dangerous type, he'd come over and get some dirt off his liver, some of his crookedness against the world; he'd look for a fight and toy with the blade of a pocketknife to back up his menace.

Whatever type he was he was queer in the nut.

Macauley saw his fire glimmering, and saw him sitting back from it hunched forward. He boiled a billy of water and washed his greasy plates, and rinsed the mugs. He sat back and idly smoked a cigarette. Tomorrow he would go after those jobs. He didn't want to waste any time approaching the contacts Varley had given him. If there was nothing doing with either, he'd scout round and feel the rest of the town out, and if nothing came up he'd get on his way.

He'd have to give some thought to the kid, too.

'Where's the man now?' Buster said.

'What man?'

'Over there, that man.'

Macauley peered through the darkness at the glowing fire and its reflections on the nearby trees and its jumping red shadows on the ground. He saw no sign of the swagman.

'Where's he gone?' Buster wanted to know.

'He's bedded down, I suppose.'

'Does he go to bed early like me?'

'I don't know. Just go to sleep.'

'Can I go over and see if he's there?'

'No,' snapped Macauley. 'You keep away from him.'

He stood up and put his coat on against the nippy air, and threw another stick on the fire. He went back to sitting on the log, smoking reflectively, palms over the blaze.

There was a sudden quick rustle of candlebark. Macauley spun round. The man just seemed to appear from behind the gum.

'She'll talk to you if you'll let her,' he said, by way of introduction, jabbing a thumb over his shoulder in the direction of the river.

Macauley felt the man had been eavesdropping, had overheard him. Though unafraid, he felt the sweat start on his brow. There was a bit of a shock in his materialising like that.

'You might knock your teeth together next time,' Macauley said.

'Eh?'

'What's the bloody idea of sneaking up on a man like that?' He made himself clear.

'Sneaking? Bless me heart and soul, friend, I wasn't sneaking. Can I help it if my feet have taken on the silence common to the shy denizens of the bush and so on? Is it not natural for a man to become a part of the night and the very surroundings and so on when that man has been all his life a traveller in nature's wonderland, as I have?'

'Have it your way,' Macauley said, offering the newcomer no encouragement. 'But blow your nose next time. Otherwise, I'm liable to hit out first and ask questions afterwards.'

'I see that I have startled you, friend, and I give you my apologies. It was not my thought to make an enemy when I came to your fire, but a friend.'

He walked into the glow of the firelight, and Macauley conned him quickly and thoroughly. He stood saggily as though inert and suspended from an invisible wire. He was slightly stooped in the apparent attitude of bending over handlebars, likewise invisible. He had a puckered mobile face, grizzled eyebrows, a large nose and one scarlet eye. He spoke with a quick, glib fluency as though he hadn't much time to voice his thoughts, before the world folded up and men were denied the benefit of hearing what he had to say.

'Yes, I like to listen to that water running,' he said, squatting down on his haunches and matily helping himself to the warmth of the fire. 'That water'll talk to you if you let it. She'll tell you stories, friend, stories that'll put you to sleep or make your hair stand up. And stories to make you laugh. And so on.' He raised a red-ended twig to light the trumpet-shaped cigarette in his mouth and sucked rapidly to draw the ignition. 'And she'll go on telling 'em for years. She'll never run out. She can't. If she ever runs out of her own she'll pick them up from the Darling and she'll pick them up from the Barwon; from the deepest south to the farthest west she'll pick them up, and she'll never let you down. She's the king of them all, the Castlereagh.'

Macauley sat down on the log, still eyeing him, sorting him out. How did they get like that? Too long on their own. Too long on the backtracks. Too much sun and too much space and not enough human voices. A pocket for everything like a filing cabinet. A set of habits like a tool chest and equally necessary. A pet phrase, a fixed row of words. A name for a pannikin and pals with a billycan. Tender with knick-knacks and touchy over trifles. The old maids of the bush.

'What do you wear that thing on your head for?'

The swagman turned his head, peering first with his blood-shot eye, then with the other. He chuckled puckishly.

'What is that I see? A little girl is it? Yes, a little girl.'

'What is it called?'

'That, my dear, is an eyeshade. Why do I wear it, you ask. For many reasons. To get the full benefit of the sun. To avoid the risk of having sweat rot what hair I have left. To scratch my head the easier. See?' He demonstrated. 'And so on. Now, if that was a hat I would have to take it off. I wear it to shade my eyes, that's all, for my eyes are not what they used to be.'

From the look of it, Macauley thought, he had been wearing it since he was Buster's age.

The swagman stood up, stretched himself, and slumped again. 'You know me, of course?'

'I've never seen you before,' Macauley flattened him.

'You know my name, though?' The swagman said, and he said it, Macauley thought, as though it was on jam tins all over the country.

'I might if I heard it.'

'Desmond,' said the swagman.

Macauley shook his head. 'No, I can't say I have.'

'I take it, then,' said Desmond, after a pause, 'that you are not a great reader, or perhaps your memory is not as retentive as it might be.' He leaned forward. 'You can read?' he asked hopefully.

'Sort of,' Macauley said.

'Oh,' said Desmond with a disappointed air. But he cleared his throat. 'My name often appears in the pages of the *Farmer and Settler*, *Country Life* and *The Bulleteen*, and so on. I write verses, you know. You know what verses are? Poetry. That's what I write, friend. And I just sign my name Desmond. Of course, my full name is Desmond Aloysius Thomas O'Dowd, and so on, but they can't get it in, and besides a single name is easy to remember. Now does that recall anything to you?'

Macauley shrugged negatively. 'Maybe it's because I don't read poetry,' he said, easing the blow.

'Oh, you don't know what you're missing, friend.'

'Yes, I do,' Macauley said. 'That's why I don't read it.'

'Well, I can't understand that. Perhaps you will change your mind when you read my scrapbook. I have it among my things. Remind me to show it to you tomorrow.'

'I'll do that.' Macauley couldn't have been less interested.

'They pay you for it, too. I do all right. I'm not too clever on the spelling, but I don't worry about that. They've got some good spellers down there, and they always fix it up and so on.'

'Fine,' Macauley said.

'But I can't understand it, no, I can't. It must be what one might say a bugger when a man can't appreciate poetry.'

'You mustn't say that word,' Buster piped up.

'Word? What word, and so on?'

'That word you said. It's a bad word. My daddy said so.'

'Go to sleep,' Macauley said loudly, chafing with embarrassment.

Desmond cocked his head to one side like a cockatoo, and the firelight glistened on the eyeball of his one red eye. He tapped his forehead, muttering, raking his memory. Then he straightened up with an expression of shocked enlightenment.

He swept his eyeshade off his head and bowed, slightly but quite sincerely.

'Neither I should,' he said. 'Leastways not in the presence of a lady. I beg your pardon, young miss. It is very rarely that I make such a forks pass, and so on, I assure you.'

Macauley yawned. He had made up his mind. He thought the old bloke was all right – definitely kinked, but harmless. Still, he didn't want him around, magging his head off. He'd had enough of his gab for one evening. He wanted to shake him off. And he wanted to do it without hurting Desmond's feelings. He exercised every hint he knew, stretching, yawning, everything, but Desmond was only getting wound up. He had a whole lifetime of knowledge and experience, and a pillar of lore, opinions and comment the diameter and height of a jarrah, and so far he had only knocked a splinter off it.

Macauley thought a mug of tea might do the trick. He went down to the river and filled the billy. When he came back Desmond was perched on Macauley's bit of log and leaning forward talking to Buster sitting before him.

He broke off and glanced up at Macauley. 'Did she talk? Did she tell you a story?'

Macauley shook his head. 'No,' he said dryly. 'She's fast a bloody asleep, like everybody else ought to be.'

'She's not asleep,' Desmond denied. 'She never sleeps. She'll talk if you let her.'

'One gab artist at a time is enough for me,' Macauley said, meaningly.

The shaft whistled over Desmond's head. He went on to tell Macauley how you had to put everything else out of your mind and listen with all of your soul. He told him of the stories the river had told him: of the drover's horse that whickered in the moonlight, galloping along the river bed, under the surging waters that played music in its nostrils and teased out its tail like a golden bush: and the ghost of the drover following after; he told of the fat Chinaman at Menindee: Hop Chick with the fat jolly face like a face nicked in a pumpkin by little boys, and how when he died they put him in a coffin they knocked together from bits and pieces, so that you could read on it: This Side Up; Handle With Care; Keep Away From Engine, and Powdered Milk, One Gross. There seemed to be no end to the tales of this quick-fire raconteur.

'Here, get that into you, Des,' Macauley interrupted the flow.

'Desmond,' Desmond corrected him politely. 'I don't care for the abbreviation. Some people may be misled by it and so on; might think it short for desert, dessert or even dessatisfied. You see what I mean?'

He lifted his mug and took a loud schloop of tea. He continued with a further rigmarole about his name. Buster knocked on his leg like a door to distract his attention.

'You know any more stories?'

No, moaned Macauley to himself. Aloud he said, 'Didn't I tell you to go to sleep?'

'I know just the story for you,' exclaimed Desmond with great vigour. 'Wait till I roll meself a smoke and I'll tell you.'

Macauley put a hand to his forehead and pulled it down over his face. He shut his eyes, feeling the daze of words. Desmond joggled a mouthful of tea, swallowed and began:

'There was an ant who was dopey and half deaf, and because he was half deaf and dopey all the other ants treated him bad. One day the ant came scurrying into the nest full of importance. He had heard a great sound, he said, and it meant danger. They must move. He described the sound. It went like this: "*Glup-glup-gleep. Glup-glup-gleep*". And so on. All the other ants laughed. And one said, "Our brother has heard a grasshopper drinking, and he fears it is a bad omen." They laughed till it was like a little carnival in the ground. And the poor dopey half-deaf ant, he felt very downcast indeed. He was no good to anybody. He couldn't do anything right. He put his head in his paws and cried. Then another day he heard another sound, but he only laughed and said to himself he was not going to make a fool of himself again. And so on. But all his brother ants told him to get out of the way. They shoved and jostled him. He saw them all making for high ground, and taking their bundles with them. He didn't catch on. He only felt superior. In a little while he was all alone. The thunder rumbled and the rain came and knocked him flat. It washed him this way and that and pelted him about so that when it was gone he lay unconscious and half dead. He didn't care much. He was too sick of himself to care about anything. Then he heard thunder. *Boom-boom-boom*, and so on. And the thunder was God. And God was talking to him, and this is what God was saying, "Lift up your fiddle-face. Throw back your shoulders. You are one of mine as much as the rest. And I have work for you. Go into that house and wake that sleeping child." "Why," said the ant, "why pick me for the job? I'm sure to make a botch of it." "Who else shall I call upon?" said God in a boom of thunder. "There is not an ant left in the place, save you, and you are the one to help.

Go into that house, I say, and wake that sleeping child." And the half-deaf dopey ant staggered into the house not knowing what it was all about. But he soon saw. There was a child asleep in a basket on the floor, and at the foot of the basket was a great fierce tiger snake. The ant went pale. How was he to wake the little babe, and so on? He could only think of one way – bite the child. So he crawled into the basket, and worked his way along the chubby leg and up under the baby's napkins. Then he braced himself and bit the nice warm flesh. And when the baby woke with a yell and squirmed and kicked the little ant nearly died with fright. He scrambled up the napkin and had a grandstand view of a man racing with a great stick and beating the snake till it was dead. Then a woman came and lifted the baby, and as she lifted it she saw the half-deaf dopey ant, shaking stupid with terror, and she said, "Oh, look, this little ant must have woke our baby and made him cry; it's just as well, for if we hadn't been roused our baby might be dead this minute. What a good little ant." And she picked him up, and they kept him in a jar and gave him sugar and nice things to eat, and made a fuss of him and so on, and in that jar he lived happily for the rest of his life.'

Desmond stopped and stayed silent, savouring the hypnotised look on Buster's face. Macauley, too, had observed the raptness of her expression all through the story.

'Did the river tell you that story?' Buster asked.

'No,' said Desmond, 'my mother told me that story. For, you see, I was that baby in the basket.'

Macauley laughed loudly. He couldn't help it. The prospect of this old bundle ever having been a baby seemed too ridiculous for words.

'What's the matter?' cried Desmond, with some indignation. 'It's true.'

His sedateness only sharpened the ludicrous picture in Macauley's mind. He burst into renewed laughter, stood up and staggered under its impact. Desmond looked cut to the quick. Macauley wiped his eyes.

'It's joy,' he said. 'I'm laughing with joy that you escaped.'

Desmond was satisfied.

'Tell me some more.'

'All right, I will.'

Macauley butted in firmly. 'Not tonight, old-timer. No more. Save 'em up. She's got to get some shut-eye now. I'm turning in, too. Good night.'

'Oh, don't mind me.' Desmond blinked. 'Go ahead.'

He turned round to the fire and pulled his seat nearer. Macauley got under the blanket and pulled it over his head. Desmond sat there a long time, talking to himself, or anybody that cared to listen. The fire burned down. Macauley dozed, conscious of the birl of sound drifting across to his suffering ears. He was about to yell, when he heard Desmond tell himself it was time all men were in bed, and he glimpsed him walking away towards his camp still talking.

Macauley approached his contacts next morning. The sawmiller said he could use him right away; the building contractor couldn't give him a start until Thursday. Macauley thought it over, and took the second job. It was a job in which he felt himself freer to handle Buster. She could come along with him. Besides, it would keep him going for four weeks. The sawmiller only wanted a temporary hand and could not hold out anything for him after a week. He wouldn't take him on for the few days until Thursday. To conserve his money, Macauley decided to camp on the river bank until he started work. Then he'd get into a boarding house or hotel room somewhere. The idea repelled him, but it was the best way out with the kid. On his own, he would have camped on or close to the building job.

He didn't see Desmond all day, but at nightfall he was back on the same site. He saw him mooching over the flare of his fire, having his tea. It looked, Macauley thought, as if he wasn't coming over tonight. Probably he had talked himself hoarse; or the novelty of new faces had worn off. He was back in the cupboard with himself. Not a bad old cow, he thought, but, hell, what an ear-basher.

Macauley was wrong. Desmond came over, all right, and he was all geared for action. He was in fine fettle, having just dined, he said, off the carcass of a chook kindly given to him by the cook at Tattersall's Hotel. He had his scrapbook of cuttings which he took great pride in showing to Macauley. It was a sixpenny exercise book, stained and dog-eared; the cuttings were secured to its leaves by little strips of gum paper stuck across each corner. He got his gum paper free at any post office. Once the officials heard the purpose for which it was to be used, Desmond said, they were more than pleased to oblige him. They were honoured.

He insisted on reading some of his jingles. Macauley honestly thought they were not bad, and told him so. Buster was anxious to hear more stories, and Desmond was only too happy to tell her. Macauley left them to it, becoming no more than a thinker and a listener on the outskirts. He watched Buster listening entranced, creeping closer and closer to Desmond until she was sitting at his knee.

Macauley swung the billy when the moment came. By the time he had made the tea, Buster was yawning, but fighting against her weariness. Desmond was only getting his second wind.

'You don't know what a boneyard is,' Buster said.

'Everybody knows that,' Desmond responded.

'It's where they put people when they get dead.'

'That's right. And so on.'

'I seen a boneyard once.'

'I've seen plenty,' capped Desmond.

'What's people got to get dead for?'

'They don't get dead. They die,' Desmond taught her. 'They die, see? Die is the word. Well, now, why do they die? Well, it's a habit, just like anything else. Like eating and sleeping. They're habits, when it's all boiled down. When you get sick or worn out, and so on, it's the habit to die. There's nothing else left for you to do.'

'Does everybody die – every everybody?' She was struggling with the incomprehensibility of the notion.

'Everybody in the world,' Desmond said with great certainty.

'Will you die?'

'Yes.'

'Gooby won't.'

'Gooby, too.'

'Will I?'

Desmond seemed stumped for an answer. The subject

possibly was getting too much for him. He looked at Buster, and after a pause patted her on the shoulder. 'You look tired, young miss,' he said. 'You'd better lie down now and go to sleep.'

'Will you tell me some more stories tomorrow?'

'Yes,' Desmond promised. Buster crawled under the blankets, yawning loudly. She settled down, and Desmond, his gnarled hands cupped about the hot mug of tea, kept looking at her, seemingly unaware of Macauley's presence. He might have been alone in the solitariness of his camp going on with one of his soliloquies.

'Yes,' he said. 'Even you. Even you with all your beauty and cuteness and charm; all your spirit and loyalty. The stars die and the greatest of the great trees; the fruit that comes in the gush of summer, and all the living things, great and small. The hills break down and the rivers change their courses. The beautiful women, the good men, the sweet children, the best pony you ever had, the prettiest houses, the dog on the tuckerbox – they all die.'

He said it with such feeling, with such mystified wonder that Macauley felt embarrassed as though he had no right to be there. He emptied the slops out of the billy, appearing not to have heard. To his surprise, the old swagman stood up and, ignoring him, walked away in the direction of his camp, mumbling, as in a trance.

Macauley found the restlessness stirring in him the next day, and he thanked God that he would have something to occupy himself with on the morrow. He and Buster went for a long walk down the river in the morning. They returned and had some dinner. Desmond was down on the bank with a couple of fishing lines. Buster spent her time running backwards and forwards between him and Macauley. Finally she stayed with Desmond while Macauley shaved.

About four he was ready to go into the town. It was only ten minutes' walk away. He had to buy meat and bread, butter and milk. The milk wasn't for himself. He also had to make arrangements for accommodation. He planned to move in tomorrow evening after he had put a day in on the job. He wanted to be certain there was going to be a job and that he was going to stick to it. No point in being premature.

He called to Buster. She didn't come. He walked down to where she sat with Desmond. He seemed engrossed in his pastime, moving his lips but saying nothing, his eyes intent on the water. He had handed over one of his fishing lines to Buster.

'Come on,' Macauley said.

'Where to?'

'Town.'

He sensed the reluctance in her; the careful questioning.

'What for?'

'Never mind what for,' he said impatiently. 'Come on if you're coming.'

'You coming back?'

'Of course. Hurry up.'

'I don't want to go,' she said. 'I want to stay here with Desmond and catch fish.'

Macauley searched her, not sure that she was serious. She was, he saw, and he felt faintly piqued. He didn't think she'd let him out of her sight.

'Don't you take your swag, will you?' she told him frowning.

It was both a statement and a question, and immediately he realised that she had more to go on than an intuitive trust in him. She knew he wouldn't have told her to come with him in the first place if he planned any treachery. He would have been trying to get her to remain behind. And she knew that so long as his swag stayed behind she had a grip on his coat-tails.

But Macauley wasn't sure about letting her stay.

'You'd better come,' he said.

'No, I want to stay here.'

'She'll be all right with me,' Desmond said during a lull in his introspection. 'She's enjoying herself. You won't be long and so on, will you?'

'Can I?' Buster pleaded.

Macauley thought it over for five minutes before he consented.

When he got into the town he had a nag of doubt. He wasn't sure whether he had done the right thing in leaving Buster behind. He tried a couple of boarding houses; both were full, but a man gave him the address of a woman, a widow, who took in boarders now and again. Macauley went to see her, but she told him she hadn't been well, her brother was having domestic trouble; her sister married at the age of sixty, she had a son killed in the war, she couldn't get the best out of her beans at all, the weather was changeable and she didn't feel up to coping. Quite aware that he was lining himself up as a target for another ear-basher, Macauley talked her into letting him have a double room, and said he would be back the following evening. He couldn't help but notice the gleam in her eyes when he left: a token that he was an event dropping into the dullness of her life.

He hurried to pick up his provisions and get back to the camp. He had a couple of shops in mind. The trouble hit him completely unexpectedly. He didn't walk into it. It surged into him. The first indication he got of it as he passed the pub was a sudden outburst of shouting, a swell of voices; the next instant a jumble of men scrambled through the open door and barged into him, knocking him to the footpath. He stumbled out of the way of their trampling feet and kicking legs. There were three of them, all snorts and grunts and flailing arms, and two were on to one.

Macauley grabbed the bigger man by the coat and pulled him away, twisting him round and clutched his biceps, playing the role of soothing peacemaker. The man swore drunkenly and furiously, struggled to free himself and lashed out with his boots at Macauley's shins.

The next instant Macauley found himself grabbed from behind, and his right arm jerked and twisted up his back. He jerked his head round. There were three, four, policemen, grim, and down to business, two of them wielding truncheons. Macauley protested astonished, but the only response he got was an extra sadistic upward thrust on his arm.

At the station Macauley rapped out to the sergeant, 'What the hell's all this? You've got nothing on me. I wasn't in it. I was trying to break it up. Ask them. Ask him.' He turned to the one he had manhandled. 'Tell him.'

'Ah, get stuffed!' The man grimaced with a drunken loll of the head. Macauley drew his fist back, glaring savagely, but he didn't throw the punch. He turned back to the sergeant. 'Listen, sarge, there must have been a dozen witnesses to say I wasn't in that blue. Have a go at my breath. I haven't had a lemonade even. I wasn't in the pub.'

'Lock 'em up,' the sergeant said.

'Listen,' Macauley persisted. 'Listen, I've got a kid . . .'

'You listen to me,' the sergeant said gruffly. 'You're in here on a charge of drunkenness. If you don't shut up it'll be worse than that. Lock 'em up.'

Fuming though he was at the injustice, and bridling as he was with anxiety, Macaulay realised the futility of arguing further. He was as sober as the sergeant himself, and if he had an eye in his head the sergeant must see it. But they had pinched him and they wouldn't back down now; they wouldn't acknowledge a mistake. But they'd keep. That three-striper would keep. So would the young sharp-faced snipe with the candle-grease skin who had twisted his arm. There was a time in the future for them.

All four men were thrown into the one cell. Macauley stood with his hands on the bars. The others grouched and mumbled and found resting places for themselves. One of the two who had attacked the third was making overtures to him, asking what had happened, and what was it all about: and the third man said he was damned if he knew; it just seemed to start over nothing.

This third man lurched over to Macaulay after a while. 'You're a mug, mate,' he said.

'Who are you telling?' Macauley snarled.

'No offence, no offence, cobber.'

'Get away from me.'

'Fights,' said the man with a sore-boned sigh. 'They're good things to keep out of. I always keep outta fights. You oughta take a tip — '

'Get to bloody hell, I told you.'

'Okay, okay.' He turned on his heel. 'Thanks all the same, mate.'

In a little while they were all asleep, snoring and blowing, but not Macauley. He got away from the bars. He started to walk about. He started to wind his hands together. His eyes never lost their stony glitter. They were the eyes of an eagle.

There was no way of knowing time in the darkness. The darkness was a block and it stood still.

Four hours – they'd come in four hours. If they thought he was sober then – sober: what a bloody laugh – they'd let him bail himself out.

The rage he felt against them subsided under the press of the anxiety that was ravaging him, coming up stronger and more provocative of hideous images. One of her shoes by the stream; a wisp of her dress sticking up through the earth of a shallow grave; a roaring fire and that crazy old hatter stoking and feeding it.

Macauley grabbed the bars and shook the gate. Shook it and shook it, but no one came.

There was a sickness of fear in his belly. His breath came in a savage panting. He felt the tension in him would snap his bones. He wished for the power of God to push the walls down like paper and trample out of there.

How did he know what he was like underneath? Underneath all that blab, all that yarn-spinning that could get a simple child in? How did he know he wasn't acting? How did he know it wasn't a front of simpleness and harmlessness to hide an animal, younger, stronger, cunning and dangerous?

But he didn't have to be that. He only had to be what he was. That was enough.

A door opened and light sliced the darkness. They let Macauley out, and when they let him out he was like a tiger. They made him mark time in a desperate ritual of squaring his account and handing back his personal effects. Then they told him he was lucky. He ran from the police station. Down the road, and on, away from the huddle of lights; desperate for speed, frightened with conjecture. And he came within sight of the camp in an agony of dread. There was only one fire burning, and he didn't stop running till he was on the fringe of its glow; and he stopped short, staring.

'Shush!' cautioned the hunched man rising and appealing for silence with his lifted hands. 'Be quiet. She's just gone off.'

Macauley darted round to the other side of the fire, looked down, then dropped to his haunches, searching the small form under the wagga, scrutinising the face with the eyeshade on it pulled down to the nose. Slowly, he rose to his feet.

'She's all right?'

'Well, you're a nice one, I must say,' rebuked Desmond. 'Leaving the poor child all this time and so on. Got on the booze, I suppose!'

'Booze me tit!' Macauley snapped, angry now in his relief.

Desmond looked at him from under his craggy brows. He seemed to be deformed without his eyeshade.

'It's none of my business, I know that, but there's no woman should keep you away that long. She could have died of the shock and so on.'

'Ah, stop going on like an old nannygoat. You and your woman. I had no woman. I was jugged. And if you'll cut out the cold-shouldering for a minute I'll tell you how it happened.'

'She caught two fish, too,' Desmond barked. 'And she kept one for you.'

'Well, do you want to hear or not?'

Desmond conceded and sat down. Macauley felt suddenly weary with the weariness of exhaustion. The throbbing was still in his chest, and he could still feel the fading pound of blood in his temples. His voice was hoarse. He paused often for breath, though he didn't take long to tell the story. Now that it was all over he was overwhelmed with a sense of foolishness; an angry despair for his weakness, lack of control, and distorted judgement. He couldn't objectify the man in the lock-up and the man sitting here as one and the same. This was the reality and that other was the nightmare; yet a little while ago that other had been the reality and this the nightmare.

'Don't you believe me?' he said. 'Well, I suppose it doesn't matter a damn, anyway, what you believe. I don't blame you for being a bit sour. You must have had a time with her.'

Desmond squatted and threw a few sticks on the fire. He had a saucepan on the coals lidded with an enamel plate and over that another plate face down. Water bubbled, and steam curled from round the edges.

'You must have been very worried,' Desmond said. 'And you do me wrong, and so on, to say I'm soured by the experience of comforting a grief-stricken child. I'm not used to such things,

I'll admit, but I managed. I told her stories till stories were no more good. She thought you'd run out on her, tricked her. She wanted to go after you. I had to restrain her with force, and so on. Her strength astonished me. I almost lost my nerve the way she went on, but I managed.' He seemed modestly proud of himself. 'I sang her songs, I gave her my eyeshade; I lied like the Devil himself about you, and so on. Finally I got her to sleep.'

Macauley looked at this old man with the firelight fluttering on his shaggy face, the hooped shoulders shrinking with time, the hands worn and polished like the stones on the gibber deserts; he saw the kink in his brain, the spark in his spirit, and the good in his heart, and he felt a pang of compassion.

He put his hand on the frail shoulder. 'You're all right, Desmond,' he said.

Desmond seemed to be instantly activated by the warmth of the approbation both physically and lingually. He fussed round the fire, and said enthusiastically, 'You must be starved. I've got some nice steamed fish here.' He lifted the plate off its mate and Macaulay saw reposing in the cavity four succulent fillets. 'You won't say no to that, I can see by the look on your face and so on. There's bread and fat in the tuckerbag behind you. Help yourself. I'll go down and get a billy of water for the tea.'

Macauley ate with relish. Then he sat back enjoying a cigarette. Desmond suddenly said to him, 'Do you know where you're going?'

'Going?'

'I don't mean going away tomorrow, or the day after, and so on. I mean do you know where your life's going?'

Macauley looked puzzled for a moment. He shrugged. 'Who does? Do you?'

'I have a fair idea. But I don't think you follow me. I'll put it this way: Why do you move about? Carry on the life you do?'

'Here and there and all over the place like a fly, you mean?' Macauley sighed, gazing into the fire. 'Some people can move slow and get on all right, I don't know, I never could. All my life something's been biting me – urging me on.'

'Yes, but where to, that's my point.'

'How do I know?' Macauley said. 'Does it matter?'

'Listen!' Desmond exclaimed. 'Hear that river? There's water coming from somewhere and going somewhere and so on. It flows on a set course for thousands of miles. It's not only getting away from something, it's getting to something. It's getting away from the mountains and it's getting away to the ocean. Well, I'll tell you something. That's the way a man's life ought to be and so on.'

'Why?' Macauley asked.

'Well, otherwise there's no purpose. A man is right to get away from evil, from trouble, and the things that are bad for him. But he can spend all his life running away from them. He should stop and think and so on. Then he should pick something that will better him, that is good for him, and try to achieve it. Then he's running towards something. See what I mean?'

Macauley nodded his understanding. 'But who's talking?' he said.

'What I just said,' Desmond replied, 'I never thought of till just a few months ago. It took me all those years and so on to find out. And it's too late for me to start doing anything about it now.'

He cocked his head and directed his one red eye at Macauley. 'But it's not too late for you.'

'I like things as they are.'

'Well,' Desmond said, 'you know best. If you're satisfied you're getting to something that's all right.'

'I'm satisfied,' Macauley said, but he vaguely wondered. What was it drove a man to this kind of life and kept him at it? Some said it was a nomadic instinct. Some said it was a sense of inborn irresponsibility. Some said it was the same thing that made a fighter want to keep coming back after he was washed up. Whatever it was, it was there inside a man and could not be denied because it could not be explained.

'Wouldn't you be better off with some mode of conveyance like mine and so on?' Desmond suggested.

Macauley threw back his head. 'Ha, me a push-bike swaggie? Turn it up.'

'There is no reason, my friend, to be snobbish about it. People have laughed and sneered at me, too, but they wouldn't know why if you asked them. I can do sixty miles a day on that bike, and I don't have to worry about anybody. I'm independent. And what's more I can carry all the belongings I want. I don't have to jettison and so on. Why, there's a whole house on that bike.'

'Soon you'll have to get off and walk,' Macauley chuckled.

'Anyway it doesn't have to be a bike,' Desmond said. 'What's wrong with a horse and sulky, and so on?'

'A horse and sulky?' Macauley echoed, more to himself.

'Yes. Cost you nothing to run it except shoes for the horse. It would carry all your gear and more. Save you boot leather and a lot of stress and strain and so on. Just the thing for you and your shiralee.'

'What?'

'Her,' Desmond nodded.

Macauley knew whom and what he meant, but he was surprised that the old man, too, had seen Buster as a burden to him: a swag to be taken, and often carried, wherever he went. Odd as he was there was nothing the matter with his insight.

'That's what I'd do if I were you and so on.'

Macauley shook his head. He stood up. He knelt down beside Buster and gathered her into his arms. She only mumbled. He said goodnight to Desmond and turned away towards his camp.

'I'll cop it when she wakes,' he said. But there was a pleasantness in his voice.

Macauley settled down to the job and the boarding with Mrs Weiss. She was a record that never ran down. He learnt about everybody in the family album and all their associations. There was the little dog she used to have that ran messages and killed and brought snakes to her for grilling on a backyard fire; there was the bantam hen called Rickety Kate, because it had a broken leg that she mended and which caused it to get about with the appearance of using an invisible walking-stick; then there was the pet magpie that could talk as well as some people she knew; and there were a thousand other things she had drawn unto herself to fill up the emptiness of her lonely widowhood.

He had little trouble with Buster. She came on the job with him, and amused herself with stones and pieces of timber, nails, bricks, sand, and cement. In between playing she ran quiz shows with all the men. They made her billy boy, second class. This meant that all she had to do was keep an eye on the billycan and tell them when it was boiling. When she got her first-class ticket she would be allowed to make the fire and light it, but that wouldn't be for some little while yet. They all thought she was a bright kid.

Sometimes, at least once a day, she would seek variety in her routine by going for a short walk down to the end of the street in either direction or in both. The house being built was on the only vacant allotment left in a street full of houses. It stood roughly about the middle of the block. When Buster went for these walks she always told Macauley first. He had no objection. He was pleased with her behaviour all round. No matter what he might do he knew there was unquestionably no chance of her running away from him. Still, he always cautioned her not to be long, and to stay on the footpath.

It was during the fourth week with the job coming to a finish that Buster went for one of these sightseeing strolls and didn't come back. Macauley forgot about her for half an hour. Then when he looked around he remarked casually on the length of her absence. When another thirty minutes had elapsed he walked on to the footpath and looked up and down the street.

'That kid's a bloody long time away,' he said again. 'I wonder what's holding her up?'

'Ah, she's probably got herself into a game somewhere. She'll turn up, Mac. She always does.'

He let it go for another ten minutes. He was not so much concerned as curious. He didn't think of her as being able to get up to much harm, and the suspicion that she might actually have come to any harm was a long way from his thoughts. Then he remembered he had only seen her going in the one direction. He couldn't recall having seen her to go down the other way.

'Better go and have a look, I think,' he said.

He walked right round the block, looking over people's fences, down their backyards, increasing his pace as he found himself coming back to his beginning. She was not back at the job. He walked down the street again in the direction he remembered her taking. At the corner he stopped, frowning. He was starting to feel worried. He stood there, looking down one way and up the other.

He saw an elderly woman come out on to the verandah of the corner house. She walked down the path, saying as she came, 'Excuse me, but are you looking for someone?'

'Yeah,' he shrugged. 'A bit of a kid, about so high. You haven't seen her by any chance?'

'The little girl, do you mean? Her father works up there on the new house?'

He nodded.

'Buster?'

'That's right, that's her name.' He was impatient.

'Oh, we're old friends,' she smiled. 'She comes and says hullo to me over the fence nearly every day when I'm about.' She rambled, seeming to have forgotten why he was asking. 'I saw you looking, and I wondered if it were — '

'I've lost her. I can't find her. Did you see where she went?'

'Oh, yes!' She looked at him in surprise. 'I saw her going along there not long ago. She was with a woman.'

'Woman? Where?'

'Why, what's the matter? Is there something — ?'

'Listen, which woman, and where?'

'I didn't know her. I never saw her before. They were walking down the street. That way. Towards town.'

'You must be mistaken,' Macauley told her edgily. 'My kid wouldn't go anywhere with anyone. Only me.'

'Well, it was Buster, and there's no doubt about that. I saw her with my own eyes.'

Macauley licked his lips. 'What'd she look like, this woman?'

'Rather small, slender. Nice clothes. Of course I didn't see her face.'

The description, except for the nice clothes part, fitted Mrs Weiss. Maybe the old duck had been passing and taken Buster home on an impulse. She was one person he could think of that Buster might go along with.

'Young?'

'Well, I couldn't tell, looking at her from behind like that, but she had a young woman's walk. Yes, I s'pose I'd say she was young. Has there been — ?'

'How long ago?'

'Oh,' the woman looked into the air, calculating. 'I'd say about half an hour. Didn't you know her, the — ?'

But Macauley was gone, jogging towards the town. He flung open doors in the boarding house. Mrs Weiss came in from the back. She hadn't seen Buster. Macauley hastened through the streets, down past the post office, back, along the main thoroughfare. He stopped people, asking them roughly, quickly, brusquely if they had seen a woman and a kid in overalls and a straw hat. He met nobody who had. A staid couple, man and wife, thought by his appearance that he was drunk, and walked away without answering.

He ran back to the job. The men were on the verge of knocking off. Buster hadn't returned there. They asked him what had happened. He told them. He picked up his gear. Cody, the boss, drove up in his Hudson. He walked on to the job.

A man said, 'Some half-witted chook's got off with Mac's kid.'

'Some bloody stunt,' said another.

'That's ridiculous,' Cody said when he took it all in. 'That sort of thing doesn't go on round here. We're not down in the city now.'

Macauley out of his reflection shot him a wild glance. 'Say what you like, that kid's gone, and she didn't go herself. Some slut took her.'

Cody believed the look on Macauley's face more than he believed the words. 'Get in the car then, and I'll drive you down to the police station if you think it's as serious as all that.'

'No, no police.' Macauley waved a hand. 'Don't bring those bastards in. Not yet.'

He asked a man named Mick to drop his togs and billycan into the boarding house on his way home. Then he rushed off. He went back to the house on the corner. He tried to get more details from the woman. She said she did not actually see the woman accost Buster and pick her up. She strolled down to the front fence and that was when she saw the woman and the child going along the street. The woman was holding Buster's right hand. Buster, recalled the elderly woman, was holding and swinging that toy animal thing in her other hand.

Macauley went back into the heart of the town. He downed two beers in the pub. He walked up and down streets, looking, inquiring. The darkness deepened and the lights came on. He went back into the pub and stood before a schooner and thought, drumming his knuckles on the counter.

He couldn't get past the premise that Buster wouldn't go away with anybody she didn't know. He knew his own kid better than anybody, he thought, and she wouldn't do that. The person must have been known to her. Yet who could it be? She had made no mention of meeting anyone who had tickled her fancy. She talked about this one and that one, names and funny noses or queer eyes or ways of talking that she met over fences on her stroll up and down the street, but he couldn't think of anybody among them who had received special attention.

Settle for that. The person knew her. They knew one another. Okay. Get to the next point. Was this somebody who knew her just waiting around? Was she there just by chance when Buster walked along? No, that was out. That didn't sound right. She must have known the kid's movements. Must have known she was in the habit of strolling up and down the street two or three times a day. She knew that and when she was ready she struck. There was no speculation about it.

And a woman – slender, small, nice clothes, a young walk . . .

Macauley went on thinking, deducting, and then he thought he had a lead that might prove to be the answer. He went to the post office, got a handful of pennies from the exchange, and rang every pub in town, asking if a Mrs Macauley was staying there. He rang two boarding houses. He drew a blank. But he didn't go away. He thought. Then he rang them all again and asked if they had a guest by the name of Margaret Andersen. At the last pub in the book he hit the mark.

They had a Margaret Andersen there. The voice wanted to know if it would call her to the phone. Macauley told him no, he would come around. 'You'll have to make it soon, sir, if you want to catch her. Mrs Andersen is booking out. She's leaving on tonight's train.'

'When does that go?'

'About forty minutes, sir.'

Macauley slammed the receiver on its hook. He thought hard. He might miss her at the hotel. He wouldn't take the risk. He'd catch her at the railway. He pelted along the street, crossed a paddock, ran along the sleepers and darted round the end of the platform. He burst through the gate and came round to the station entrance, watching.

Travellers and farewelling relatives passed him carrying luggage and blankets. He watched them walking up out of the darkness. He knew their shapes before the light touched them. He saw cars slide in and he saw them get out.

The time dragged on. He thought he must have missed them. Panic started in him. He was thinking of rushing onto the platform and canvassing the train. Then he watched a taxi glide in and turn and he saw Buster's face at the window. He was at the door before the driver was out. He jerked the door open and the woman gaped at him with a look of guilty consternation.

'We're going in the train, daddy,' Buster said, excited,

scrambling forward and throwing her arms round his neck. 'I thought you mightn't be here, but mummy said you would.'

He lifted her out onto the ground, distracted in his rage, not knowing what to say or where to start.

The woman put a foot out of the door and moved her body forward.

'Get back in there,' Macauley said.

'We're catching the train.' She tried to make her voice firm.

'Get back or, so help me Christ, I'll kill you on the spot.'

The taxi driver put a hand on his arm. 'What's the matter?'

Macauley shook his arm free. 'Keep out of it, you.'

The woman, taking advantage of the diversion, scrambled across to the other door and thrust it open. Macauley flung himself round the back of the car and caught her, standing, but with her back to the open door.

'Get in!'

She glanced round nervously. Suddenly she waved a hand and called in a loud voice, 'Oh, officer!'

Macauley flicked a look sideways. The policeman standing at the entrance door started to lumber across to them.

'If you want a fuss,' Macauley ground out, clutching her arm, 'I'll give it to you. I'll turn it on proper. Get rid of this flatfoot.'

He stood back from her as the policeman advanced. Macauley clenched his fists. His eyes glittered, but they were on her. She looked down at Buster hugging his legs, and staring up at her unruffled, but bewildered.

'What's the trouble?' said the policeman.

There was a silence. The taxi driver sat in behind the wheel like a dummy, only his neck listening. He knew what was good for him.

'Well?'

'I didn't call you,' Macauley said to the policeman. He looked stonily at his wife. She glanced from him to Buster to the policeman. A little nervous smile twitched her lips. 'It's all right, constable. I — I'm sorry to have bothered you.'

He was a young man with a thick neck and hard eyes. Macauley hadn't seen him before. He seemed to take a time to consider the situation. He looked at them all in turn. Then he nodded impassively and walked away.

Macauley pushed Buster into the car and got in beside her.

'Back to the pub,' he told the driver.

'What about my train?' the woman protested with a cover of anger for her fear.

He didn't answer. He wanted to talk to her and he wanted somewhere he could do it in private. There was no place at the railway. She would have walked away. There would have been a scene. He couldn't take her to the boarding house. He didn't want his affairs broadcast and handed down to posterity. The hotel was the only place.

She walked ahead of him docile with fear, obedient to her instincts, and he carried the single suitcase. He told the attendant Mrs Andersen had changed her mind; she wouldn't be leaving until tomorrow or the day after, and maybe never.

The attendant looked him up and down in his workman's clothes, but only nodded.

At the top of the stairs the woman turned left, and walked down the corridor. She stopped at Room 14. The door had no lock or key. She turned the knob and went in. She tried to slam it shut before he entered, but he was too quick for her, wedging the suitcase in the opening.

He closed the door behind him and dropped the suitcase on the floor and stood there. Buster grabbed at his coat and started to prattle. He told her to shut up and sit down on the chair in the corner and look at a book. It was a wicker chair on which lay a pile of magazines under a cushion. He waited until she had settled herself with a magazine on her knee. He was in no hurry. But the tension was working in the woman's face. Macaulay turned his eyes on her again.

'What are you going to do?' she said, with fear.

Nice clothes all right, Macauley thought. Snazzier than the sort she had put on out of his payroll. The figure to wear them, too. Still as slim as ever, still as attractive; still built, she was, to catch the eye, and hold it. She hadn't lost the pretty face, either; the lustrous dark eyes, the full red lips, the striking white skin. Her dark hair was cut short all round, parted on the side and brushed back close to the head like the sleekness of a swan. But there was something different about her; something changed. There was a hardness, a shadowy controlled malice: the look of a woman, he thought, who had been around and was no stranger to any experience.

'Don't be frightened,' Macauley said. 'I've never touched you yet and I'm not going to start now, though God knows I ought to.'

She was satisfied he meant what he said, but suddenly she

put her head in her hands and cried. He wasn't fooled by the weapon.

'What a sneaky bitch you are,' he drawled with scorn.

'What's so sneaky about taking my own child?' she shot back at him tentatively, now with her back turned and still weeping.

'Thought you'd get away with it, didn't you?' Macauley said. 'Hanging round here, spying out the land, working the nut. How long have you been here? A week? How'd you get on to me? How'd you know where I was?'

She didn't answer. Buster threw down the magazine with a bored air. She climbed on the bed and lay on the pillow, humming to herself, holding Gooby out before her.

'You don't have to tell me,' Macauley said. 'I'll tell you. Mrs Callahan, Mrs Callahan. That's where you got the drum. Mrs Callahan told you. Mrs Callahan went to see you while she was in Sydney. She spilt the beans over the teacups. Didn't she? Told you I was looking extra good. Told you the kid was fine. Told you where I was heading. Wasn't hard for you to pick up the trail. Wouldn't have been hard if I'd have left here. Only what'd you come for?'

She turned to face him. She took off her hat and turned it in her hands. 'You know why I came. For my child.'

Macauley gave a grunt of amused contempt.

'It's true,' she flashed. 'She's mine and I want her.'

'So you come all the way up here to steal her – steal her like a lowdown sneak.'

'That's the way you took her. You stole her from me. Or maybe you don't remember that night.'

'Remember it? I remember it,' Macauley said. 'It reminds me of a French postcard every time I think of it.'

Her lips quivered with fury. Her eyes were cold and hard with hate. Her fear had drifted away, both the real and the spurious, and she was giving herself over with growing confidence in her antagonism.

'Of course,' she sneered, 'you're so clean and holy. You're such a saint.'

Macauley stood up, and for a moment she felt a momentary fear. He pulled up the eiderdown over Buster's sleeping form. He walked round to the woman and stood looking into her face.

'Listen,' he said quietly but with a cold anger. 'I'm no saint. I'd be the last man to claim it. I've had women. I've had 'em from one end of the country to the other. And that's not the skite of a eunuch, or some poor galah that can't get it any more. But I played the game by you, and it wasn't easy.'

'Huh!' she gibed. 'Are you trying to tell me you didn't go round sleeping with other women all the time you were away?'

'That's what I'm telling you. Bloody mug, wasn't I?'

'You've got a nerve – expecting me to believe that. What do you take me for? A fool?'

'I married you and I did the right thing by you,' Macauley repeated, grimly emphatic. 'In the whole five years I never touched another woman.'

'Oh, that's wonderful! That's marvellous! You ought to tell the world about it. You must be mighty proud of yourself.'

He ignored the heavy sarcasm. 'I am,' he said. 'I had no complaints to make about you. You suited me.'

'Yes,' she snarled, her voice shaking with rage and hostility.

'I'll bet I did. Someone to drudge while you had the good time. Someone to come home to when you felt like it. Someone to sleep with at your convenience. I run the house while you have the holiday.'

'I had to work. I wanted you all right.'

'Yes, your way. On your terms. That's how you wanted me.'

Macauley bridled. 'I sent you money. I kept you. You never knocked that back. You had clothes, pictures. You never starved. You never went short of the rent. I was your breadwinner.'

'So you should be. It was no favour. That was your responsibility.'

For a moment the illogicality of the remark confused him. 'Was it?' he said. 'Then it was your responsibility to see that you deserved it.'

She gave him a look of satirical pity for his blind selfishness.

'A cheque every week, and I'm supposed to be grateful. Do you think that's everything?' She faced him, storming. 'Do you know how much married life I had with you? Do you?'

He stared at her raging bitterness, unable to frame an answer, knowing that she was plucking at the heart of his guilt.

'I'll tell you,' she said. 'Six months. Out of that five years. Six months' married life. How do you like that?' He didn't answer. 'No, it never struck you like that, did it? Three, four days home and you were away again. I counted those days. I had plenty of time to count them. And add them up. Six months! And you wonder why I went off the rails.'

'You never let on it was that bad, if it was that bad.'

'Not much I didn't. I was always at you to get a job so we

could have some life together. You used to laugh or get cranky and say you couldn't stick it in the city. How many letters did I write to you telling you how I wished you were home and wouldn't you think about settling down?'

'Right,' Macauley snarled, facing the truth, 'maybe you did. Even admit I was at fault. People don't bust up their lives over things like that.'

'Don't they? That's all you know.'

He knew differently. He knew people did, and for less than that. But he had to fight his guilt, and defend himself against her knowledge of it. The mockery made him sick at heart. The way he had been sick at heart that night he discovered her perfidy and recalled with a jolt how he could agree smugly that this sort of thing could happen to people, and did, and ruined their lives, looking at people as though he was not one of them, forgetting about that, and never dreaming of it happening to him. He sat down and rolled a cigarette.

'You're selfish to the core,' she went on. 'Any woman would do what I did if she was married to you. You're not a husband at all, and you were never meant to be one, and that's all there is to it.'

He agreed with that, too, in his mind: marriage wasn't for him any more than becoming a politician was; or running a music academy. He had made a mistake, and had tried to make the best of it; that was the sum of it.

'When she was born – you weren't even home for that. I went off alone. I had her, and I came home alone. To a lonely house. To nobody.'

Yet couldn't a man have helped it? What did this making the best of it mean? Why did it have to be a mistake?

'You think a woman has a child and it's nothing. It's just tossed off like peeling the spuds or hanging out the washing. What do you know about how it feels to be getting around like a balloon? Sickness and pains and discomfort – not for a day but for months. Months on end. You think you're tough. You couldn't stand it ten minutes.'

It was a mistake because a man had found the way of life he was happiest following, and he wanted no interference with that way of life: he was not prepared to sacrifice it for anything or anyone; nor even prepared to test his willpower to see if he could do without it; flog his willpower into abandoning it.

'The terrible pain when it's born – what do you know about that? When you scream with the torture, and nobody gives a damn whether you live or die, when your body feels like it's being torn apart, and all for what?' She lowered her voice, looking away from him, not seeming to care much whether he heard or not. 'What did I get out of it? Nothing. Only more to put up with, more trouble, more responsibility, more work, another mouth to feed. And nobody to give me a word of appreciation.'

Macauley raised his head. 'And yet you want to take her back with you. What happened to Donny boy? Walk out on you, did he?'

She glared at him. 'You'd like to think so, wouldn't you?'

'Don't tell me he's all keen on having the kid, too. Why, can't he get one for himself?'

'He'll be a much better father to her than you ever were.'

He strolled idly over to her and clutched her shoulders, squeezing the flesh. A sensual feeling stirred in him at the touch.

He relaxed his grip. 'You've had a hard time,' he said. 'I feel sorry for you. The way you must have worried about that kid, how it was eating, whether it was warm enough. You couldn't expect me to take good care of it, could you?'

His sudden softened attitude aroused a flicker of suspicion in her eyes, but she couldn't fathom his motives. 'How could you blame me?' she said. 'You never took any interest in her. You saw her about as much as you saw me.'

'Naturally, you'd fret, too.'

'Even when you were home for the few days she got on your nerves. She broke your sleep. You were always moaning about her getting under your feet. You never played with her. You were completely indifferent.'

'True enough,' Macauley admitted. 'I hardly noticed her, you might say.' He walked back to the chair casually, straddled it, folded his arms on the back, and rested his chin on them. His eyes were half shut like a cat's in the sun.

'I'll give you this, Marge,' he said. 'You're a good trier – but you don't fool me.'

'What do you mean?'

'You don't want that kid,' Macauley said. 'You only want to get your own back on me.'

She was ruffled only for a moment. 'Don't be ridiculous!' she snorted derisively. But he knew he was right.

'You wrote me a letter, remember? You spilled your guts in that letter, and I haven't forgotten a word of it.'

She flushed uncomfortably, unable to think of anything to say.

'You meant everything you said. You hoped like hell that I

was having a tough time. You had about as much concern for Buster as that wall.'

'That's not true,' she blustered.

'When Mrs Callahan gave you the lowdown you couldn't believe it. You couldn't imagine the kid looking a picture, better than she's ever looked. You couldn't imagine me getting by with her as good as any old mum, could you? It maddened you. You got steamed up all over again. You boiled. And you couldn't rest until you came up here and took that kid away. By God, you must have it in for me.'

She pleaded guilty in every line of her face, and was furious with herself for not being able to disguise it.

'No, you don't want the kid,' he purred. 'You just want to use her to twist the knife in me. It doesn't matter a continental to you as long as I get hurt. And she's the best weapon you've got. That's it, isn't it?'

She felt humiliated by his perception, like a child being found out, and she tried to conceal it. But she couldn't. She only succeeded in confirming it with an aspect of baffled rage; all the venom and hate she had for him was in her eyes and lips. She watched like a cheated victor as Macauley went to the bed and took Buster into his arms. 'Where's her clothes?' he said.

'I'll tell you something now,' the woman said desperately. 'She's not your child. You're not her father.'

'Where's her clothes? Get them!'

'You've got no right to her.'

'Get her bloody clothes when I tell you!'

The woman pulled open the wardrobe and snatched out Buster's straw hat, shirt, and overalls, which, apparently she had intended leaving there. Sullen, chagrined, she thrust them into Macauley's hand.

'I guess she can keep the dress you had all readied up for her. This.' He flicked at the frock Buster wore. 'You don't mind giving her that, do you? A present from her mother. I can't say that you're not that.'

The woman's feelings broke in a torrent of sobbing words caught up with rage and bitter loathing. 'I'll get her back. You just see. I haven't finished yet. I haven't even started. You're not going to do this to me and get away with it.'

At the door he put up a hand motioning to her for silence.

'You know when your mouth is parched,' he said. 'You know what it feels like to bite into a warm wet pear? You used to be like that. Go to bed,' he said. 'And wait for me. I'll be back later. When strangers can help themselves to what's mine I don't see why I can't help myself to what's mine for a change. Do you?'

He went out. He felt no bitterness and no sense of victory. He wished it could have been different. But there seemed no help for it. The situation and its instigation seemed to be the work of an immutable cause beyond and even unrelated to him and her: it was on another plane and mere human power could not hope to control it.

He walked down the street squeamish with all the violence of that unpleasantness. He put the child into bed. He didn't go back to the hotel. He had never intended to. It was just the gesture of belittlement, a last cruel flout. He undressed, climbed in beside Buster and lay awake for a long time.

From Coonamble Macauley went south to Gilgandra and worked for three days in a wood yard there. He pushed on east to Dunedoo, and put in a week poisoning rabbits for a wheat farmer. It was at Dunedoo that he bought Windbag. He was glancing idly through the *Dunedoo Chronicle* when he saw the notice giving a description of the impounded horse. It seemed to him to be a nudge of fate. He went round to the pound, and the horse, still unclaimed and apparently not even wanted by a few bidders at the sale, went to Macauley for a song.

When he led it away, to the great excitement of Buster, he wasn't sure whether he wanted his head tested. It was a bony animal with a long, sad face and dolorous eyes, and looked as if it might fall over any time without warning. It was quiet and gentle, with a disposition to laziness: and Macauley couldn't make up his mind whether it was born that way or had been ill-treated into an obsequious stupidity.

He didn't expect to come by a sulky in the same town, but he did. With the engine of his future mode of transport in hand it was only natural to look for the body to put it in. He found the sulky among a sargasso of derelicts in the blacksmith's yard. There were wagons, buggies, buckboards rusting and falling apart, their wheels sunk into the ground with long standing and the weeds growing about their fellies.

The sulky had a wheel-wobble which, when it was going, made its tail waggle like a bustle on a chorus girl. One of its shafts was broken, snapped off in the middle, but Macauley, with the help of the blacksmith, who was glad to get rid of the antique, at a profit, too, repaired it with a smooth sapling bolted to the shortened limb. The blacksmith greased the axle and went clinically over the invalid testing for general soundness. He said he thought she'd do for a few years yet.

The whole deal set Macauley back $15, and the harness cost him the most of that.

He went out over the green hills and down the red roads. He had no set plan. He kept on going, working here and there, where the job was practicable as well as suitable. At Guyra he added a tent to his gear. He went over to the plateau of Dorrigo and camped out a mile by the Dangar Falls. But there was nothing to hold him there and he took the mountain road north to Grafton.

This was the road he had taken when he first left Sydney and made for the Rivers, and it put him in mind of many things. He had traversed it perhaps six times since then, and it was always the same: always filled him with pleasure for the beauty and the magnificence of its scenery. He had worked in the potato paddocks in the winter with a fire bucket to warm his freezing fingers and a sack like a monk's cowl on his head and shoulders and back to keep off the sleety drizzle: the valleys were full of milky vapours; the forests howled like stormy seas. And you could come here in September, say, in the mystery of September, feeling good, and all about you a ripeness and purpose; the creep of the beetle, the bursting buds, too silent for human ear, and the touch and strength of daylight, and the long-lingering sun, and all of it like the sound and the radiance of God passing.

Coming into Grafton he passed where old Tommy Goorianawa had sat on his throne in the anchorage of his years. The shanty was gone now, gone a decade ago, and a modern house, fenced, with children playing in the backyard, stood on the site.

He passed the door-front where he and Lucky Regan had hugged each other in the pleasure of mateship, munching their fish and chips; and he saw the pub, still in the same spot, where he and Lucky had fought each other stiff and sore and then shaken hands for better or for worse.

And with the past vividly in him he thought of Lily Harper. And he didn't know why but he thought he would like to see her. In all the times he had been here since that night seventeen years ago, he had had no wish to contact her, though he knew where she was and who she was now. He might have felt a curiosity about her, had a whimsical chuckle at the possibility of running into her in the street, but he had never had the desire to approach her.

He went on to Ulmarra, and the wish became stronger. He examined it for its audacity, decided he was a fool and then scrapped the decision. But he would check first, and besides, he didn't think he could pluck up whatever had to be plucked up to face her directly and personally. He'd pave the way first, find out how she felt. What made him think that she might want to see him?

While Buster minded Windbag and Windbag minded Buster, Macauley went into the post office and looked in a telephone book. He went to the phone booth. When the voice answered he stammered and hesitated, and then managed to say coherently who he was and add any necessary details to establish his identity in her memory.

He heard a gasp. There was a silence. When the voice came back it was excited and incredulous. Where was he? He must come round to see them. And right away. Good Lord, and fancy, and how was the world treating him, and quick, I'll make some scones, and keep a lookout for you.

Macauley went round, but each of them was shy when they met. Each of them looked the other up and down, and commented, and laughed. Macauley found Lily still beautiful, still vivacious, and none of the matron about her though she had three children, all going to school, and a schoolmaster husband. She had a settled, contented look about her. All that flightiness was gone, and the cultured guyver. She found him so subdued she couldn't believe he was once the wild character she knew.

There was room there for him to stay, she said, but Macauley declined. It wasn't that he couldn't trust himself – and he wasn't too sure about that, either – but he didn't think it would be in good taste, and he didn't want to start any trouble. But he was mistaken about Lily's husband, Harry Macready. He was a gentle, genial fellow with a honey cowlick and golden eyes. He was full of good sense and bad jokes. He knew what was the matter with the country, but he didn't bore you with it.

Macauley, camped down by the river, paid them a couple of nightly visits, and they prevailed on him to spend the last Sunday with them. In the evening, while the children were entertaining Buster with their books in another room, Lily and Harry and Macauley sat about the lounge fire. Macauley was aware that Lily and Harry had something they wanted to say to him, and he had a shrewd idea what it was. He saw Lily look at Harry and urge him with her eyes. Harry cleared his throat, and started filling his pipe.

'Mac,' he said on a ponderous sight, 'we've been thinking . . . Maybe you find it a bit hard the way things are. I mean, with the sort of life you lead . . .' He said quickly. 'Don't think I'm reflecting on that, I'm not, but don't you find it . . .' He left the sentence unfinished.

'With Buster, you mean?' Macauley helped.

Lily leaped in. 'Yes. That's what we mean. We'd like to help you, if we could, Mac. Buster, too . . .'

'It won't be long before she's going to school,' Harry chipped in. 'Be no trouble for us to make provision. We've got it all at our fingertips. She'd have a good home, and playmates. Well, you saw how she played with those kids of ours today.'

'We'd treat her just like one of our own,' Lily said encouragingly. 'I'm sure she'd stay.'

'She might,' Macauley said, preoccupied with his thoughts. A few months ago he wanted to get rid of the child; wanted to give her away. 'It's real good of you, and I couldn't think of a better place for her to be in or better people to be with. I know she'd get on fine. But I don't know — '

'I do.' He looked up and Lily was smiling perceptively at him. 'You don't want to leave her.'

'Well,' Macauley said, a little flustered, 'why should I?' He found them both smiling at him, understandingly. He stood up, and stood with his back to the fire. 'No. I've got plans for that kid.'

'You can't keep her with you all the time, Mac,' Lily told him.

'I've realised that,' he said. 'And I don't intend to.'

'You've got to think of her future,' Harry said.

'I've thought of it,' Macauley said. 'I'm going back to Walgett. I'm sweet for work there with a building contractor; any amount of it. I've got friends there. I've got it all worked out. I'll put in two years there – I think I can stick it that long; I'll have to, anyway. I'll get some dough together, and when Buster's seven I'll put her in a boarding school.'

'That's a good idea, Mac,' Harry said. 'But will you carry it out?'

'Nothing'll stop me,' Macauley looked doggedly at him. 'Nothing. She'll understand things better then. She won't mind going into boarding school.'

'You might settle down in Walgett,' Lily pointed out, 'and let her go to school there.'

Macauley shrugged. 'I might at that,' he said.

When the supper was over, and Buster was asleep on his shoulder, Macauley took his leave. Harry and Lily followed him out to the gate. They shook hands. When Macauley took her soft hand he said, 'I'm glad you're happy, Lil.' She pressed his hand warmly with both of hers, and gave a little smile, and he felt himself blushing in the darkness – blushing in shame for a deed seventeen years old.

Macauley moved off early next morning, north to the Tweed. Strangely enough, he awoke with the presentiment, and it was with him recurrently all day. It became so acute towards evening that he looked all about him, wondering what was waiting or watching for him. If it only made itself more apparent physically he might be able to rationalise, foresee, and forestall. But it was nothing physical. It was the same vague sense of something impending that a man had in a pub when he felt the presence of someone behind him ready to pick him and put in the bounce for a loan; the same awareness of danger a man had leaving a pub in a strange town on a dark night with a roll in his pocket.

At twilight he pulled off the road between Rappville and Casino. And strangely enough again, the feeling left him suddenly when it had most right to be with him.

'Time to put the nosebag on,' he said. 'You go and gather some sticks while I unharness the nag.'

He heard the car, but even then he didn't look up until it screeched. And then he looked up in a shock of fright. He heard the one piercing scream. He stood like a rabbit paralysed on a hill. The car thirty yards away, a bulk of darkness in the darkling scrub, seemed to be slowing. He started to run, his legs unfreezing. Then he heard the engine roar and the car shot away accelerating rapidly, disappearing in a whine of sound and a fade of red tail-lights.

Macauley found Buster limply by the roadside. He felt her heart, her pulse. He didn't move her. Her eyes were still open in terror. The snapped-off scream was still on the gaping lips. He stood up. He was shaking. His stomach was a plate of iron. His entrails coiled. He turned to run, swiftly to put the horse in the sulky, swiftly to rush her to a doctor. But he stopped in his stride. That was no use. He couldn't move her. He mustn't move her. They moved old Bill Gogarty when the tractor struck him and they killed him because they moved him: they completed the work of the tractor.

And yet time could kill her, too; time could finish her off. But what could he do? Wait and watch in the darkness; listen in the darkness; hope in the darkness and get Christ there beside him to help him hope.

He ran back to the sulky and lit the hurricane lamp. He covered her with a blanket. And he waited. It was an hour before a car came, but it came from the south. And that was good. It was only ten miles to Casino. He waved the lantern. The car stopped. Macauley pushed his face into the driver's with the urgency of his message and the frenzy of his command. The motorist seemed to absorb both, judging by the speed with which he tore away.

Macauley waited. He was anxious lest the motorist be delayed, lest he decide not to go to the hospital and report. Then he heard the sound from the north like a faraway sawmill. The ambulance men told him nothing. He went with them.

He waited again. He waited amid the smell of waxed linoleum, linen, and antiseptics. A doctor came, frowning. He asked Macauley if he was the father. He looked away. He said they would have to operate. He looked away again.

Macauley lost his temper. He snarled, 'All right, don't be a bloody granny! Tell me. What's the betting?'

The doctor said quietly, 'She's in pretty bad shape. If there are any other relatives you want here I think you'd better inform them.'

Macauley grasped the doctor's lapels. 'Listen, sawbones, you're licked before you even start. Do something! You've got her in her coffin before she's bloody well dead. Do something, can't you?'

He pulled his hands away, dropped them at his side. His voice sounded harshly unnatural even to his own ears.

'We'll do all we can,' the doctor said, unruffled, assuring. 'All we humanly can.' He touched Macauley's arm. 'I'll get the nurse to give you something to settle your nerves.'

'I'm all right,' Macauley snapped. 'Never mind me.' He

suddenly gripped the doctor's arm as he was about to go. His voice was lower, trenchant with appeal. 'Go your hardest, doc. Give her a chance. She'll do the rest. She's tough.'

He went out into the darkness. Two policemen were getting out of a car at the kerb. They called him. They asked him who he was, and was he the victim's father, and he answered them. They questioned him. What he saw. How much he knew. He told them. He couldn't be sure of the colour of the car, it was too dark to see, and he was so distracted he didn't take much notice. But it wasn't a light colour. It looked to be a heavy job, modern shape, but he couldn't describe the design. It could have been anything from a Chev to a Plymouth.

'What about your gear?' one of them said. 'Well run you out there if you like and you can bring it in.'

'It can wait till the morning,' Macauley said.

They drove off, and Macauley went down the street. He thought about it for ten minutes before he sent the telegram to his wife. He said briefly: 'Buster Casino Public Hospital. Not expected to live. Mac.' He sent it urgent.

Then Macauley set about looking for a man, or what passed for one. He didn't know whether his quarry had gone straight through and on perhaps to Lismore or Tweed Heads, and because he didn't know he meant to make sure he had or hadn't vanished. Somewhere in the warren of this town maybe there lurked a cur – a cur that wrapped forty hundred-weight of steel round himself before he boxed on, and boxed on with fragile flesh and bone, and even then ran when he struck the blow, ran like a craven whelp with its tail between its legs. This was the man Macauley wanted, this hit-run driver, the dingo of the highway.

Up and down the main street he walked, first on one side and then on the other. He looked for dented mudguards. He looked for bent fenders. He looked for blood on bonnets and windscreens. He looked at the faces that passed. He looked for strain, nervousness, guilt.

In restaurants and cafes he looked around him, sniping off the diners.

He walked down back streets, side lanes. He went right round the town. And when he came back to his starting point he started all over again. Doggedly he retraced his steps, alert, scrutinising, proving that his quest was futile, disappointed to prove it, but gratified that he had proved it.

They'd catch him, Macauley thought. They'd do what they had to do. They'd give him his medicine, some medicine, not half enough. They'd play around like poofters, with the kid gloves and the soft soap. A kid's life, like the life of an old man, had little value. They'd send him up for a year, maybe two. The day he came out, Macauley would be waiting for him. And then the real trial would start, and the just sentence pronounced, the fit punishment inflicted. And if they didn't find him, if he got away as some cunning dingos do, time might fall down on the job but eternity wouldn't; or if it did the stars swung blind in their courses, a man's soul was dirt, there was no God.

He was feeling the strain when he got back to the hospital. There was a fatigue all through him. It came not so much from physical exertion as from an ordeal of spirit. Buster was still unconscious. They were fighting for her life. Macauley sat inside, walked about outside. There was no change.

In the dewy dawn he walked out and got his things together.

He found Gooby beside the road in the grass where it had been flung from her senseless hand. He unstrapped his swag. His eyes clung to the books he had bought on raising children, diet, nursing care, diseases. They seemed to ridicule him. His mind was in a turmoil of recriminations. If he had left her with Bella, if he had left her with Lily, even if her mother had succeeded in abducting her . . . she wouldn't have been lying in there now; this wouldn't have happened.

He took the sulky and Windbag back into town. He did nothing but wait round and inquire. In the afternoon he saw the doctor. Fitzmaurice by name, and he seemed to notice him for the first time; a tall, well-built light-skinned man with gingery hair and freckled face.

'Still unconscious,' he said, 'but she's hanging on.' He said it as though he found it remarkable and encouraging.

Macauley plucked at his arm. 'Last night,' he said. 'I didn't mean to cut up rough. Don't hold it against me.'

Fitzmaurice only smiled, and patted his shoulder. 'That's all right, old man.'

Macauley got through the night with little sleep. The next day was like the day before. Buster was still in a coma; everything was being done to save her. Macauley waited about. He thought, half expected, his wife would appear any moment. She didn't turn up. But he had an answer from her.

In the afternoon a portly man with a heavy face threaded with little red veins ferreted him out in the hospital yard, introduced himself as Bathgate of the local firm of solicitors, and served a notice on him. Macauley took it unsurely and read the contents. They told him stiffly and formally that his wife had made application to the court for the custody of their child, and that the case was listed for hearing on a date two days hence.

For a moment Macauley was utterly bewildered. 'Where did you get this? How?'

'We received it in the post today,' Bathgate replied, freeing his fat neck momentarily from its catch in the tight collar. Seeing Macauley's confusion, he went on. 'It had to be served on you personally. You know about that sort of thing, don't you?'

'Yes, but who — ?'

'It's a firm of Sydney solicitors,' Bathgate explained. 'Our colleagues advised us where you could be located and begged us to serve you with the notice.'

'Whose solicitors are they?'

'The petitioner's, of course.'

'They must have known I was here,' Macauley muttered.

'Obviously.'

'But it says this case is to be heard Friday. Today's Wednesday. They're not giving me much time.'

The fat solicitor looked at him with an officious aloofness as though averse to consultations without a fee. 'Probably it's not a rush job, if that's what you are thinking. Our colleagues have probably been chasing you, strenuously trying to discover your whereabouts, and now they know. The application in question was probably filed a month ago.'

Macauley seemed to have difficulty in taking it all in. 'What do I do about it?'

Bathgate shrugged. 'That's your headache. If you wish to contest the claim you've got to be present in court. If not, if you don't want representation, then you just forget about it.'

'What happens then?' Macauley said. 'If I don't appear, I mean?'

'What do you think?' Bathgate jerked up his neck. 'The court will simply make an order giving the party to the application custody of the child. Provided, of course, the court is satisfied with her ability to take care of it. And it usually is.'

'She's living in adultery,' Macauley exclaimed.

Bathgate merely lifted his eyebrows. 'That is not a serious objection. In fact, it has nothing in a sense to do with it. She might be an excellent mother. And that is all the court is concerned about. Its rulings are made in the sole interest of the child's welfare.'

Macauley looked away reflectively for a moment. 'You've got all the drum about this,' he said. 'Can you tell me – will the case come off on Friday if I'm not there?'

Bathgate wasn't so prompt with his answer this time. 'I'm not sure,' he said. 'But most likely it would. For instance, suppose I hadn't been able to find you. Your wife' – he corrected himself – 'the alleged applicant or petitioner could inform the court that you cannot be traced, and the court has power to dispense with the formality of serving notice on you.'

'You mean that would give her open slather?'

'In a sense, yes, more or less.'

'But listen,' Macauley cried. 'That kid's in hospital. It's touch and go whether she'll live. My wife knows that. How could she come at a thing like this when she's a full wake-up to what's going on?'

Bathgate gave his neck a decent jerk so that he instantly became an inch taller.

'Not knowing the circumstances and not knowing the party,' he said, 'I'm afraid that's more than I can tell you.'

'Okay,' Macauley said, absently, but in a tone of dismissal. 'I'll buy you a drink some time.'

He had to think and think hard and fast. The news had jolted him out of his torpor of shock and impotence into the old fire of rebellion and pugnacity. The challenge picked off his nerves, every one, and his nerves bristled in goading and readiness. Yet the reality of that message jarred with his sense of human decency, and his knowledge of her, his wife. He couldn't see her just cold-bloodedly rushing off to inform her solicitors the moment she learnt his address. It was an inaction incompatible in his mind with the character of any woman, let alone a mother whose child was dying. It had come to this, the two of them wrangling over a scrap of humanity, like dogs wrangling over a bone; only dogs wrangle for the same reason: her reason and his were totally different. He was sure of that. But if the child died, what use was it to her then? What was the winning of a court case then but a hollow victory?

And that thought gave him another, and insight gave him reasons, and reshuffled the picture to try to convince him; it flared his emotions, but his mind could not readily accept it.

One thing he knew, though: the challenge was there and he had to fight.

He went into the hospital, and he told them he was going to Sydney. He didn't know for how long, but he'd keep in touch. The attendant gave him a telegram. Outside he opened it, and read: 'Terribly sorry. Please tell us if we can do anything. Lily Macready.'

It warmed him.

He went to the police station, briefly explained his trouble and asked them if they would keep an eye on his things. They told him to bring the horse and sulky and leave it in the police paddock, and his swag, they said, would be in nobody's way at the station.

He took what he needed out of it – a shirt, a pair of socks, a handkerchief, a bottle of hair oil and a toothbrush – and wrapped them all in a sheet of brown paper tied with a string.

In the train he could think of nothing but what lay behind and what lay ahead. He could not get away from the torment of his imaginings. He should be back there. He had to be down there. And still he was here, shackled to space and handcuffed to time and both of them calling the tune. The train talked to him.

It said, 'You won't get away; you won't get away . . . She'll die in the night; she'll die in the night . . . You gave me no life; you gave me no life . . .'

It chattered and rocked and hammered and gnashed. It pricked him hard and told him this, 'Hang on to your guts; hang on to your guts . . . Pull yourself together; pull yourself together . . .'

He dragged his mind away from the mirage of cleanliness and white starched uniforms and hospital smells and looked in on the bleak dignity of a courtroom: the high windows and the cold polished floor: he could see people like people at a funeral and he could hear the voices; and then it was his turn and they were waiting and he didn't know what to say. The judge, the lawyers, they looked strange; they looked as if they were not the sort of men who could understand what he had to say; the sort of men who would make what he had to say seem weak and foolish, even to him.

But he was saying something, out of the compulsion of his stubbornness, because if he had to lose he needed to lose with his teeth in their throats; and what he was saying was the truth, and nobody could say anymore.

I've never hurt that kid. Maybe I've been rough and hard, but I've never ill-treated her. She came as a stranger, and she grew on me. I didn't want her, but she wanted me, and I was wrong. She pulled me up. From her I found this out: to live is not easy and often by the time a man has learnt how to live his life is over. She had a home with me. It wasn't much, but she didn't grumble. She put the hobbles on me. She had a rope round my neck and she wouldn't let go. I didn't have to be frightened of her getting away from me. She was frightened of me getting away from her. You know what a dog's like. He knows you're the boss. He respects your authority. It shows strength. He feels protected. He knows that, and that's all that matters. You can dress him down, but he holds no grudges. You can beat that dog and he'll forgive you. That kid's the same, just like a dog.

I mean no disrespect, but all this – strangers sitting in on a man's life, ready to lay it out for him. It doesn't seem right to me. I've had all the bush lawyers and all the bush Solomons talking to me and they've had the world's problems carved up and solved in two ticks on a deal-board table, but their own lives were slung together like a crow's nest, and they didn't know how to put order in them. Look, if a bomb fell and a man had to gather the few things he had and his children with him and take them away; if he had to go through hell, and his kids with him, who'd point a finger? Men would help where they could. They'd understand. There'd be sympathy, not condemnation. They wouldn't think hard of him.

I've done my child no wrong. I'll admit this: I took her out of spite, and it turned out to be a good thing for her. It was sour soil she was growing in. It was rank. I don't want to see her back there. But I don't want to see her in a home, either. If you're dead set against giving her to me then give her to her mother. Maybe it's not right that any mother is better than none, but the way I see it any mother is better than a home. You ever see kids in a home? They crowd you when you go there. They think you must be their mother and father. You don't eat too good for days after coming away from a place like that. Your sleep's not too hot, either.

That was all he could say, and he'd leave it at that.

The first thing he did when he arrived in the city was to go to the post office and put in a long-distance call. Dr Fitzmaurice spoke to him. Macauley asked for the truth. He got it. Still pretty low. He came out, turning the words over in his mind. Still pretty low. Hanging on. Hanging on to what and what with? Not three feet tall, not three stone weight, soft flesh and gristly bones, shot nerves and somebody else's blood, fractured skull. Four years on the earth: knowing so much and yet no chance to know anything. But hanging on to something and with something.

He booked in to the hotel, and walked about the city. He drank one beer. He had a cheap meal in a hamburger. It nearly made him vomit. The noise belted his eardrums. The grime covered his face and he wiped off dirty sweat on his handkerchief.

People jostled him, scurrying with a strained look in their eyes or an easy acceptance. This was like being in the belly of a dragon. It was like being in a box and struggling for light and air. This was the city and he wanted no part of it. Too many strangers. Too many hard roads. Too many fences. It was a circus he'd never join.

At nightfall he rang Casino again. A nurse answered. Precise and formal like a stone figure talking. The child was out of the coma but still in grave danger.

He wouldn't have got that from her if he hadn't told Fitzmaurice he wanted no punches pulled. He would have been fobbed off with that old line of bulldust about the patient doing as well as can be expected. They made a bloody man sick with their queasy hypocrisy.

Standing on the kerb in the uncaring city, in the loneliness of lights and people; thinking of a car screeching in the darkness and a pulse of life in a hospital bed; thinking of the wire he had sent, and outraged by the despicable response to it, Macauley decided, was driven by his feelings, to confront his wife then and now and not in the morning.

The residential was the same, only older and shabbier. There was still a scoop in the sandstone step from the abrasion of feet. The fly-specked oniony bulb still fought the darkness on the staircase. There was a strip of light under the door. The doorknob still lolled dejectedly.

Macauley didn't knock. He opened the door, and the moment he stepped in the room, the moment he saw her, his angry heartsick bafflement vanished. He was glad in a way that there was an excuse and a reason for her apparent inhumanity, glad though he condoned neither. He was caught up in an anger of disgust; words of opprobrium rushed like gall into his mouth, but he held them back at bay, sensitive to their futility.

'Oh,' she sneered. 'It's you.'

Her head swayed. She turned it away and let it droop. She was sitting at the small kitchen table. There was nothing on it but the few home comforts – a white glass half red with wine, a bottle three-quarters full, an ashtray full of stubbed cigarettes, and one fresh cigarette burning away to a cylinder of grey ash.

'You're in a pretty mess,' he said.

She sniggered, and the sound filled him with contempt. Nothing looked more silly, more degraded, than a woman with too many under the belt. They couldn't take it. A man looked bad enough stripped of his self-respect, reduced to a pie-eyed clown, but a woman looked ten times worse; a witless hag.

'Pretty mess,' she muttered. Her eyes found him. They gleamed like black water. Her lips quivered before the words came. 'Who did it? Who did it, eh?'

'You're a fool,' he said. 'You're a weakling.'

'Am I?' She fixed him with an expression of determination and abhorrence. 'That's what you say. But I'll beat you, Macauley, if it's the last thing I do.'

'A court'll never give you that kid.'

'No?' she jeered. 'You know nothing. You ask my lawyer. It's a cinch, it's a cert. You haven't got a look-in.'

She stood up, pointing at him with a look of triumphant disdain.

'You thought I'd come running, didn't you? You thought

you'd break me down. You thought I'd be on tap with the help and the comfort.' She grimaced. 'I wouldn't move ten yards for you.'

He repressed his exasperation, aware of its uselessness. He said quietly, 'I just thought you'd like to know, that's all.'

'You just thought,' she said scornfully.

'Where's it going to get you, anyway? You know that kid might die. It's on the cards she will.'

She shrugged.

'You won't get her then,' Macauley added.

'Neither will you!' she shot back. And he realised positively then that that was all she was concerned about. He was talking to a stranger to whom he meant nothing, not to a wife, not to a woman he had loved and who had loved him. There was no reason why she should feel any sentiment for him or a child that had long ceased to be a part of her life. No reason at all. Any good that was in her, and there was much, had been seduced by antipathy; and it wasn't just a kernel of hatred, it was a poison all through her, going the rounds with her blood, feeding her brain, filling her with zeal and despair.

'You don't want that kid,' Macauley said. 'All you want is revenge.'

'Ah, you're getting smart,' she praised him mockingly.

'Is that why you feared nothing from me? Why you gave me a chance to appear in court? You reckon I haven't got Buckley's?'

'Mister,' she said, 'I wanted you to turn up. I want you to be there. It's going to give me the greatest pleasure I can think of to hear you babbling your piece, trying to get yourself out of the fix I can put you in; and I can't wait to see your face when they hand that kid over to me.'

He looked at her steadily. 'You'll never get that kid,' he said. 'You and your tin-pot court. There's no court in the world big enough to make me give her to you. The Almighty himself couldn't make me do it. Go for your life. See where you get.'

There was no more he could say to her, no more he wanted to say. He walked to the door. Then he turned, with a pang of hope. 'I'll be at the Met, if you want to talk to me – but make sure you want to talk sense.'

'Get out!'

He had his hand on the knob. He heard the quick steps on the stairs, and the knob was turned from the other side. He swung back as the door opened and was behind it.

'Hell, Marge, you still on it.'

The man slammed the door, and then he saw Macauley, who stood against it. His face whitened. His eyes flicked in fear.

'Don't get the wind up, Donny,' Macauley said. 'Nobody's going to hurt you.'

Donny relaxed slightly. He looked bewilderedly at Marge, and gestured slightly with his thumb. 'What's he doing here?'

The woman was suddenly quiet. There was a look of momentary sobriety on her face. Macauley didn't miss the way she glanced with cautious trepidation round the room. He was curiously interested by the change in her.

'Get out!' she said.

Macauley spoke quietly. 'Donny wants to know why I'm here. Tell him.'

'Get out!' she shouted, rising. 'Get out!'

'She doesn't want to tell you, Donny. Why?'

Donny looked blank. He squirmed like a man who feels he's being made a fool of. Then his forehead crinkled slowly. He swivelled his eyes round on her. 'But you said he wouldn't be here. You — '

The woman looked uncomfortable as though she had been caught in a guilty act and was trying to shrug it off as being of no consequence.

'I got word from her to come, Donny. She asked me, in a way.' Macauley knew the cards to play now.

Donny shot him a glance of disbelief, then transferred it to the woman. 'Is that true, Marge? What's going on? Are you crazy or what?'

'He's lying, he's lying,' she said wildly.

'Looks like she's been putting it over you, Donny,' Macauley said. 'And I can't be lying. I'm here. And I'll be in that courtroom in the morning, fighting her every inch of the way.'

'You said he wouldn't be here,' Donny repeated accusingly. 'You said it'd be walk-over. Nothing to it.'

'Like the time she tried to kidnap the child,' Macauley said. 'Is that what she told you then? And you sort of didn't mind as long as there wasn't going to be any trouble. You wanted to see me get it in the neck too, and that was a nice and easy way to do it.'

Donny held up his hands placatingly, absolvingly.

'You gutless bastard, don't try to tell me any different. You've got no more time for me than I've got for you.' Macauley walked a few steps away from the door. Donny flinched and moved back. 'You didn't intend to keep the kid, either, no more than you intended to keep it this time. What were you going to do with it?'

Donny looked at the woman, trying to get his cue from her, but she only looked at him with the same notion.

'Tell me,' Macauley snarled, advancing. 'Tell me, or I'll make it willing. What were you going to do with her?'

'Get her adopted, an orphanage, we didn't know . . .' Donny blurted in fear.

Macauley stood still, staring at them in the rage to destroy that possessed him. Then he shrugged. 'Well, what are you going to do now, Donny, now that you've found out she wants to have her cake and eat it, too, now that you know I'm here ready and bloody willing to give you the trouble you don't want?'

Donny looked about him, cornered. Then his temper flared. 'You had no right to do this,' he snapped at the woman. 'I came in with you. I give you a fair go. You didn't have to do this.'

The woman stood up, frightened, flustered heat in her face.

'Donny, listen — ' There was a note of panic in her voice.

'Listen, nothing! I told you how I stood. As long as there was no fuss, I said. I don't want my name dragged through the scandal sheets. Why should I for a bloody nobody? And now you go and do this on me. Well, that's the finish.'

The woman ran to him. 'No, Donny, don't say that. It's not finished. I don't want anybody but you.' Her voice broke in supplicating sobs. Macauley backed to the door, hating the harsh abject tones.

'It's not as if you wanted the kid,' Donny said in a softer voice, gesturing. Then he braced himself again, the sense of hurt coming strong in him. 'It's too late now to be sorry,' he said. 'Well, I won't be here. I'm going. I want nothing more to do with you.'

'No, no, Donny.'

'It's not too late,' Macauley said ruthlessly, his back to the door.

Donny shot him a glance of incomprehension that slowly faded. 'You mean you can call it off?'

Macauley shook his head. 'Not me. I've got nothing to do with it.'

Donny looked slowly away from him to the woman, with her hands to her face, sobbing, the savagery and desperation of the trapped animal gone. Donny seemed to be waiting for her answer, but his impatience ran out. 'Well, how about it?' he rapped out. 'It's in your lap. You started it. Make up your mind. It's that kid or me.' He stared at her, vehement. 'Hurry up.'

Macauley took one searching look at the woman, and he knew what her answer would be. It was written in every shudder of her flesh, in every twinge of her grovelling submissiveness. He spared her feelings, he made it easier. He had seen the piteous disintegration; he didn't want to be in at the kill. He closed the door softly and went down the stairs. But he went like a guilty man leaving his crime behind him. There was compassion in him and a bitter sickness of remorse.

He put through another call, and was told that Buster's condition was still the same. He could go back now, though. There was no point in staying in the city. It was all over in the city. He rang the railway, found he would be able to catch a train in two hours' time.

He went back to the hotel, and there he found it wasn't all over, not for him.

They caught him right off guard. There was just the short swift knock on the door. He opened it, and a fist shot through. It dazed him and sent him back on his heels. Then they were in the room. The tall one grabbed him, twisted his arms back while the nuggety one pummelled him. Macauley freed himself and fought back, and it was boots and all in. They grasped him again. The big one held. The short one pummelled. But they didn't get him again. He backed, ducked, and a fist crunched on the stone wall behind him. He hit out. He felt the jerk in his shoulders. They swung in together. They fought with the ferocity of panthers. The fight lasted ten minutes. At the end of that time nobody moved.

Macauley stirred first. He crawled along the floor on his hands and knees and pulled on the bed. He dragged himself upright. He sat there. He put his hands to his face and drew them away in stupid puzzlement, for they met his face before they came to it, or so it seemed. He had no side-sight from the left eye. It was as though he wore a blinker. He had to turn his head at right angles to his shoulder before he could see the wardrobe mirror. He staggered towards it. A man, a visage he didn't recognise, came towards him. He stared at it close up, turning his head this way and that.

When he washed away the blood and combed his hair, it looked no better. It looked worse because it was getting worse. He had a blinker on the right eye now. But the face was his all right. He changed into a clean shirt. He got the blood spots off his clothes as well as he could. He tied up his brown-paper parcel and was ready to leave. Then he saw his two assailants. But they were in no condition to worry him. The tall one with the rugged sloping shoulders lay back down on the floor with his head propped up slightly against the skirting board. The nuggety one lay drawn up near the head of the bed, starey-eyed, agony frozen on his face. He was still clutching his testicles.

Macauley went on down the stairs, and out into the darkened foyer. He caught the sudden flick of movement and instinct spun his head around, and he lurched sideways and thrust out a rigid arm, pinning the squirming man hard against the wall. The surprise at seeing Macauley when he expected to see his hirelings, the surprise of being caught unawares and which forced him to draw himself inconspicuously up against the wall, was still in Donny Carroll's face, but fear was chasing it now.

'Now, listen, listen,' he cringed, licking his lips. 'It wasn't my idea — '

Macauley jerked him forward.

Donny put up his hands. 'No, don't! Don't!'

Macauley peered at him, still grasping the handful of shirt. 'No,' he mumbled. 'I'll leave you alone. You're all she's got. And you're not much.'

He dragged the craven wretch closer.

'Take a good look,' he said. 'Go back and tell her what you saw. Make it good. She'll feel better. Maybe it'll cure her. Maybe she'll be satisfied then.'

He let the silk go with a flinging motion, and Donny Carroll stepped quickly away and then he ran.

Macauley didn't miss the train. He got in a dog box and stretched out on one seat with a paper over his face. He rode most of the way without company. The company who entered at Coff's Harbour was a taciturn pasty-faced man with round hat and a briefcase. He couldn't help staring. Macauley asked him if he was jealous, because if he was, Macaulay told him, it wouldn't be much trouble to make his face match. The company went out of its way to avoid staring and found it an unnerving ordeal.

It was noon at the hospital when Macauley arrived. The horrified nurse skittered away after the doctor. Fitzmaurice came, showed his dismay and started to ask questions. Macauley shut him up. 'I know I look like a bloody clawed-up tomcat; so do you. Leave it at that. What about her?'

'You want it straight,' Fitzmaurice said. 'I don't know. The crisis is approaching. If she makes it she'll be a sick little girl, but we'll get her right.'

'What's this crisis?'

'Think of a thread,' Fitzmaurice said, bluntly, 'with death pulling on one end and life on the other. And there you've got it. We've done all we can. We can do no more. It's all up to her now.'

All up to her – all up to that bit of a scrap of flesh and blood, with a ticker no bigger than a two-bob piece, a waist you could slip through a bangle, a neck you could circle with your finger and thumb.

The nurse handed Macauley two letters and a small parcel wrapped in a piece of newspaper. She said an old man left it. He went down to the park, away from people, and read the letters. One was from Beauty Kelly with a blue five-pound note enclosed. Beauty said he read all about it in the papers, he hoped they'd catch the low bastard, he wished him the best and thought he might make use of the enclosed spin. He added a P.S.: 'Don't laugh, but I'm on the wagon.' The other letter was from Lily. It was full of warmth and sympathy and generosity. He unwrapped the parcel. It was a packet of fine-cut tobacco. A pencilled scrawl on a tatter of paper told him: 'I was passing throo when I herd. Sorry to heer. But don't worry. She's got yooth on her side. I owe you this. Im no bludja. Sam Bywater.'

Macauley drew warmth into him from these tributes, but they worried him too; as if they were an appeasement for the blow that might yet befall him. He thought he had better go back to the hospital. Then he thought they must be getting tired of him mooching about there. He'd leave it for a while. And he remembered his face and he felt self-conscious about it.

He thought if he slept for a while, to forget, to refresh himself, he would feel better. But he couldn't sleep. Not even in the cool green grass with the warm air and the sun on his hands stretched back beyond the rim of the shadow.

The pictures tumbled in his mind, and they were morbid and premonitory. He saw himself sitting there, waiting. He was listening for steps. The nurses were drifting quietly about their work. They had homes to go to, friends, parents, sweethearts. They had things to do. This was none of their worry. This was routine: the sick, the dead coming and going.

But he was sitting there, and he saw it clearly: the doctor coming out, coming down the polished corridor, the way his trouser legs flew round with each step, the verdict on his face before he opened his mouth; he heard the clods on the coffin; he saw the open road and himself alone.

It was all so brutally real that it brought out a chill sweat on his face and screwed up his nerves so that he craved some outlet for their relief. His swag was still at the police station. He thought he had better put in an appearance there. He decided he had better not – not yet. His face would be on show; all the questions; there might be some kickback; the tall man and the nuggety man, he didn't know how they came out of it.

With shaking fingers he took out the piece of pocket mirror from inside his coat and looked at his face.

If it belonged to a man at all, that man lived in the jungle in a time gone by. It was swollen and lopsided. The lips were pumped up and protuberant. The neck just below the jawline was a green-and-blue bruise like a birthmark. The left cheekbone was split in a brown scar. The nose as well as being enlarged was thrown out of line by, and so contributed to, the whole disfigurement of the face.

He waited and he went along in the dark and by that time the tension in him was almost beyond his endurance. Haggard, worn, his shoulders slumped like the shoulders of an old man, he sat down and waited. It was just as he imagined. He saw the doctor come out. He watched him coming down the corridor. He tried to read his face, but he couldn't. He stood, keyed-up, panting.

The doctor saw him. Instantly he smiled and shook his clenched hands above his head in the gesture of a prize-fighter.

The doctor was before him and he couldn't look at him then. The words seemed far away. He only caught one or two of them. His hands were shaking. He clenched his fists.

'She keeps asking for something . . . or somebody by the name of . . . well . . . it sounds like Gooby. Does that make sense to you?'

Macauley's throat strained, tightened like hawsers after the rain; the ache started in his belly.

'I'll go and get it,' he muttered.

He turned away. Fitzmaurice looked after him. He thought he heard him sobbing.

'Poor bastard,' he said.